PRAISE FOR FINDING US

"For readers who love small town romance, tough guys with big hearts and sassy heroines, it's perfect"

" I love the humour you put in this book, and I think you have a real talent for it—
you made the sex scene funny and hot"

"I loved how easily you could connect with the characters and their relationships, meaning it was difficult to put the book down."

"What memorable characters, and what a fun, layered and emotionally resonant story!"

"It's sure to be a favourite with your readers!"

"I'd forgotten just how freaking talented you are!"

i

ALSO BY CAROLE BRUNGAR

The Nam Legacy
The Nam Shadow
Going Home
Loving Summer
The Return

A Tide Too High
Caught in a Riptide

Brock
Lucy
Jaxon
Aiden

Finding Us

A fun small town romance

Carole Brungar

CAROLE BRUNGAR PUBLISHING

Finding Us

Copyright © 2025 Carole Brungar

Carole Brungar is a New Zealand author and British English spelling is used in this novel.

To Janet Elizabeth Henderson,

my weird Scottish friend who writes the best rom coms and romantic suspense,

and who inspires me with her strength and determination.

(Go check out her books!)

1

REID

WHEN I HAULED MY sorry arse out of bed this morning, I had a feeling today would turn to shit, and now, here we were. "You're doing *what?*" I bellowed. The last thing I wanted was some righteous stranger telling me how to run my business.

Connor, my older brother by two years, reached for the radio and dialled More FM up a few more decibels. Outside on the workshop floor, the two mechanics we employed looked up before quickly returning their attention to whatever the hell they were working on.

"Calm down," he growled.

"Don't tell me to calm down!" I thumped the desk. Things bounced.

"Well, I've made an executive decision to hire an office manager so at some stage, you have to learn to trust again. Not everyone is scheming to ruin you."

"You reckon? It wasn't *your* reputation that got dragged through every damn newspaper in the country and destroyed."

"It was messy, not to mention embarrassing, and we know it was a setup, so you need to put it behind you and move on."

"Yeah, well, easy for you to stand there and be all fucking virtuous."

Connor took a step towards my desk and brushed the assortment of invoices and flyers I'd been trying to put in order for the last two hours further under my nose. His dramatic sweeping motion started a mini avalanche, sending papers cascading over my knees to the floor. I made a hurried grab for them but had to admit defeat and threw up my hands in frustration. Connor raised a brow at me, giving me a look that told me I'd just proved his point. Smug bastard.

"It's simple. We can't do this. You've been playing with this pile for long enough, and it looks like it's grown bigger, not smaller. I'm over it, Reid. Neither of us wants to do it, neither of us is any good at keeping the records, and both of us would be better off spending our time out there," he said, with a nod to the workshop. "So, we're employing someone who can."

I growled my disapproval and, grappling with sheaves of papers, shoved back my chair with more force than intended. It toppled. My hands grasped at thin air while the chair hit the metal filing cabinet behind my desk and bounced onto its side. It struck the floor with a loud crash before coming to rest on top of the paper-littered floor. I ended up on my arse.

I grudgingly accepted his offered hand and let him haul me to my feet. "Trust has nothing to do with anything. At all."

"Bullshit." Connor perched on the corner of my desk. "And there's no point getting mad at me. We're both on the same team." He crossed his arms over a Hamilton's Automotive T-shirt that was years old and looked two sizes too small over his sculpted chest. "I'm sure the tax department will love calculating the interest if we're late paying our dues."

"Why did you let it get so bad?" I demanded. "It's a wonder this place is still open."

"Yeah, well, doing the accounts isn't exactly my idea of fun."

"We all have to do things we don't enjoy doing." I righted the chair and pushed it back under the desk so I could retrieve the papers scattered all over the floor. I'd just spent the past twelve months of my life doing something I hated, and my brother was whining about a few bits of paper. "All I'm saying is we don't need to employ someone. Give me a bit more time, and I'll get this filing sorted."

"You know as well as I do this isn't a one-off situation—things were getting bad before you were carted off. We need permanent help keeping all this in order."

If there was one thing I hated, it was admitting my brother had a point. I was more interested in working on the vehicles that came into our garage than spending hours pushing paper. But I was worried we couldn't afford another staff member—not yet, anyway. Our business was at an all-time low in terms of customers, and it was going to take a miracle to build it back up to what it once was.

"You could have at least warned me you were doing interviews," I muttered as I dumped a fistful of papers on my desk. Defeated, I yanked open one of its drawers and rummaged for the pack of cigarettes I kept hidden at the back, next to my emergency flask of JD. I'd given up the smokes while incarcerated, but now that I was out again, I was chewing through almost a pack a day. Despite repeated declarations that I'd quit, today was not the day.

My brother and I ran an old-fashioned auto garage, the sort of place you brought your car to if it was pre-electric, pre-computerised, and still performed well on good, reliable 91 fuel. We loved it when a real good customer rolled through our door and gave us the chance to modify a classic car into a souped-up hot rod. Connor's paint jobs and my workmanship with motors had gained us a nationwide reputation within the hot-rod community, and we'd had more than enough business to keep us busy and employ two mechanics. But now, most of our jobs comprised warrant-of-fitness checks and minor repairs.

I'd made some modifications to a very nice Holden a customer entrusted to us just over a year ago; a car I'd failed to notice had its engine number ground off—apparently while in our care, although both Tyler and Liam swore they hadn't touched it. My brother and I had never been involved in anything illegal; we ran a clean shop and were proud of our work. Unfortunately, that didn't help me, because the customer turned out to be an undercover detective, Tony fucking Selgrave. Someone, at some stage, had planted two hundred grams of coke inside one of the car's door panels. Of all the unoriginal places to hide it. *Drugs.* I've never touched that stuff and never will. What annoyed me the most, apart from being locked up for a year, was that I'd done a fucking great job on the car, even if I did say so myself.

Someone stitched me up so well that I hadn't seen it coming, and if I ever found out who it was, I'd take a great deal of fucking pleasure in making them pay.

The cops went through our garage with a fine-toothed comb, leaving no tool drawer or filing cabinet untouched. They seized hard drives and purchase orders and, not satisfied that everything was legitimate, went to my place and then Connor's and turned them upside down, still finding nothing except a half-used packet of paracetamol in a kitchen cupboard.

Despite them having established no motive for why I'd use or deal, I'd gone down for five years on circumstantial evidence. I'd drawn a judge set on cleaning up drugs on the streets, and he needed to prove he meant business. After one year, against all odds, I managed to convince the parole board I wasn't a liability to the community and got released on good behaviour. I've never felt so damn happy in all my life as when I walked free of those concrete block walls. Now, I was suspicious of everyone I met and every customer who came through our door.

All credit to Connor: he'd held the business together when customers stopped dealing with us in case they, too, got caught up in shady dealings that would result in their vehicle being impounded. But if things didn't pick up soon, it would be a case of last in, first out.

I flipped open the packet lid, prised out a cigarette, and lit it. As the smoke made its way into my lungs, calm washed over me. I saw no reason to change the status quo. If I had to, I'd put aside one day a week to do our paperwork.

"Admit it," Connor said. "It would be nice having a pretty face here, making the coffee." He glanced at the notepad in his hand. "Anyway, the first candidate will be here—"

As if my brother had somehow conjured them out of thin air, there was a knock on my office door.

"Hello?" a woman's voice called, and Connor got up to let her in.

I stood and took in the interviewee's appearance. She looked like she'd just come from a garden club meeting. She had to be in her late sixties at least, and she carried a large straw bag stuffed with bits of shrubbery. Her fingertips peeked out from the sleeves of an oversized brown woollen coat that covered everything except her sensible black shoes. With her hair pinned back and an angular, bare face, her orange lips stood out. Orange. Jesus, who wore orange lipstick? I rolled my eyes at my brother. She looked like she'd be a barrel of laughs first thing on a Monday morning.

"Gloria? Come on in and take a seat." Connor pulled a seat forwards for her. "This is my brother, Reid. Thanks for being so prompt."

He reassumed his position on the corner of the desk, and I pulled out my chair and sat, resigned to the painful process of being trapped in an interview.

"Thank you," she said. "If everyone prioritised punctuality, society would run so much more efficiently."

I smirked and she eyed me as if I'd just farted and blamed it on her. I'd picked up some bad habits during my stint inside.

I could tell she was making judgemental notes in her head as she glanced from me to my brother and then around the office. Her gaze lingered on my vintage poster hanging behind Connor, the iconic 1976 red swimsuit photo of Farrah Fawcett I'd had framed about eighteen years ago.

"Would I be working in this office, or would I have my own?" she asked. Her demands prickled. Or maybe it was the orange lipstick.

"Whoever we hire would have the slightly smaller office next door," Connor told her, pointing through the window separating the two offices. "This is my brother's office. Mine's at the far end. We have the waiting room for clients, a small kitchen for staff use and, of course, bathroom facilities down the end." He glanced over his shoulder, and her eyes shifted to the corridor.

"Of course." Her gaze returned to me and narrowed as she continued. "I couldn't work in an office with a smoker. Are you aware that second-hand smoke does just as much damage as actually smoking the cigarette? It interrupts the normal functioning of the heart and increases your risk of having a heart attack."

I reached over to my tyre-shaped ashtray and stubbed out my cigarette. She lifted her chin. She might think she'd won that battle, but I'd win the war. There was no way in hell we'd be employing her.

"What would I be required to do?" she asked.

I crossed my arms over my chest. She could walk back out the door for a start.

Connor cleared his throat. "You'd be our office manager, so some filing and keeping the accounts in order. Payroll. Some general cleaning. Answering the phone, making coffee."

I hoped it sounded boring as hell to her, but knowing my luck, she'd thrive on *boring*.

"And the hours are nine till three, three days a week?"

"Actually, I think we'd decided eight to five, five days a week," I said before Connor could correct me. "And Saturday mornings." If the job itself didn't put her off, maybe the hours would.

She switched her attention from Connor to me and then glanced at the state of my desk and the floor beneath it. "I thought it was part-time?"

My brother glared at me. "We're still finalising the hours."

She turned to Connor. "Is your desk as bad as this one?"

"Not quite," he answered meekly.

She nodded. "I don't enjoy working with loud music, and those calendars will need to go. I find they don't promote a professional atmosphere in the office. And there'll be rules for using the bathroom—no leaving the toilet seat up."

"Noted." I'd had enough. I pushed out from behind my desk and stood.

Connor slipped off the desk and turned down the radio until it was merely a quiet bass thump in the background.

"Well, thanks for coming, Gloria." I flashed her my most charming smile. "We have a few applicants to get through, so we'll be in touch in due course."

She picked up her bag and stood. "Thank you," she said in a matter-of-fact voice. "You can reach me on my home phone number every day except Wednesdays, when I'm helping at the St Mary's Retirement Village." And with that, she turned and walked out of the office.

"Wait for it," Connor muttered. We stood there, waiting for Gloria to make her way through the workshop, past the two mechanics. A second later, a wolf whistle pierced the air, followed by laughter, and I shook my head. Whoever we employed would have to have a sense of humour to cope with Liam.

"Nope," I said as my brother turned the radio back up. "She reminds me of a prison warden."

"Fair enough," Connor said.

The next candidate was also a non-starter. He looked like he hadn't seen the sun in forever and would scurry away and hide if a client spoke to him.

"Can you type?" I asked.

"Sure, can't everyone?" His left eye twitched, and for a moment, I wondered if he was winking at me. I narrowed mine at him.

"What about payroll?" Connor asked.

More blinking.

"How hard can it be?" he answered, avoiding my stare.

"What type of car do you own?" I quizzed.

"Don't own a car. I use public transport. Sometimes a taxi."

Great. It would be helpful if the person we employed knew the engine from the boot.

The third candidate wasn't much better. His stomach overflowed the waistband of his pants, and he was breathing heavily when he reached the office. Beads of sweat ran down the sides of his face, and the armpits of his shirt were soaked.

"How did you get to the interview today?" I asked him, seeing as he clearly didn't walk anywhere. He plonked himself down in the chair and looked from Connor to me as though watching us rally a tennis ball.

"I borrowed my flatmate's bike." He stared at us. I suspect he wanted our approval.

"Nice." I certainly approved if he rode a motor. "Harley? Suzuki? Triumph?"

"Push."

"Push?" I asked before it dawned on me what he meant. Impatience surged to the surface.

"Do you own a car?" Connor asked quickly.

"No, I don't. No need in this town. What's that got to do with working in an office?" the man added.

Fair point. "Nothing, but it would be an enormous advantage if you knew a bit about motor vehicles."

"Isn't that what the internet's for?"

"Right," Connor said, after fifteen minutes of back-and-forth questioning. "We'll be in touch."

We interviewed four more people, each of whom either Connor or I disliked for various reasons. The last one was only sixteen—far too young—and when all her questions were about meal breaks, toilet breaks, how many holidays she'd be entitled to during the year, and if we paid sick leave, Connor thanked her for coming and escorted her out, signalling to Liam to zip it.

"Listen, I'll come in early tomorrow morning and create some sort of order out of all this," I said.

"I'll cut you a deal."

"Does this deal involve beer and food?" I asked, ever hopeful.

"No. I'll stay late tonight to sort paid and unpaid, and then you can pick up with what's left in the morning."

"Okay. Suits me. Do you want to hit McCarthy's first?"

Connor shook his head. "Can't if I'm going to make an honest start on this mess." He glanced at the clock on the wall. It was already five-thirty. "Say hi to Annie if she's working."

"It's about time you said hi to her yourself," I grumbled as I shut down my computer. "I'll grab you a burger."

Since it was a Thursday, McCarthy's wasn't busy. Just a few patrons having a quick beer or ordering a takeout meal on their way home. I'd opened the door looking for a friendly face and, when I came up short, took a deep breath before stepping inside. Silence swept through the pub like a Mexican wave going around a stadium. It used to be my haunt, but it seemed the locals had reassessed their loyalties to the Hamilton brothers—me in particular, Connor by association. Well, they could get stuffed. What was it with these folks? Most of them had known me since my school days. Some since I was a baby. They knew I was as honest and clean as the day was long.

I noticed the high and mighty Detective Inspector Tony Selgrave sitting at a table with some bloke I didn't recognise. I turned back to the bar with the feeling he was watching me.

"The usual?" Matthew McCarthy asked.

I nodded. Matt was one of only a handful of imports, and he owned the joint. He'd stopped in town fifteen years ago while on a road trip through New Zealand, when the radiator in his Ford truck blew up. My father had told him it would take at least four days to replace, maybe five, and by the time his truck was back on the road, Matt had decided he was staying put. Five years ago, his son had flown out and joined him and now managed the kitchen.

Matt put down a glass he'd been polishing, flung the dish towel over his shoulder, and filled it with beer for me. He threw a glance over my shoulder, and I sensed heads turning away from me. The chatter picked up again.

"Don't mind them," Matt drawled in his Texas accent. "They'll come around, eventually."

"What's that slimy bastard doing in here? It's not his regular." I nodded in Selgrave's direction.

"Minding his own business."

"Can I also grab two double chicken cheeseburgers with extra bacon, to go, please?"

"Sure thing."

I swiped my card across the machine, paid the bill, and sipped my beer while waiting for the burgers.

Annie appeared at my side and leaned into me as she slid her tray of empties across the bar and called out the refill orders.

"How are you doing, Reid?"

"Just fine. Connor says hi."

"I haven't seen him in a while. What's he been doing?"

"He's knee-deep in paperwork."

"It's about time you picked up the slack. He's been carrying it for long enough."

"Thanks for the unsolicited advice," I growled. "Where's Ellie?"

"Had something on, so we swapped shifts." She turned to look at me, her hand on one hip. "Why'd you want to know?"

"Just making small talk."

"Ellie's too good for you, Reid."

"Since when did you become everyone's keeper?" I took a long swallow from my glass.

"Since I heard you got out and might be looking for someone to cheer you up, among other things. Ellie isn't gonna be that girl."

"Well, you don't need to worry that gorgeous head of yours, Annie. I'm not on the hunt for anyone except the fucking lowlife who set me up."

"Good luck with that. I know you're a good guy under all that macho shit, and you didn't deserve bars for what happened."

"Try telling the rest of the town that."

"Just give them time, Reid."

"I'm getting sick of hearing that."

Matt slid the tray of refills across the bar to Annie.

"Tell your brother to call me." She winked at me.

"I already did."

I swivelled on my stool and, over the top of my beer, watched her walk to the far table and hand out bottles and glasses. She and my brother had been having an on-again, off-again relationship for years. They were currently in one of their off-again stages, but I suspected that was about to change. Annie claimed Connor wasn't interested in a full-time girlfriend, while she told him she was done with men. My dumb-arse brother reckoned he didn't want to be tied down to one woman, but she was the only one he ever dated. In my opinion, they were made for each other, and the sooner they realised it, the better.

Matt set a takeaway bag on the counter. I drained my glass, grabbed the food, and headed for the door.

2

REID

IT WAS ONLY SEVEN in the morning, but I'd already spent an hour at my desk, shuffling bits of paper and sorting them into piles. I needed coffee. The good stuff. On the workshop floor, the older of the two mechanics we employed was switching on machinery.

"Morning, Tyler. Liam not in yet?"

"Not yet."

"I'm going for a coffee. Want one?"

"Thanks, lad." He unplugged the diagnostic trolley and wheeled it across to an early-model Mini.

Riverford Valley was coming to life as its residents made their way to work. With a population of almost fifteen thousand, the small rural town comprised an even mix of young families, farmers and retired folks. It was a place where generations stayed. The hub of the community was the rugby club, where Connor and I played for the local team, and along with the hospital and schools, there seemed to be just the right number of businesses to keep anyone who wanted work employed.

16

The valley was well off the beaten track. It wasn't a place you passed through on the way to someplace else; you had to choose to come here. At the top was the Riverford Falls, a popular place for trampers and campers, where a decent-sized lake offered great swimming in the summer months. Most of the land was farmed, but there was still a sizeable portion in native bush, despite the growing trend to carve out lifestyle blocks for aspiring weekend farmers like me.

I had bought twenty acres, transported an old villa onto a corner of the property, and between renovations, planted the bare land in pines and macadamia nuts. Then I'd built a three-bay garage. Landscaping the grounds closest to the house was a work in progress over the last six months since I'd been released from prison.

Whereas I was ten minutes out of Riverford, Connor owned a place in town with an even bigger garage and a backyard big enough to host a game of touch rugby. He spent his weekends messing about with cars, working on projects for others, and neither of us had ever considered leaving town.

"Morning, Reid," Kate Marley called from the front of her florist shop, where she was arranging containers of flowers on each side of the doorstep.

"Morning," I acknowledged and kept on walking.

Connor loved socialising. Me, not so much. I preferred my solitude, even more so since getting out of the slammer. There was nothing more relaxing than to put on some vinyl, crack open a beer, sit outside, and let the notes wash over me while nature carried on doing what it did. I didn't feel the need to be constantly entertaining or making small talk. And there was always plenty to do on the property—like planting along the boundary fence and making a start on the cabin out the back. But the best part of my place was the privacy. No nosey neighbours.

I could smell the freshly baked pastries before I reached Hannah's place, and once inside, I was greeted by the tantalising aroma of coffee. My mood immediately lifted, and my stomach rumbled its approval as I made a beeline for the counter.

Three years ago, I'd become a silent partner in the café when Hannah's husband walked out on her and demanded his share in her business and their apartment upstairs. Hannah and I had a history. We dated for a year when we were twenty, until I realised she was more like the sister I'd never had. We'd remained close friends, and when she told me she needed finance and didn't know what to do, I invested. It was a simple decision; I figured I was doing the whole town a favour—Hannah's baking skills were too good to lose.

She had a way with sugar, butter and flour that no one could match. Her signature donuts, which she baked four days a week, always sold out before lunch. They were my downfall—especially the ones with a salted caramel filling—and the reason I had to hit the gym or the pavement on a regular basis.

"Hey, Han. How's business?" I asked, eyeing up the food cabinet.

"I've still got that apron back here with your name on it, for whenever you get sick of playing with cars." Her smile was wide and welcoming. She was one of the few people in this town who'd defended my innocence without question.

"You'd have no customers if I worked here."

"Don't you believe it! Females would pack this place, all vying for your attention." Hannah laughed. "Are you joining your brother this morning?" She nodded towards the far table, and I turned to see Connor eating a cooked breakfast with some girl who looked like a fucking sideshow freak. She had vibrant blue and orange streaks through what would have otherwise been blonde hair and wore a chunky, bright pink jumper that looked several sizes too big. Red tights and striped platform shoes completed the ensemble.

"Who is that with him?"

"Lou."

"Lou?" I knitted my brows, trying to put a face to the name. I felt I should know her, but the explosion of colour was throwing me off.

"Come on, Reid," Hannah teased. "Louise."

"Your *cousin, Louise*?" I spun around again to take another look. She was four years younger than Hannah and me, and she looked nothing like she had the last time I saw her, about twelve years ago. As a sixteen-year-old, she'd had long sandy braided hair, and she hid her body under baggy sweatpants and sweatshirts. She was always quiet, with her nose buried in a book. As a twenty-year-old, I'd been overbearing and cocky as hell. I hadn't treated her that well and had never quite got over the embarrassment I'd felt when I finally came to my senses. By then, it had been too late to apologise.

How many times had I thought of her after she left town? At first, I'd thought about nothing else. I couldn't shake the memories. Now she was here in person, I didn't know what the hell to say to her. Or if she'd even speak to me. I was probably the last person she wanted to see.

"Reid!" Connor called, motioning me over, and my stomach plummeted.

Shit.

I turned back to Hannah. "Can I have my usual to go, and a coffee for Tyler?"

"Sure thing. I'll bring them over."

After dropping a couple of notes on the counter, I swallowed the feeling of dread and weaved my way through the other early-morning diners and coffee drinkers to my brother's table.

Connor looked excited. Like he'd just discovered the atom. "Reid, you remember Hannah's cousin, Louise?"

I dragged my eyes from Connor to Louise, momentarily forgetting to breathe.

Couldn't be.

This was not the same shy girl I'd known back then. I did a quick calculation—she had to be about twenty-eight now.

Holy. Shit.

This woman held me spellbound, and it wasn't the splashes of blue on her eyelids that echoed her hair colour or the full, fuck-me red lips that curved upwards as her eyes met mine. Something twisted in my gut as I forced my tongue around her name and then remembered I needed to breathe.

"Louise." It emerged as more of a squeaky grunt, and I embarrassedly pulled out a chair and sat in the gap between them.

Her skin was flawless. She could have passed for twenty. I wanted to reach out and touch it, slide my fingers over her cheek, press my thumb to her mouth. Reassure myself she was real. Check the gods weren't playing some cruel joke on me.

I didn't realise I was staring until she opened her mouth and spoke.

"Nice to see you too. It's been a while." Her voice skipped from her lips, flowed across the table, and dripped onto my crotch like a spilled bottle of maple syrup. Turns out my dick loves maple syrup.

"Lou-ise." Now I'd developed a stutter.

No way.

Goosebumps rippled across my skin as memories I'd suppressed came flooding back and tapped me on the shoulder. My gaze dropped lower, but it was hard to make a call on the rest of her body with the jumble of oversized clothing she wore. Her face and voice told me she was all warm-blooded temptress, while her clothes told me she was hiding from something.

Or someone.

"Louise. You look... You've changed." I stumbled over my words. But, hell, wasn't that the understatement of the year? Gone was the timid little mouse who'd spent much of her time hiding behind books and following Hannah and me around like a puppy. In her place was a woman who could ruin a man.

"So have you." She gave me a quick appraisal before returning her attention to her coffee. It felt like she'd just passed judgement, and I hadn't made the grade.

"Louise is staying with Hannah for a while, and I've just employed her to help in the office while she's here."

I dragged my attention back to my brother. "What happened to *We own this business fifty-fifty*? You know, where we make decisions jointly and democratically." I didn't know whether I should be relieved or worried. This wasn't some nerdy kid. I hadn't known her that well back then, and I've never asked Hannah about her in the years since she'd left.

Connor cleared his throat. "Louise needs a job, and we need someone to take care of us."

I gritted my teeth. I didn't need anyone taking care of me.

Something flickered in her eyes that told me working with me wouldn't even make the bottom of her wish list.

"So"—Connor turned back to Louise—"how does three days a week sound? Nine to three?"

Louise licked one manicured finger and ran it along her plate, squashing crumbs onto it. My dick found this an excellent form of entertainment. She slid the finger into her mouth, and as I watched her lips close around it, my blood pressure pounded in my temples, and things got uncomfortable under the table.

"Perfect," she said, giving me an encouraging grin.

Oh, Jesus. How on earth was I going to work with her? I turned on my brother, trying to distract myself. "I wish you'd check with me before making these decisions," I growled.

"Did you just forget your manners?"

"Did you just employ someone without consulting me?"

"Get your head out of your arse, Reid."

My patience was wearing thin. "Well, does she have any experience?"

He leaned into my personal space. "We're not a multi-national fucking company here, Reid. We're a couple of small-town mechanics, and we don't need some hotshot with a PhD to answer the phone and file some invoices."

"How do you know we can trust her?"

"Hello? I'm sitting right here, you idiot," Louise interrupted.

I turned in her direction. Attitude and sass stared right back at me. That's all I needed. The sight of Connor clutching his stomach as he laughed sure didn't help.

"I think I can manage to answer the damn phone and do some filing. But, hey, if you want someone more experienced and way more expensive, I totally understand."

At that moment, Hannah appeared at our table and deposited a takeaway tray with two coffees nestled in it in front of me, along with two paper bags containing my breakfast.

"Everything good?" She glanced around the table before her gaze settled on me.

"Sure is. Louise has just agreed to come work for us," Connor confirmed, while I glared at him. He ignored me. "When can you start, Louise?"

"Monday... If that's okay with Reid."

All eyes focused on me. "Fine," I muttered, outnumbered. Hannah patted my shoulder, but for some reason, it was no comfort at all.

Connor reached across the table and shook Louise's hand. "Brilliant. Mondays, Wednesdays and Fridays?"

I narrowed my eyes at him. Was he gloating?

"No problem," Louise said, reaching out her hand to me. It was small and looked like it would break in my grasp. I hesitated, my eyes swinging from my brother to Hannah and back to Louise. Anyone would think she was offering me a grenade minus its pin.

I pushed back my chair and stood. I had things to do. Places to be. "See you at the garage." I had to escape the café before I ran out of oxygen. Turning, I made a beeline for the door without looking back.

"Sure. I'll bring Louise over soon and show her where she'll be working." Connor's voice raced me across the room and made it to the door before me.

Smug bastard.

I stalked back to the garage, thrust Tyler's coffee at him, and stormed into the inner sanctuary of my office, a stream of curse-laden air flowing in my wake. I wouldn't bother finishing the accounts. Louise, with all her sass, could sort them herself on Monday—after all, that's what we'd be paying her to do.

With my feet resting on my desk, I chowed down on my steak pie and finished with a donut. The crispy, deep-fried ball of dough oozed the salted caramel filling I craved. I washed it all down with the last of my coffee. Then, with no paperwork to do, I got up and wandered out to the backyard, where our latest restoration project sat. Connor had found this '56 Chevy about three weeks after I'd got put away. It had been rusting in a paddock over in Greenhill, a neighbouring town about thirty thousand people bigger than Riverford. He'd visited me to show me a photo. He wanted to buy the body—reckoned we could turn it into something we'd make a decent profit from. At the time, I didn't care if I never saw another vehicle again. All I wanted was to get out and go home.

Walking down the hall, past the offices, heading to the staff bathroom to change into my overalls, I still remembered that first visit. Connor said he planned on offering the old guy who owned it five hundred bucks to take it off his hands. The old guy told him it was ours free to take on one condition: he wanted to take a ride in it when we'd returned it to its former glory—*if* it didn't disintegrate first.

It was my brother's way of keeping me invested in the garage, but I flipped out. There was no way I wanted to touch another motor to repair or restore, but every prison visit, Connor turned up full of shit about what we could do with the car, how he'd seen a custom paint job in a magazine that had given him ideas, or how he'd found a motor we could put in it.

When I got out, the first thing Connor wanted to do was take me to see the car that was waiting for me in our garage. The first thing I wanted to do was grab a dozen donuts from Hannah's, then head home, take a shower, and sleep in my own damn bed. But I humoured him and eventually had to agree it had potential.

In the bathroom, I peeled off my shirt and hung it beside my overalls. With my boots unlaced, I toed them off, then took my overalls from the hook and shoved my feet into the legs. Leaving them hanging at waist level, I replaced my boots. Moments later, I stepped into the corridor... and walked straight into the fluffy softness of a woollen jumper with a smash of pink.

Louise.

My thin tee might as well have been non-existent in that second when her face compacted hard against my chest—before she bounced backwards. My hands shot out in reflex, and I grabbed hold of her arms to stop the trajectory she was on. A jolt of energy shot through my body. Her breath hitched, and for a fleeting second, our eyes locked. And in that tiny window of time, I glimpsed something I couldn't understand before she raised a protective shield.

"Why?" she demanded, glaring at me.

I released her as if she were contagious, sidestepped the woman, and marched back down the corridor and out to the car. I knew she wasn't asking why I'd grabbed her, but I didn't know how to answer.

With my head full of a fragrance that reminded me of the wild honeysuckle that grew around our house when we were kids, I wondered how long she'd been waiting to ask me that question?

3

LOU

I WAS NOT PREPARED to feel so much of Reid's body pressed against mine. It short-circuited my defence system and almost buckled my knees. I jerked a hand out to brace myself against the door frame. I knew I'd have to face him sooner or later, but I was still preparing myself. Riverford was a small town, and once news that I was here staying with Han had got out, it would have spread like a wildfire in summer until it reached Reid Hamilton.

I stood, staring after his retreating form, unaware my mouth was gaping open like a fish out of water. He almost broke out into a run as he left the building, sucking all the air out behind him, and now my chest felt crushed. I breathed in the remnants of his pine-forest scent. The solid, immovable wall of grumpiness was even more swoon-worthy than what I remembered from all those years ago, although the Reid from back then had longer hair, and was clean-shaven and lean with muscles in all the right places. The twenty-year-old Reid was cocky and fun and intimidating. I knew because I'd spent so much time hanging out with him and Hannah. I had ogled his body under the pretence of having nothing better to do than follow them around.

Now he'd filled out in lots of other places, too. My heart skipped and fluttered and settled back into a normal rhythm.

What the hell was his problem, anyway?

I wasn't a teenager anymore, either. The infatuation I'd had with Reid as a sixteen-year-old had worn off long ago.

I hoped.

I'd moved on. I was more experienced in the fine art of being a grown-up in normal relationships. Or I should be, but actually I wasn't. Who was I kidding? I was a total failure when it came to men. I'd gone from one inappropriate relationship to another until I'd hit the motherload of bad men.

Jayden Carter had played me like a conductor leads an orchestra. Before I knew it, we'd moved into a new flat together that I was paying the rent on. He'd convinced me that his car needed upgrading because it had a lot of repair work to be done on it—replacing it was the far cheaper option. Of course, I offered to help him out when he told me he couldn't afford it. Oh, he'd pay me back, he'd said. He didn't care that I'd been made redundant at the web agency where I had worked for the last three years and was living off my savings. No. He was only concerned that I'd be able to meet the repayments. Then he'd told me he'd resigned from his job because he'd been shoulder-tapped for something much better paying.

Turned out that was me.

I discovered by accident that Jayden had actually been fired for sexual harassment and was secretly seeing the twenty-four-year-old girl from the flat downstairs. When all my savings ran out, a week later he did too—with the new girlfriend. I guess I'd lost the shine and appeal I once had, and unlike my neighbour, I definitely didn't have parents who could buy me holidays in the Greek islands.

After spending a week on my best friend Ed's sofa, I decided to head north and start my life again. I'd stopped in at Hannah's and let her talk me into staying for a while. I'd left Wellington and my old life behind, determined to be a better, stronger, aggressive and more progressive version of me. I didn't need a man in my life.

I certainly didn't need Reid.

Nope. Not even a little bit. I was taking control. The new me was living life with no manipulative men to suggest what I wear, how I act and what might be good for me or otherwise. I was going to put all that baggage in the bin and slam the damn lid on it.

Languishing in self-affirmation, I brushed myself down. I took a deep breath and inhaled the lingering woodsy smell of Reid, thinking how lovely it would be to take a walk in that forest, then shaking my head in disgust.

The twenty-year-old Reid I remembered lived in rugby shirts, shorts and runners. He would arrive at my cousin's place in a beat-up Ford and take Hannah on dates while I accompanied them in the back seat like a third wheel. I discretely looked away when they kissed, but he caught me watching him one summer up at the lake, my head full of images of what it would be like if he was kissing *me*.

When Hannah, Reid and Connor went swimming. I preferred to sit and read—was too embarrassed to get into a bathing costume and join them. When Reid climbed out of the lake and stripped off to change, I couldn't tear my eyes away. Every muscle on the length of his body rippled and glistened, right down to his pale arse cheeks that peeked over the edge of his towel when it slipped.

Then he'd glanced up and caught me staring. I can still see the grin that spread across his tanned face as I scrambled to my feet in embarrassment and stumbled my way back to the car. I had seen boys before, but Reid was no boy.

A wave of heat crept up my neck with the memories, and I fanned my face with my hand. Back then, I must have seemed immature to Reid. And now here he was, looking more... well, more of everything. And I was no longer naive.

The man set the bar really high in the sex-god stakes. He had a way of wearing casual clothes that I doubted anyone else could pull off. This morning, his belted jeans rode his hips in a way that would make a porn star drool. His hair was styled well above his collar and lightly gelled into place. He was still clean-shaven, showing off the rigid set of his jawline, but there were shadows that made me want to sleep over to see what he looked like in the mornings. In my tallest heels, I reckoned my lips could reach his without...

Wow! *Big mistake!*

Fantasising about Reid Hamilton would not get me anywhere except in trouble. Anyway, surely he was married or had a girlfriend by now. Hell, he probably had kids.

My insides somersaulted at the thought I'd be working with him. My skills lay in web design and marketing, and I'd even done a paper at university on computer forensics, but how hard would it be to do some filing and answer the phone? Besides, thanks to Jayden, I needed the money right now.

While I was lost in my thoughts, a door somewhere in the building slammed closed, startling me. Connor appeared at my side.

"I take it you found the bathroom." Connor grinned at me. "I saw Reid sprinting out the back door like he had a hive of wasps after him."

I put my innocent face on. "Nothing to do with me."

"If I didn't know better, I'd think he was afraid of you." He chuckled to himself while I gulped down the knowledge there was no way *Reid* was afraid of *me*.

"This is you," he said, opening a door on the opposite side of the hall.

I nodded and followed him in. My desk was in a shoebox of a room. Windows took up most of both partition walls, giving me a view into the rooms on either side.

I did a quick stock-take of my space. There was a computer, a phone, a big-arse stapler that looked like it'd been fashioned from the remnants of a shipwreck—possibly the Titanic. Three filing cabinets sat against the windowless wall, and a lengthy set of cupboards ran the length of the other. A thick layer of grime coated everything. I had a chair that didn't have wheels, and there was a matching chair on the other side of my desk, which I guessed was for clients. An old 2015 calendar featuring a scantily clad woman was pinned to a wall, one corner curling down over the woman's face. Overall, the office was dismal and stark, and smelled like a urinal in a pub. *Ugh!*

"The door just past the kitchen on the left will take you out the back of the workshop where we have a spray booth and plenty of lock-up space for vehicles we're working on. So, think you can bring law and order to our office?"

"I'm not backing away from the challenge. I'll give it a go, but can I make a suggestion?"

"Sure."

"It would be better if I was out there in reception at a desk rather than shut in an office." I pointed to the waiting room with its curved counter and small desk. "If I'm out there, I can see to customers and still handle accounts, answer the phone, and file."

Connor thought for a second. "Perfectly logical, and I like that you're being positive about interacting with the customers."

He gave me a grin not dissimilar to his brother's.

"I'll get the boys to help me shift things, so you're good to go on Monday morning." He perched on the corner of the desk. "Has Hannah told you anything about us?"

"You and Reid?"

"Yeah. And the workshop," he said, with a wave of his hand at his surroundings.

"No, not really."

"We have two staff, Tyler and Liam. Tyler's been with us for years, Liam has been with us for two. They usually arrive between seven and seven-thirty. We lock up around four-thirty. Reid and I are here most of the time. Now and again, one of us might disappear for a while—run errands, get some exercise—that sort of thing. But usually there's always one of us here if you need help."

"Okay. Will you want me to process the pay?"

"Do you know how?"

"Show me the program, and I can take over while I'm here."

"Great. I'm looking forward to Monday morning. Why don't you and Hannah come down to Mc-Carthy's tonight for a celebratory *welcome aboard* drink?"

"With you and Reid?"

"Maybe."

"I don't know."

"He won't bite," he teased.

"It's not his bite I'm worried about."

Connor laughed. "His bark is all show. Ignore it."

I followed Connor through the workshop, to where an older man was doing something with a drill on an oil-smeared, stainless-steel bench.

"Tyler, meet Louise. She's our temporary receptionist slash admin person."

"Well, this is a turn up for the books," Tyler said. "About time we had someone pretty to look at around here. I swear you two lads are getting uglier by the day." He wiped one age-wrinkled hand down his overalls and held it out to me. "Lovely to meet you, lass. You're new in town, aren't you?"

"I arrived yesterday," I told him, accepting his hand then checking mine for grease smudges. Surprisingly enough, it was clean.

"Louise is Hannah's cousin," Connor informed him.

A second, much younger guy rolled himself out from under a car and got to his feet.

"Liam, this is Louise."

We went through the same cleaning of hands and shaking routine.

"I like your colours," Liam said, nodding at my hair.

I gave him a smile of thanks. The colours were a confidence-building exercise. I had been advised by a counsellor to work on doing things that made me feel in control and happy, and to ignore what others thought. Adding colour to my life did exactly that.

"How about I take you out for a drink tonight?" Liam suggested. "We could go to McCarthy's. You can meet the locals, sample the food. Keen?"

"No, she's not," a familiar voice rumbled close behind me. Every tiny hair on my body tingled and stood to attention.

I spun round and gave the monster that had been my teenage heartthrob my fiercest glare, at exactly the same time as one of the false eyelashes I'd been wearing—as another confidence booster—came unstuck and fluttered from my eyelid. "I'll do exactly what I like," I continued, trying to breathe through the unlashing and hoping no one had noticed. "And I'd like to go out for a drink with Liam."

Reid scowled at me.

"I think you're having some sort of malfunction. You look ridiculous. Get back to work, Liam," he directed as he eyed me possessively.

I *humph*ed and headed back inside to use the bathroom. Peering in the excuse for a mirror, through the crazing and grime, I saw my wayward eyelash was stuck to the side of my nose. I stifled a laugh and fiddled with it until it was securely back in place. Satisfied it was going to stay put until I was out of Reid's sight, I turned and stepped into an immovable wall.

"You're in my personal space, Muscle Head."

"Don't call me that."

"Well, stop puffing your chest out and acting like a gorilla."

His nostrils flared, and his eyes widened. I raised my brows to illustrate my point and rested my hands on my hips.

"I am not." His eyes shifted to my lips.

"What's wrong now?" I asked, running my tongue across them.

He diverted his eyes. "I'll call past and pick you and Hannah up at six."

"No, you won't."

"We'll see."

"Listen." It was my turn to reach up and grab his arm as he turned away from me. I couldn't hold him; trying to hold his bicep was like trying to cling to a slippery pole. When did he change to a grumpy-arsed Mr Universe?

"I know you don't like me, but working here was not my idea. I'll help you and Connor as much as I can. If you don't want me here, fine. I'll go find a job someplace else. What'll it be?" I put my hands behind my back and crossed all my fingers he wouldn't fire me before I'd even started.

He mumbled something I wasn't sharp enough to catch and his eyes dribbled down the front of my jumper, which I instantly felt too hot to be wearing. Why had I chosen to wear the thickest piece of clothing I owned? I knew it was the last days of autumn, but it wasn't that cold yet.

"Up here!" I ducked and positioned my face in his eyeline to pull his focus up from my boobs. His eyes flicked up to mine. "What's it to be? I stay and help put some order back in this place, or I go find employment elsewhere?"

He sighed as if he'd lost the battle. "Han'll kill me if I don't keep you on," he said grudgingly. He mumbled something unintelligible and crossed his arms over his chest. It was like staring at the bull bars on a freight train.

"Pardon?"

"Okay. Please stay," he said louder. "We desperately need your help."

"Fair enough." I squeezed past him, my shoulder connecting with his. I tried to ignore the increasing heat levels under my jumper.

4

REID

I'D MANAGED TO TALK Louise into coming for a bite to eat and a drink if Hannah came too. I buzzed the street entrance to Hannah's first-floor apartment, then leaned back against the building's white wall and watched traffic cruise past. Liam drove up the street towards Mc-Carthy's and gave me a salute. I lifted my chin in acknowledgement.

In the lock-up, I'd kept to myself. I didn't want to get involved in anyone else's trouble. I'd wanted to keep my head down and get out as soon as I could. Nowadays, my two closest friends were Connor and Han. They were the only ones I trusted. For the first weeks of freedom, I'd watched both Tyler and Liam, sure that one of them had stitched me up. But Tyler had been a friend of my father's, and I was sure that if he was going to set me up, he would have done it years ago. That left Liam. He liked to call in sick on a Monday, hungover after a hard weekend. And if he got the chance to leave early, he would. But as a mechanic, he was quick to learn, and he'd improved a lot since he'd first started. I'd checked and double-checked his work, and I'd asked Tyler to keep an eye on him, too. But at the end of the day, I couldn't find any reason to suspect him, either.

Connor was out of the question, and so was Hannah. Out of the cops, I refused to believe that Gaylene Dewinter, the local cop, had set me up, which left Tony Selgrave and I didn't know if I'd ever be able to prove he had something to do with it. I'd gone over a list of anyone else in town who might hold a grudge against me and come up with nothing—which made me more pissed at everyone and everything.

I don't know how many times Connor had told me to let it go and move on, and I was trying. But it was hard to let go a grudge.

I went to work, did my hours, plus some, then went home and enjoyed my freedom by watching whatever the hell I felt like watching on the TV and eating all manner of shit. I didn't need people like my brother did. He loved nothing more than having friends around for dinner or to watch rugby games with a house full of mates. But I'd become a hermit, happy on my own, and it was a tough habit to break. The most socialising I did was a quick trip to McCarthy's, or stopping in at Hannah's for something to eat or coffee.

The door opened and Hannah stepped out onto the street, followed by... My smile dropped.

"Is that aimed at me?" I asked, trying not to stare at the curves under the damn writing on her tee. The gravel-grey, figure-hugging T-shirt had *He's cute but psycho* written across the front in white lettering, with emphasis on the *psycho*. She wore it tucked into her high-rise jeans, accentuating her narrow waist. Electric blue two-inch heels elevated her to my height.

Her hair was blue for the most part, and she wore oversized cherry earrings that bounced around her cheeks and led my eye to her glossy lips.

Louise smiled sweetly at me, ignored my question, and followed Hannah to my Hilux. By the time I'd opened the door for Hannah, Louise was already in the back seat, making herself comfortable.

Fine.

I rounded the front of the truck to the driver's door, climbed in and turned the key in the ignition. The scent of honeysuckle had already infiltrated the interior and was starting to meddle with my rational thought processes.

I indicated and pulled out onto the road. My glance in the rear-vision mirror was met with Louise's smug grin. I turned my attention back to the car in front. What I wouldn't give to be back home, flicking the cap off a bottle of Export Gold and edging myself into my comfy old sofa to watch a provincial rugby game on the Tube. Instead, I was going to expose myself to a torturous night full of glares and judgement. I was losing my freaking mind.

Friday nights were one of the busiest at McCarthy's. There was only one other bar in short driving distance from Riverford—The Greenery, a boutique place on the road to Greenhill—and tonight, the whole fucking town seemed to have squeezed itself in here.

I noticed Connor was already seated and leaning across the bar, beer in hand, talking to Annie as she filled orders. There were only two stools vacant. Hannah claimed the one next to Connor, and I pulled the other out for Louise. She came up beside me, placed one butt cheek on the seat and leaned on the counter.

"Well, well, we've got the whole team here tonight," Annie said, as her eyes skimmed the row of us and settled temporarily on Louise's shirt. "Even the psycho member, I see." She laughed and her eyes darted to mine.

"Yeah, thanks for your support," I muttered.

She reached a hand across the bar to Louise. "Welcome to McCarthy's. I'm Annie."

"Louise—Hannah's cousin," she replied.

"I think I remember you. Didn't you come and stay here when you were younger?"

I watched as a flicker of embarrassment touched Louise's face and a second later, it was gone.

"I try to forget that visit," she told Annie.

"Well, you look a lot different from how I remember you. I love your hair, by the way. I tried to be adventurous once—my hair turned an angry shade of orange and most of it fell out. Had to run over it with a number-two comb and hope to God it grew back in its natural colour. So, what'll it be?"

"I'll have a rum and Coke, please."

"Hannah?"

"House white for me, thanks."

"Psycho?"

I narrowed my eyes at Annie. "If you're going to call me that, I'm leaving."

"You're so easy to wind up," she teased. "Usual?"

I grunted.

Beside me, Louise spun around on her seat and scanned the room. I saw her wave to someone and my eyes shot to the recipient of her attention. Liam. Of course it was.

He excused himself from his drinking buddies and made his way towards us. Great—now *he* could wear the psycho label. I backed away and took a place on the other side of Connor. Liam greeted us with a far-too-cheery *hello*, casually elbowed himself in next to Louise and put his arm on her shoulders. He didn't even know her—what made him think he could drape himself all over her? I felt a protective growl rise up from the pit of my stomach that was obviously audible, if the nudge from Connor was anything to go by.

"You hungry?" Hannah asked.

"Hilarious." It was hard to concentrate, with Louise laughing at something Liam had just said. That soft, caramel voice infiltrated my body and made my dick stir again. Just what I needed. Annie placed Louise's drink in front of her and turned to Connor.

"You all eating tonight?"

"I think I'll have the Valley burger." Hannah picked up her drink and took a long sip.

"Connor?"

"Green curry mussels for me."

"Reid?"

"Steak."

I reached for my card and remembered I hadn't asked Louise. "Hey."

She glared at me. "I have a name."

"Do you want something to eat? I'm ordering for us." I slid the menu down the bar to her.

"Chicken burger, please," she said to Annie.

"Thanks, Annie," I said.

Annie tapped the orders into the computer, I waved my card across the machine, and Annie moved down the counter to another customer. I kept my eyes on Liam's roving hands. Who knew how many beers he'd already consumed?

"Hey," Hannah nudged me. "I was just thanking your brother for taking Louise on. The job will help take her mind off what happened in Wellington."

What happened in Wellington?

"She'll make a great addition to the team," Connor said.

"As long as she stays out of my way, we'll get along fine," I grumbled.

"You're a barrel of laughs tonight," Hannah said.

Annie's sister, Rachel, hit the bar for a drinks order. They were all working tonight, even Ellie—and Matt's son, Stuart, was running dishes between the kitchen and the bar.

"Reid. You're looking... What's the word?" Rachel paused for effect and lifted her eyes briefly to the ceiling. "Rehabilitated." She shouldered me in a friendly gesture and unloaded her tray. We'd been out on a couple of double dates with Connor and Annie, but the magic wasn't there for either of us.

"Very funny. From what?" I asked.

"Your former drug-dealing days. You also look like you joined the Mob while you were away." She made a show of squeezing my bicep. "Nice. Have you got new ink too?"

I growled and she laughed, moving in to give me a hug. It was nice, but I felt like I'd become the town's only source of entertainment these last few months, and the jibes were wearing a little thin.

Meanwhile, behind her, Louise slipped off her stool and followed Liam across to his table. I could feel a surge of something that might have been jealousy, except I couldn't be jealous of Liam. He introduced her to everyone and dragged a chair in for her from a neighbouring table.

Great. I turned my attention back to Rachel, who was talking to Hannah about something that didn't matter, and Connor was busy making those stupid fucking eyes at Annie as she leaned over the bar towards him. I was starting to feel like a fifth wheel.

"There's a table," Hannah suddenly said, getting up. We all threaded our way through the patrons to a table just vacated by an elderly couple. Ellie was clearing empty glasses and dishes as we made ourselves comfortable. I took a seat that gave me the perfect line of sight at Liam and his mates as they laughed and drank and shared plates of hot nachos and loaded wedges. And one cherry-red earring as it bobbed and swung with each word and movement. I pushed back and stood. Louise could come and sit with us.

"Sit down," Hannah said, reaching out to catch my hand. "I want to talk to you."

Resigned, I sat down again. "What about?" I knew what was coming. Hannah was my conscience.

"You."

"Me? You know everything there is to know about me. I'm an open book."

She smiled. She knew damn well I was blowing it out my arse because in truth, the opposite was true.

"Tonight, my friend, you are also acting like Lou's T-shirt suggests. But ignoring that, I want to know how you're doing."

"This is not the place nor the time, Han."

"It's as good as any. Spill." She took a sip of her wine.

"There's nothing to tell."

"I know you, Reid Hamilton. You're bottling it up. I want the old Reid back."

"You're imagining things," I told her, keeping my eyes on the neighbouring table.

"I don't think so. The Reid who got out is bitter, twisted and reserved. Not to mention a grumpy shit."

"Gee, thanks, Han. Prison changes people. It's a cold, hard fact." I was far more interested in Liam and the arm he had casually laying across the back of Louise's chair. He had his hand resting on her shoulder again.

"So, when are you going to ditch the attitude?" she continued.

"I don't have an attitude."

"Hello?" She waved her hand in front of my face.

I dragged my eyes from Liam's table back to Hannah.

"It's me you're talking to, and I can see right through you. I suspect you're also harbouring a grudge."

"I'm not," I snapped.

"Mars to Reid?"

"I don't think Louise should mix with Liam and his mates, all right?" I was beyond rational conversation now.

"Why on earth not?"

"She's only known him two fucking minutes."

"Stop swearing at me."

"Sorry."

"He's one of your employees. You know the man. If he was dodgy, you wouldn't have employed him."

"Doesn't make any difference."

"She's due some harmless fun and if I didn't know any different, I'd think you were jealous."

Jealous? Of Liam? I doubt it. Or did I? "I'm just looking out for her," I mumbled.

"Getting back to *you*—you realise holding a grudge and carrying that attitude around will eat you up and make you a sad old man with no friends except me."

Liam's chair had inched itself right up beside Louise's. His leg was now touching hers. I grunted my displeasure. Now who was in whose personal space?

"Reid, you've got to let stuff go."

"Han, I'm fine. I'm back at work. Sleeping in my own bed. I'm eating whatever I want and not some predetermined menu of tasteless shit they pass off as food. And I can run whenever and wherever I want, instead of the confines of a prison yard under the watchful eye of some over-zealous guard. What more could I possibly want?"

"How about inner peace? Calm? Happiness? Someone to share a bed with at night? Friends you'd trust with your life?"

"They're overrated. Besides, I have you."

"I'm really worried about you, Reid."

"I don't see *you* with anyone special."

"I don't have time for relationships. Anyway, don't turn the situation around, this isn't about me."

Our meals arrived, and I was relieved when she shifted her attention to the burger in front of her. I knew she was just looking out for me. That's what she did—what we both did. But I was just looking out for Louise, too.

"We all need friends," she continued after a few minutes.

"If I need another friend, I'll get a dog." I took a bite of my steak. It was cooked to perfection. "I know you mean well, Han, but I don't need your psych evaluation." Over her shoulder, I saw Liam lean into Lou's ear and whisper something. The woman threw her head back in laughter, and Liam's free hand reached out, and then his beer was knocked over and spilling over the table and over Louise. A rumbling deep down inside me clawed its ugly way out. "That's it." I pushed my chair back and marched over there.

A hush descended over the table. "Come on, Louise, we should leave. You don't need drunks spilling their drinks on you." I took her arm and pulled her to her feet; her chair tumbled over backwards as she stood.

"Let go of my arm," she demanded, trying to right the chair. "It was a simple accident."

Liam stood. "Hey, boss. It's all good. I'll see she gets cleaned up and home okay once she's finished eating."

"That's what I'm afraid of," I muttered.

"Hey, bro." I felt Connor's hand on my shoulder.

"This has got nothing to do with you, Connor."

"You're messing with my staff."

I stood my ground, facing off with Liam. I might have been doing the nostril flaring thing again—I couldn't tell. Lou pulled her arm free from my grasp at the same time as Connor pulled me back a step.

"Thanks for your concern," Louise said, "but I'm old enough to choose who I want to talk to, and you know what?"

I eyeballed her as if she'd just suggested I should get my dick pierced.

"I can also get myself home."

"We're leaving," I ground out. An expectant silence had settled over the entire bar as everyone waited to see what was going to happen next. "What're you all staring at?" I shouted at the room. Heads turned away as patrons pretended not to be interested in what was going down.

Matt appeared at the table. "Reid, buddy. Sit back down and finish your meal or take off. I don't want any trouble in here tonight."

My brother still had his hand on my shoulder. "Sit down and act like a grown-up."

"Fuck off, Connor."

"Reid." His voice dropped an octave in warning. "Louise is a grown woman. She doesn't need a minder."

"You can take me home," Hannah said. I hadn't noticed her appear at my side with two takeaway bags. "Let's go." I felt her fingers curl around my hand as Connor sidestepped to let us past.

Liam sat back down, but Louise stepped towards me, arms crossed over her ridiculous T-shirt. "If this is how you're going to act, then the job's off."

"Ignore his behaviour, Louise," Connor said. "He's picked up some bad habits while he's been away. The garage needs you. We both really need you."

"Right now, I'm finding that hard to believe," she said, staring me down.

Hannah pulled at my hand. "My burger's getting cold, Reid. Let's go."

I turned and high-tailed it across the room, and out into the night.

"That's exactly what I was talking about," Hannah said, clicking the seatbelt into place a few moments later. "You've got to ease up on yourself, Reid. Not everyone has an ulterior motive."

I kept my eyes on the road, my knuckles turning white on the steering wheel as I drove.

"Not everyone needs protecting, either. Lou is having a friendly night out. You should have just let her just enjoy herself."

Was she ever going to drop it? I pulled the truck to the kerb.

"I know it can't be easy trying to slot back into life. This is a small town, and sometimes, small towns can be smothering. But you've got good friends. It doesn't make you any less of a man to relax a little with us."

"Just give me the damn bag," I muttered, taking it from her.

"Do you want to come up for a beer?"

I sighed. "I'm sorry, Han. I don't deserve your friendship. Sometimes I think I lean on you too much."

"Nonsense. You're not getting rid of me that easily—just ease up on Lou. Okay? She had a shitty time of it, and she needs all the friends she can find."

"I promise I'll be the best version of me from now on."

She grinned. "Just be yourself. That's the version I love."

5

LOU

MONDAY MORNING, I WOKE at an ungodly hour. I couldn't sleep. The fact that I was starting work this morning with the incredibly moody, and far too sexy, Reid Hamilton, certainly didn't help.

I'd heard the door to the flat squeak open and close around four-thirty, and knew Hannah had gone downstairs to start work. If I couldn't sleep, I might as well go down and help, or just keep her company.

I rolled out of bed, showered, and wrapped myself in a towel. Then I added gel to my hair, followed by green and purple chalk, and scrunched it. Satisfied with the look, I applied various shades of green eyeshadow and my smiley-face earrings.

Ready for whatever the day had to throw at me, I was finally taking charge of my life and being the real me—not some snivelling people-pleaser who worried about what everyone else thought. Today might actually be fun.

I was wearing another one of the T-shirts my BFF Ed had made for his online store. I'd known him since high school days; he was much more entrepreneurial than me. He'd started printing T-shirts in his parents' garage before he'd left school, and they'd become so popular he had to rent space. After I'd got my degree in web design and marketing, he employed me to make him look professional and develop a social media presence. We had this agreement where if I gave him a great slogan for a tee, he'd give me a shirt for free when they rolled off the production line. Ed-E's Tees was making a name for themselves now and he employed eighteen staff across his small factory and three stores, and I had a case full of shirts—one for every occasion.

It was quarter past five when I let myself into the café; Hannah's didn't open until six-thirty, and I had almost three hours to kill before I started work.

"Morning," I yelled, interrupting Han's singalong to the radio. I helped myself to an apron off a hook by the back door.

"Morning," Hannah called over the whirring of a large cake mixer anchored to the floor, its gloopy contents in a synchronised dance sequence with a large wire beater. "You're up early."

"Couldn't sleep. What can I do?"

"Can you lay out the four pie trays and put the tins in them for me?" She pointed at the large wooden trays sitting under the far countertop.

"Sure." I was done in five minutes, so I went through to the café floor, took the chairs down from the tables, and put sugar shakers and small jars of daisies on each one. Then I turned the coffee machine on, filled the grinder with beans and went back to see what else needed doing. Hannah was rolling a large sheet of pastry across the empty pie tins.

"I'll leave you to do these. You'll find four labelled containers of various fillings in the back fridge. There should be just enough to do one tray with about a cup of meat to each pie case." She turned the mixer off and lifted it onto the only bench with space. The pies would last for two days, if it was quiet, before she'd have to make more.

I finished filling the pie tins, then made a flat white for Hannah and a latte for me. I prided myself on my ability to make a great coffee. Before Jayden had bled me dry, I'd bought a high-end coffee machine to use at home and had become proficient at churning out great coffee.

Watching Han, I marvelled at how competent she was. She had everything organised like clockwork. Things went in and came out of the three big commercial ovens with precision timing. She had sausage rolls and other savouries cooling on the large metal racks, the pies were gone from the bench, and she had the donuts proving on wooden racks waiting to be cooked in hot oil. The whole café was filled with the aroma of freshly baked goodness. My stomach rumbled.

The back door opened and the tall, slim figure of William Sadler stepped into the kitchen. At least ten inches taller than Han and six years older, Will took charge of deep-frying the donuts and making some of the sandwiches and slices. Although he officially only worked Mondays, Wednesdays and Fridays, he could be found here more often than not.

"Morning," Hannah and I called in unison.

"Morning, ladies," he replied, dropping his car keys on the small table in the staff alcove as he aproned up. "I heard you had a visitor, Hannah."

"Will, meet my cousin, Louise. Our mums are sisters."

"It's nice to meet you," I said, offering my hand. He took it, his large, soft fingers curling around mine. His eyes sparkled despite the early hour.

"Nice to meet you, too. I heard you're staying with our Hannah for a while."

"For as long as she'll have me."

"Well, you're safe in this town with us. We'll kick his butt back to where it came from if he shows his face anywhere near here."

I caught the look that passed between Hannah and Will before I turned away to hide my embarrassment. Only Hannah knew why I was here, so I'm guessing she had given Will the lowdown.

"Let me know if you need an escort anywhere," he offered.

"Thanks—I think."

Rolling his sleeves up, he turned his attention to the deep fryer before inspecting the trays of proving dough. "They look good." He moved to the basin and washed his hands. He acted as though I was an everyday occurrence in the café's kitchen.

"I heard it's your first day at the garage today," Will said, making himself at home.

"Sure is." I'd almost forgotten about it until now.

"Not nervous about working with a hardened criminal?" He checked the temperature of the oil in the vat and switched the production line on.

"Will..." Hannah cautioned.

"Just joking."

"I don't believe Reid was guilty of anything," I told him, "except perhaps, of being a stubborn mule." I leaned on the end of his bench with my coffee and watched him.

"Oh, I don't know," Will continued. "There are some around here who would say his good looks and all that sex appeal are illegal." I caught him wink at Hannah.

"Very funny." I rolled my eyes and ignored how flushed I suddenly felt. "Those people probably all wear corrective lenses and have never met a real man."

He gave a hearty laugh as he began to drop the dough into the hot oil. "You're quite the expert, aren't you?" he said.

"Not with my terrible track record." The donuts smelled divine as they started to turn golden-brown and move through the oil. Will retrieved a large plastic container of cinnamon sugar and slid it into position at the end of the machine. The first batch flipped over with the help of an automatic arm under the surface. Slowly they exited the oil and dropped into the tub of sugar and cinnamon. My stomach rumbled again, and I thought it wise that I head for the sink and make a start on washing the growing stack of dishes.

"None of us are experts when it comes to relationships," Hannah said, having deposited a tray of melting moment biscuits in the oven.

"What about the high-school sweethearts who get married, have kids and live a long and happy life together?"

"They're few and far between," Hannah answered, collecting the ingredients for a batch of her famous brownies. She made them every day. There were rumours that if you were in the right frame of mind, Han's triple chocolate and caramel brownies could give you a food orgasm—a food blogger had once said so in a rave review: *"Every mouthful sent thrills through me until I was a quivering mess. These brownies will spoil you like no man can, and I dare you to eat more than one!"* Now, random strangers called in on a regular basis to test the theory, but I hadn't tried them yet. I wasn't brave enough, in case I exhibited signs of the fabled climax and embarrassed myself in public.

"When you get to the stage where you think you know everything there is to know about someone, that's when you start taking them for granted," Will stated, as he jiggled a batch of donuts in the sugar and replaced them with a second container. "You miss things—little things."

Hannah started cracking eggs into a jug. "Totally. It's the opposite of when you start a relationship, and you notice all the charming things about each other."

"What was your wife like, Will? Did you know her, Hannah?"

The eggs slid into the mixer and Hannah handed me the empty jug for washing. "I met her at the tennis club one summer when I was in my early twenties. We used to meet up and play a game now and again, but I didn't really know her that well. She was such a lovely person. Never said a bad word about anyone and I remember her infectious laugh."

"She had the ability to read people," Will added. "If she sensed you'd had a bad day, she'd have you laughing in no time, and the day was forgotten." He'd lost his wife seven years ago and had never looked at another woman since, even though the reports from Han over the years suggested he'd been on every eligible woman's hit list.

Hannah walked past Will and stopped, running her hand down Will's arm. "Losing someone hurts more than you realise."

He nodded. "It sure does, but it was a long time ago. The hurt's gone but I have plenty of memories. It was a little different for you, wasn't it?"

Hannah unhooked the mixer bowl and lifted it onto the bench. "It was. By the time things were settled, I was pleased to see my ex go."

Interesting. I was getting the sense I was the third wheel again as they exchanged looks of compassion and... something else I couldn't read. I think for a moment they forgot I was even there. Was there something going on between these two? Han had told me she was sworn off men. I sat my coffee on the windowsill above the big double sink and plunged my hands into hot soapy water. There was lots to think about.

The back door opened and Grace, Han's other staff member, stepped into the kitchen, shoulder bag in one hand, two copies of the *Riverford Valley Morning Post* for the café in the other. I checked the clock above the door. It read quarter past six. I still had over two hours until I needed to head to the garage—not that I was counting.

"Grace, meet Lou," said Hannah. "She's staying with me for a while."

"Hi, Lou. I think I met you once before. Many years ago."

"Really? When?"

"I was working part-time as the librarian, and if I remember right, you came in and borrowed books with Hannah's library card."

Ah—the book borrowing. I couldn't remember her at all. She looked to be in her late forties, with a smiling face but her grey hair pinned up in a bun at the back, made me think she was older. Greenstone drops hung from her ears. She looked the type you'd want to spill your secrets to. I made a mental note to keep her at arm's length and went back to washing the dishes.

"Grace looks after front of house," Hannah told me, trying to reach a tub of something from a top shelf.

"Here, let me get that," Will said, rushing to Hannah's rescue. He slid a plastic container down and handed it over. I thought I noticed a look flicker between them again. Maybe I secretly wished there was something. My cousin deserved a second chance at happiness and, by all accounts, Will Sadler did too.

"Thanks for setting everything up out here, Lou!" Grace called from the café floor. "Old Mr Taylor is already outside waiting for his coffee and the morning paper. I swear he gets earlier every day."

Everyone worked in an unspoken order. I finished drying the dishes and helped Grace fill the cabinets with mouth-watering trays of goodies. There were five customers waiting in line when she unlocked the front door and shifted the *Open* sign out onto the pavement. While she sorted customers and their orders, I set up a couple of tables outside. Then I manned the coffee machine.

By eight-thirty I'd made around twenty-seven coffees and Grace had already sold an entire tray of donuts plus two dozen pies. I peeled off my apron, hung it up and grabbed a sandwich to eat on the way to work.

"Here," Han said, handing me a brown paper bag.

"What's this?"

"Donuts for the boys' morning tea," Hannah said.

"They'll think I'm greasing up to them for something."

"No, they won't. They'll think it's a nice touch on your first day."

"Good luck!" Will called as I headed back upstairs to put lippy on and grab my bag.

I stopped off at the florist and bought a small bunch of chrysanthemums. I was going to need something to help pretty up the environment.

Liam waved at me when I entered the workshop and made my way towards the reception. No sign of Reid or Tyler. Connor was working on a car, hoisted high above him.

"Morning, Connor," I called. He looked down from whatever it was he was fiddling with, laughed when he noticed the flowers, and gave me a cheery good morning. "Anything you want me to make a start on first?"

"You might like to arrange your desk how you'd like it."

I snuck into the customer waiting room and came to a stop. Over the weekend, the guys had moved the furniture and placed an ugly pasta sauce jar on my desk with a bunch of carnations in it and a note that said, *Welcome, Louise.* I noticed their welcome hadn't extended to cleaning the desk.

Deciding to add my flowers to the jar, I searched drawers and cupboards, but found nothing I could use to cut the stems. Somebody here had to have scissors. On my way to drop off the donuts in the kitchen, I walked through to Reid's office to ask him for some—but it was empty.

The left-hand drawer of Reid's desk was stuffed with papers, which sprung out at me when I pulled it open. *Shit.* I hurriedly squashed them back into place and squeezed it closed. What a frigging nightmare. How he ran a business, I did not know. The drawer underneath held what looked like car parts. As well as spark plugs and batteries, there were spanners, a couple of paint tester pots, a large padlock, various keys, plus other stuff I had no idea what it was. With still no scissors, I moved to the next drawer. It slid open with ease to reveal an excess of stationery, more spark plugs, a packet of Pall Mall, three cigarette lighters, a bunch of keys, Sellotape, a king-sized bar of Dairy Milk chocolate and two old lotto tickets. You could learn a lot about a man by what he kept in his drawer. As I rummaged, I kept my fingers crossed that there were also a pair of—

"Having fun?"

I slammed the drawer shut, completely forgetting my hand was still inside it.

"*Fudge!*" I quickly pulled it back open and took my fingers out, flicking them about to relieve the pain. "Do you have to sneak up on people?"

"When they're snooping in my office, I do."

"I was looking for scissors." My fingers were throbbing. Great.

"You could've asked." He gave me a lopsided grin until his eyes dropped to the words on my T-shirt. *This shirt belongs to your brother.*

His eyes narrowed, and the smile fell away. He reached out, took my hand and checked my fingers, one by one. My gut burned and I felt his energy flood my body. My fingers pulsed painfully for a totally different reason. His eyes lifted to mine, and thankfully, he dropped my hand before I combusted.

"You'll find them over there." He nodded towards an old cardboard box—the type reams of photocopy paper came in. It was sitting on the only other piece of furniture in his office, a filing cabinet. "Maybe hold your hand under the cold tap for a minute or two. What's in the bag?" he asked, spying the bag on his desk.

"Donuts." I searched in the box. It was also full of tools: hammer, Stanley knives, stapler, an assortment of screwdrivers, a measuring tape, spanners and, at last, near the bottom, scissors. I took what I wanted and left the room, feeling like I'd escaped an electrical storm. In the hall, I paused and sucked in a deep breath. It was like there hadn't been enough oxygen in the space for both of us. I couldn't even remember what I wanted the damn scissors for.

I went to the kitchen, held my fingers under the cold water and then hunted the cupboards for cleaning products. Nothing except a bottle of washing-up liquid.

I remembered the flowers and headed back to reception. I would walk to the town's only supermarket and get fresh milk, some Spray and Wipe and a clean dish cloth. I grabbed my bag.

"Louise."

I could feel lightning strike the walls of my stomach. I turned to see Reid standing behind me, arms crossed over his packed chest.

"Leaving already?"

"I'm going to the supermarket to buy supplies. I won't be long."

"For the garage?"

"Yes."

"Then I'll take you."

I rolled my eyes and watched him push his overalls down his body to reveal a chest-hugging tee tucked into his jeans. A man who stripped wherever he felt like it. My heart rate stumbled and I felt heat spread across my face. Turning, I fled the reception before he could see it.

6

REID

"LISTEN, LOUISE. IF YOU need cleaning products for this place, then I'll run you to the supermarket and the business will pay for them."

"I'm perfectly capable of going by myself. I don't need any hand-holding."

She was the most stubborn woman I had ever met. "Did you bring your car?"

"No, but—"

"Yeah, so it's going to take you a good hour to walk there and back. I'm not paying you to go walking all over town."

She glowered at me and stormed off through the workshop. I grabbed my keys and followed her. She was waiting beside my truck by the time I got there, arms crossed, one foot tapping. I unlocked the vehicle and opened her door for her.

"We've got to work together, so let's try to keep our relationship civil." It was the best I could do for now.

"There is no relationship." She clicked her seatbelt into place and refolded her arms across her chest. "Just get in the damn truck."

I felt like grabbing her by the shoulders, hauling her butt out of the truck and kissing those pouty lips so damn hard. "Thanks for the donuts," I finally said, a flash of guilt sweeping through me.

"Don't thank me. They're from Han."

"But you brought them for me."

"They were for everyone. Don't read anything into it."

"Oh, I won't." I smiled. We shopped in silence, and by the time we got back to the truck, I had a shopping bag full of cleaning products plus fresh milk, tea, coffee and three new tea towels.

"Let me carry those." I offered as we climbed out of the truck back at the garage.

"No, thank you," she said as we both reached for the bags at the same time, my hand closing over hers. She stopped, paralysed for a moment, before pulling her hand swiftly away. The softness of her skin and the scent of honeysuckle was messing with my mind again. She had disappeared before I remembered what the hell I was supposed to be doing.

I stalked back inside, my mind replaying the time all those years ago when Louise had been staying with Hannah and her parents. I was almost finished with my mechanics apprenticeship, while Han was studying at business college. When she managed to get time off to come home, we spent most days fooling around and having fun. We went camping up the valley, or hung out at the lake, met with friends or went to movies.

But the summer Louise arrived changed a lot of things. There was something about her that haunted me. She tagged along with Han, and every damn time I looked at her, she was watching me. She always turned her head away or pretended to be reading, but by the time she had to go home, she had my hormones raging on all cylinders.

And then that last weekend, when we'd all gone to the lake to swim, Louise and Connor had come with us. I tried to coax Louise into the water, but she preferred to read. Connor and I had stripped off and plunged in. Han kept her bikini on. And every time I looked in Louise's direction, she lifted her book a little higher. Pretended not to notice or be interested. I had to keep reminding myself she was only sixteen and I was an adult.

The next morning, I'd decided the right thing to do was apologise. I should never have taken such liberties. But that backfired too when I found her on her own in Han's parents' kitchen. Her hair was braided to the side and hung over her shoulder. She was wearing a sleeveless tank and frayed shorts that I'd never seen her wear before. The more I watched from the door, the more entranced I became. When the opportunity presented itself, I'd kissed her. I'd stood there confused and I imagine she would have been shocked, then she'd run out of the room. Looking back, I had realised at that moment, that Han wasn't the girl for me, not when I felt so messed up.

Hannah and I broke up a few months later, and then Han fell head over heels for Steve Reynes, so I obviously wasn't the right guy for her, either. The guy was a total douche bag, but Han and I had made a pact to stay best friends no matter who we ended up with. Reynes tolerated me, and I tolerated him. She went on to marry the douche bag, but I never met anyone I wanted to settle down with. I didn't blame anyone for that—I'd dated a couple of girls after Han, but in all honesty, I was happier on my own and I wondered if I'd ever get to see Louise again. The thought that I'd never got the chance to apologise to her for my bad behaviour had stuck with me.

I had a feeling the town was running tabs on Connor and me, and who would make it down the aisle first; their money was on me. The return was higher.

"Are you going to help get that Escort done?" Connor asked, leaning against the doorframe of my office.

I lifted my head from my hands. "Sure."

"What? No bite? You feeling okay?"

"I was just remembering some shit that I didn't need to remember."

"From when you were inside?" Connor asked.

"It doesn't matter." And as if on cue, Louise walked past the door in a cloud of honeysuckle, with a bucket in her hand.

"What are you up to?" Connor called after her.

"Cleaning the reception," she called back. "If I'm cleaning my desk, I might as well do the whole room."

Connor lowered his voice. "I think we've employed a monster. Hey, are those donuts?"

I did a couple of hours on the car, then took off home. I needed exercise. I changed into my running gear and pounded the streets until the damn image of Louise stopped following me. Every time I'd walked into reception, there she was, cleaning surfaces. Making our lives tidier. Each time our eyes met. Each time lingering a little longer.

I ran sixteen kilometres before I started to tire and turned back.

She was still with me.

Later that afternoon, I returned to the garage, finished the remaining work on a car, cleaned it and blacked the tyres. I had my standards; I got a kick out of knowing a car was leaving the workshop in better condition than when it arrived. If we were busy, it didn't get a clean, but we were hardly rushed off our feet at the moment.

At the end of the day, I handed over the keys to one pleased owner and packed up. It was quarter to five, the workshop was closed, the radio was off and everyone had left. I pushed the large button that lowered the oversized roller door, securing the workshop.

It was quiet in reception. I removed my boots and peeled the overalls off my shoulders to the floor. In the warmer months, I usually only wore a pair of shorts under them, but today I was wearing jeans and my normal tee.

I looked around me. Louise had done a great job of cleaning the guest lounge. It looked user-friendly again. Everything looked hygienic and the coffee rings from the table had gone, replaced by a small selection of automotive magazines. The water cooler had a fresh stack of paper cups, and the wastebasket had been emptied. The flowers sat on the reception counter alongside an array of business cards and some client satisfaction forms—God knows where she'd found those.

I gathered up my overalls and boots and walked through to my office, took a seat behind my desk and kicked the computer into life. Opening the program we used for job details, I one-finger typed the hours I had worked on the Escort, and the parts I'd replaced. It was a four-hundred-dollar job and wouldn't make a difference to our bank balance.

When I finished, I hit print and turned the computer off. We had three more cars booked in for tomorrow: two for fitness checks, and one for a water pump replacement. Simple jobs, again. Tyler and Liam could work on those while I made more headway on the restoration project.

I sighed heavily and leaned on my elbows, massaging my temples. We could do with at least ten more bookings a week, or we were going to have to lay someone off. I didn't want that on my shoulders, knowing it was because of me we were in this situation—and that the person we laid off would have to be Louise. And possibly Liam.

I pulled the drawer open and reached for the emergency pack of smokes, then thought better of it and pushed it closed again. I didn't need a cigarette. I needed to go home, eat and sleep. With my boots laced up, I grabbed my jacket from the chair it was draped over. As I flicked the office light off, there was a crash. Was someone breaking in?

I moved silently, checking for anything unusual, and then I heard it. Muffled crying coming from the kitchen. I stepped into the doorframe.

"What the hell?" Louise was sitting on the floor, gently rubbing her ankle, an overturned stool lying on the floor next to her. "Are you okay?"

"Gee," she sniffed, "thanks for asking."

"What are you still doing here? The place is locked up."

"What do you think I was doing? Breaking and entering?"

With every breath I sucked in, the tension in my head tightened. "That's not what I meant."

There was soapy water in the sink, and one of the kitchen cupboards was open. Damn it. "Were you still cleaning? You should have finished up a couple of hours ago."

"No. I was having my hair done," she drawled.

Sarcasm didn't look good on her.

"You do think that, don't you?"

"I do think what?" I had no idea what the fuck she was talking about. Maybe she'd hit her head in the fall.

"You think I was stealing something!" The pain disappeared from her face, replaced by anger. I felt a knot twist deep in my stomach.

"Don't be ridiculous. You work in a garage. What would you possibly want to steal? A spark plug gapper? Let me look at your ankle." I crouched down beside her and she flinched as I took her ankle in my hands. For a fleeting moment our eyes met, and I knew she was remembering another time when I'd put my hands on her and the kiss we'd shared. And then the memories were gone, and anger crowded her face again.

"I told you, I'm fine," she snapped. "Just help me up."

"Nothing's broken, but we need to get it checked." It was already starting to swell.

"Why aren't you listening to me? Just help me up." She grabbed the overturned stool and attempted to leverage herself up, wincing as she tried to put weight on her ankle.

Unable to stand it any longer, I scooped her up and carefully manoeuvred her out of the kitchen.

"What are you doing? Put me down!"

"I'm putting you in my truck and taking you to Accident and Emergency, that's what I'm doing."

"I can ring Han to come and get me. Just leave me here."

"No way. You're my employee, and I want to make sure you're okay." She was lighter than I'd imagined, and after lifting her into the passenger seat, I worked to concentrate on the traffic while I drove across town to the after-hours medical centre.

"Stay right there," I ordered when we arrived, swinging down out of the truck.

"You are not carrying me in."

"I'm not letting you *walk* in." But by the time I'd got to her door, she was already out and hopping on one foot. She was testing my patience. I ignored her protests and bent, picking her up with ease. My senses filled with honeysuckle again, and something else—lemon-scented cleaning products—reminding me she was in this position because she was cleaning up years of our bad habits and lack of standards around cleanliness. Things were going to change.

"Don't think you have to take care of me because I work for you. I'm not your responsibility."

"Don't I know it," I mumbled, kicking the Hilux door shut and crossing the parking lot to a somewhat quiet hospital.

"Nothing broken," the registrar on duty confirmed an hour later, after the X-ray had been taken. "It's a simple sprain, but you need to rest that foot. Stay off it. Use an ice pack on it four or five times a day and keep it compressed. That will help with the swelling. A nurse will be in shortly to strap it for you."

"Thank you, doctor," Louise said. "How long do I have to keep off it?"

"It's not too serious, so I would suggest you rest it for a week."

"A week?" Louise's face fell, and I thought she was going to cry. My guts twisted and I growled unspoken obscenities.

Both heads turned in my direction. I shrugged my shoulders. "What?"

"The more you rest it, the faster it'll heal." The doc turned and left Louise and me on our own. She didn't look good at all.

"Why are you looking at me like that?" she hissed.

"You're not sore anywhere else, are you?"

She shook her head, but her face told me there was something upsetting her, and it wasn't her foot.

I narrowed my eyes at her. "Are you sure everything's alright?"

"No, actually, I'm not," she snapped.

Whoa. I leaned back from the force of her voice.

"I don't have a home. I don't have a proper job, and I'm living with my cousin. My ex took all my savings. I'm stuck working with you. And now I've got to sit on my backside for a week." She waved a hand towards her swollen ankle, which was colouring nicely. "No, things are not okay. Okay?" She gulped down a breath and swiped the back of her hand across her face.

Oh, shit. Tears. I was allergic to them. Especially when they ran down the face of a beautiful woman. "I would have thought working with me and Connor was a consolation."

"Fuck off, Reid."

My attempt at lightening the mood obviously wasn't appreciated. I glanced around the miniscule cubicle, feeling slightly uncomfortable while she blew her nose on some tissues. Her words kept playing in my head.

"Your ex stole from you?" With everything she'd said, I was stuck on that one piece of information. Suddenly, it didn't matter that someone had locked me up for a crime I didn't commit. Or that I'd had to face hardships and humiliation like I'd never known before. Had to take orders from an overweight, uptight prison warden with a god complex. All that mattered was that someone had taken advantage of Louise. Some lowlife who deserved to be taught a lesson. I put my arm around her shoulders and hugged her to me. She blew into the tissues but didn't shrug me off.

"You'd think I would've learnt the first time."

The first time? "It's happened before?" I could feel the anger surge through my body.

"Twice."

This was going from bad to worse. "How the hell...?" I let her go. "You had three boyfriends that ripped you off? Did you go to the police?"

"I was too embarrassed." She sniffed out an answer.

"But, buttercup, these guys are nothing but criminals. They get their kicks out of preying on kind, good-natured, caring women. You can't let them get away with it."

"I'm an idiot. Besides, it's too late now. I've moved on. But all my attempts to start afresh, as a strong independent woman who doesn't take shit from anyone, are turning to rubbish. I'm failing at that, too."

"Actually, you've been pretty impressive up till now."

"Really?" She brought her eyes to mine. They were streaked with black stuff, but at least her eyelashes were still in place.

"Don't worry about work. You can still do the accounts, but maybe the cleaning has to wait."

"I'm not worried—"

"Miss Adair?" A nurse swept open the curtain and placed a roll of elastic bandage on the bed beside her ankle.

Louise nodded while I fumed. Men who preyed on vulnerable women were no better than cockroaches, and deserved to be stomped on.

"I'll strap your ankle for you. If you can follow the R.I.C.E. principles—rest, ice, compression and elevation—it should be back to normal in a week or two."

"I'll be back in a moment," I told Louise. I had to get some air and calm down. And I also had a couple of phone calls to make.

7

LOU

BY NOON THE FOLLOWING day, I was bored enough to actually want to go to the office, even if it meant I would see Reid. It had taken me a long time to try and forget the feel of his chest as I was cradled against it. The smell of engine oil would be forever stuck in my nostrils and remind me of him.

When I was sixteen, I could have sunk into his arms and stayed there. How many times had I imagined holding his hand? Hours spent wondering what it would be like to have him put his arms around me, like he did with Hannah, and kiss me.

But I wasn't sixteen now.

I needed to be doing something. I was so annoyed at myself for falling off the stool. And even more embarrassed that I'd blabbed to Reid about my previous relationship failures. I hopped from the sofa to the apartment's kitchen. It was near impossible to carry anything on crutches. I filled a glass with water and drank it, leaving the empty on the kitchen counter.

At one o'clock, Hannah popped up with lunch, and Connor called in shortly after with flowers and told me if I needed anything at all, he and Reid were there for me. Just name it, he said, and they'd see to it.

"Bring me the accounts and I'll start work on them."

"Nope. You're officially on sick leave. You need to rest."

I screamed.

He laughed and promised to come back tomorrow and go over the wages process with me. I sat on the sofa with my leg up as we talked about what they already had in place.

"I've got some friends coming around for dinner tonight. How about you and Hannah join us? If you feel up to it, that is."

"I don't know."

"There's always plenty of food. Reid will be working the grill, I'll be on music and drinks, and Annie's in charge of the kitchen."

"What should I bring?"

"Food has already been allocated, so I wouldn't worry about it. Hannah never lets us down with her supply of disgustingly good desserts. We'll see you about seven," he said, standing and heading for the door.

I nodded. At two o'clock, Will called in on his way home to say hi and ask if I needed anything. I decided Han had the best circle of friends and I was lucky they accepted me as one of them.

In need of something to occupy myself with, I reached for my phone and tapped in the keywords: *Reid Hamil-*

ton. It brought up a selection of articles and images. The photos of Reid were mostly mugshots attached to articles on his arrest. In one, Reid had turned to look at the photographer as he was being led to a waiting police car. His wrists were cuffed, his eyes dark with anger, and I imagined how furious he must have been. I knew as well as Hannah did that he was no drug dealer. His parents would turn in their graves at how their son had been treated by this community.

I scrolled down. Article after article covered the court case. A photo of Reid and Connor in suits with a third man—I assumed, a lawyer—walking into the courthouse took my eye. I enlarged the half that showed Reid. He was clean-shaven, his hair neat. The way he filled out the suit jacket—I fanned myself.

The cut of his pants as he stepped up towards the doorway left little to the imagination. I had never seen him in a suit before. It was obvious the judge had been a male and not a female. No woman in her right mind could sentence a man as sexually attractive as Reid Hamilton to time behind bars. That in itself was an injustice.

I found an article on a Lucy Hamilton winning some sort of racing award, and another on a fire in a nightclub owned by a Jaxon Hamilton. Reid was in a photo taken at a society wedding standing beside a guy named Aiden Hamilton—Connor on the other side. How the heck was *either brother* still single?

I scrolled some more, but couldn't find any website or social media pages for the garage. Link after link took me to Reid, as if the world was trying to tell me something.

Scrolling further, I found a photo taken several years earlier. Dressed in rugby shorts that hugged his arse and thighs, and a rugby shirt tight enough to give me hives just looking at it, Reid's hair was mussed and he had grass stains on his arms and legs. I raised an eyebrow. Damn, the man had it going for him in spades. "No. Not happening," I said, trying to stop my mind from wandering down the wrong path.

I scrolled back up to the original image of him in a suit. No harm in taking one more look. Remembering what was underneath those layers made my skin feel like the surface of the sun.

"What's not happening?"

I jumped at the sound. My phone slid off the sofa and I spun myself around and put my foot on the floor, grimacing as the pain shot up my leg. The room instantly closed in, with Reid in it. He crossed it with a couple of strides and put two takeaway coffees on the table in front of me. Then he noticed my phone on the floor. It was screen-up, displaying an enlarged image of him. I hoped that the ceiling would peel back and I'd be sucked up into oblivion.

His eyes went wide.

"I was just—" I could feel the flush of embarrassment creep across my face. I stood and, wobbling slightly, made a lunge for the phone.

At the same time, Reid bent to pick it up and noticed today's T-shirt slogan: *Blink if you want me.*

Reid blinked.

Probably from surprise.

His eyes lingered on my breasts.

Trying to balance on one leg and recover the phone with the other, I misjudged and was falling forwards. Before I knew what was happening, I was in Reid's arms.

My eyes travelled up over the wall of muscle to the angular lines of his face and the dark eyes that were right now judging me.

"It's not what you think," I stammered.

"Oh, so you were just checking out the latest in men's fashion, then?" He helped me back to the sofa and held out my phone. I snatched it from him like a toddler snatches a sweet.

"Something like that." My lie sounded painfully transparent and if the grin on his smug face was anything to go by, he didn't believe a word I was saying.

"I think you were checking me out. Not worried about working for a hardened criminal, are you?"

I slapped his hand away and his eyes dropped to my nipples, which were now trying their hardest to push through the thin fabric of my top. Attention seekers.

"Not that I need to explain myself to you, but if you must know, I was looking for your website." I raised my leg up onto the cushion again and pulled the throw up around my shoulders. He looked blankly at me, and I turned the phone off and tossed it on the sofa. "For the garage," I added, just to make myself clear.

"You won't find it, because we don't have one."

"I gathered that much. I kept scrolling only to find every article is negative."

"Figures," he grunted, and helped himself to one of the takeaway coffees.

"I thought I might make one." I didn't know what he'd think of my idea, but designing a website was easy for me—I'd made hundreds of them over the years.

"Do you think we need one?"

"Don't you?"

"I hadn't really thought about it."

"Judging by the number of articles, some positive links on the internet might help. I think I can set up your socials as well, spin this around and increase business while I'm at it."

"You can do all that?" I watched his lips. He was look-ing at me as though I was going to perform some sort of magic trick.

"It's what I'm qualified to do. Plus, I can set up some analytics so we get an indication of how much traffic is generated and where it's going."

"And how do you propose to do this?"

"I can build the website and have it running in the background. I'll get you and Connor to take a look at it and tell me what you like and don't like. Then we can add in extra pages if need be. I'll need photos of any custom jobs you've done—for customers or yourselves; information on what jobs you specialise in; models you like to work on; what qualifications you both have; any awards."

"Will you still have time to do the accounts and reception duties while all this is happening?"

"I need something to do now. I'm going mad sitting here." I reached for my coffee and he beat me to it, picking it up and handing it across. Our fingers touched as I took it. The energy that shot up my arm went straight to my nipples and triggered another wave of heat. Thank goodness for the throw.

His eyes lifted to mine and I knew he'd felt it too. Whatever the hell was going on couldn't be good. The room filled with an uneasy tension.

"Louise, we need to talk."

"There's nothing to talk about." Panic began to stir in the pit of my stomach.

"I owe you an apology for—"

"No, you don't." I gulped my coffee and cursed at not letting it cool down more. "Nothing happened."

"It might have been nothing to you, but I should have known better. You were sixteen."

"You weren't much older."

"It doesn't excuse what I did."

"I was old enough to know you were Hannah's boyfriend. You guys didn't need me tagging along everywhere with you." My hand was shaking. I put my coffee down before I spilled it. "I was out of my mind, and you were out of my league."

Reid inched forwards in his chair; his eyes not leaving mine. "You had no idea how I felt about you."

"What you felt for me was nothing but an infatuation with a silly, naive teenager who had a gigantic crush on the first boy who'd looked at her more than once. You saw me watching you, and—well, I made more of it than I should have."

"Is that what you think?" There was a harshness to his voice that hadn't been there a few moments earlier. "You think I was infatuated?"

"It's what I know."

He drew up to his full height and hesitated, the line of his jaw set tight, his eyes that familiar inky black colour. Then abruptly, he turned and stalked out of the apartment.

Good. I had work to do.

I reached for my laptop and booted up the software. There was a website waiting to be designed—if I could just calm the shaking in my hands.

8

REID

CONNOR PUT ME ON grill duty. He had pestered the hell out of me to come, and Hannah had attacked from the flank. It had left me with little choice but to turn up. *Why* was a total mystery, but grilling the meat gave me something productive to do, and an excuse not to mingle and make small talk.

The usual group of friends were spread through the house and around Connor's backyard: some lazing on bean bags, others sitting in deck chairs. The lawns had been mowed and my brother had strung up coloured lights—what the hell for, I had no idea. We weren't celebrating anything.

I swung a quick scan at the yard, manicured to perfection. Autumn was slipping into winter and it was getting cooler during my rugby training runs, but tonight was mild, almost warm.

Frustration still festered over the fact Louise hadn't let me apologise for what happened all those years ago.

She'd waved it off like it was some silly schoolgirl crush and she got what she was due. But I wasn't a schoolboy.

I poked at the sausages. For some reason Hannah thought having family and friends around me was good for my mental health. I wasn't good for anyone. I was continuously grumpy and I knew it. The whole town knew it. I gripped the steak I'd been prodding, and flipped it with unnecessary force.

Tyler stepped outside, followed by his wife, Julie-Ann, and I lifted my hand in a half-wave. My insides were cringing at the prospect of being nice to everyone all night. Once I'd eaten, I figured I could probably slip off and no one would notice.

I turned the rest of the steaks, then the sausages, chops, cobs of corn and potatoes wrapped in foil, then threw the bacon on. The air was full of marinade spices and garlic. My stomach rumbled and I gingerly picked at a strip of sizzling bacon and lifted it to my mouth. A lick of excitement stirred in the pit of my stomach and heat filled my chest cavity. But I knew it had nothing to do with the bacon, and everything to do with the creak of crutches on the deck.

"Hi," Louise said, stopping beside me.

She looked more subdued tonight. There were no colours in her hair, and it hung in messy curls. None of the heavy blue shadow tinged her lids, either. Her long lashes looked natural and, *Jesus*, if she didn't look sexy as hell. I couldn't help myself—my eyes dropped to her pale pink, glossy lips that begged to be kissed. *Shit*. My gaze slipped lower. She was wearing another of those

T-shirts. This one said: *free hugs*. Harmless enough, but I just hoped I wasn't going to have to watch everyone take her up on the offer. I remembered what she'd felt like in my arms yesterday. Tonight she wore a shirt with a long, billowy skirt that floated around her ankles, and although I wanted to take her up on the offer, I didn't think it was me she wanted the hugs from.

"Hi," I said, turning my attention back to the grill and the row of sausages.

"Annie asked me to check on the meat—I think she meant check on you."

She blushed.

I smirked.

She shifted on her crutches, and we fell into an awkward silence until Liam burst through the back door and made a beeline for us. Or rather, for Louise.

"Hey, boss. Need a beer?" He handed me a bottle.

"Thanks," I muttered, screwing the cap off and lifting it to my lips. It quenched one of my thirsts.

"How's the ankle?" Liam asked Louise.

"It's good. Aches a bit if it's down for a while, but it's not as sore as it was."

"You'll be back at work next week then?" He lifted his brows a couple of times and grinned at her. What the hell was that about?

"She'll be back when her ankle is better, and not before," I informed him.

"Whatever works for Lou." He lifted his bottle in salute towards her shirt. "Nice." And he leaned in and gave her a hug. He must have picked up on the hostile vibes, because he wandered off to where Tyler and his wife were sitting at an outdoor table out on the lawn.

"Reid. Lou." Will strolled up to the grill. "Nice to see you both. Need any help?"

"Nope. I'm fine," I told him.

Will was looking smart tonight in a button-down and jacket with dress jeans and boots. I suspected he definitely had a thing for Hannah, but she didn't seem to be able to read the signs. Or she was ignoring them. I liked him, though. He had sound ethics, an agreeable personality, and that smattering of grey that women these days seem to love sprinkled through his hair. He was always there for her.

"Nice shirt, Doll." He leaned in and gave Louise a hug.

I rolled my eyes.

"I'm getting a drink for Hannah. Anyone want a refill?"

"No, thanks," Louise and I said at the same time.

Connor appeared with a boom box and an extension cord.

"Hey, Louise. Loving that shirt," he said, setting the speaker down and wrapping his arms around her. *Geez*, did *everyone* have to take her shirt literally?

"Didn't you already do that?" Louise laughed, ignoring my obvious discomfort.

Connor picked up the speaker. "Once is never enough, eh Reid?" he said, sitting it at the opposite end of the deck, feeding the extension cord through an open window. A few minutes later, Lady Gaga filled the backyard.

"He's just being nice, you know," Louise said.

"Who is?"

"Liam."

"Really?" I found that hard to believe. He was young and interested in any woman who had a pulse. Just as every guy was at that age.

"You shouldn't be so harsh."

I looked over at where Liam was talking to Tyler. She was right—I should cut him some slack. Besides, why shouldn't he hit on Louise? She was beautiful and had a right to date whoever she wanted. That brought me right back to the dickheads she had history with. "I'll try harder," I grumbled, narrowing my eyes at Liam.

"I'll tell Annie everything is ready." She turned and hobbled back inside.

Fifteen minutes later, Annie and Hannah had a table set up on the deck, laden with salads, meat and breads, and Connor was rounding people up and shepherding them towards the food.

"Here," Hannah handed me a plate piled high. "Can you take this over to Lou for me?"

I hesitated.

"She won't bite."

"Very funny."

She leaned into me. "Be nice to people. And no fighting with Liam this time. Okay?"

"Okay. Okay. I'm reformed."

Louise was sitting on a sun lounger with her leg up, talking to Liam. I strode across the lawn and forced a smile while my tongue curled around her name. She glanced up at me.

"Thought I'd save you getting up." I handed Louise the plate and utensils.

"Thanks."

"Food's up, Liam."

"Thanks, boss. I'm starving." Liam winked at Louise, scrambled up off the grass and hurried off to get something to eat. I stopped myself from making some smart-arse comment and instead pulled a chair over next to her and sat.

"So..."

"Thanks for this," Louise indicated the plate.

"How's the website coming?"

"I'm almost done with the homepage."

"Already?" She didn't mess around. I'd expected it would take her days or weeks to make.

"When do I get to see it?"

"Any time you want. You know where I'll be." She pushed potato salad across her plate and speared some chunks on her fork. "Stuck at Han's with my leg in the air."

I smirked at the picture forming in my head. Louise's face flushed scarlet as she realised what I was thinking. She ate the remainder of her meal without looking at me.

Once everyone had finished seconds—and in Connor and Liam's case, thirds—Annie and Hannah cleared the table and brought out the desserts. There were two strawberry cheesecakes, a large plate of Hannah's orgasmic triple chocolate and caramel brownies, and if that wasn't heart attack-inducing enough, in the centre of the table sat a multi-layered red velvet cake, courtesy of Will. That man would definitely make someone the perfect husband.

Connor arrived at our sides wanting to know if we needed a refill on our drinks. Then Annie came over with a plate containing a selection of desserts for us to share. Louise took a piece of brownie, while I helped myself to a slice of Will's cake.

Louise lifted the brownie to her lips and took a bite. The moan that resonated from her cruised through my body and gave my dick a good nudge. She closed her eyes as she swallowed. Was she doing that on purpose? Parts of me certainly appreciated the visual. No one else here would, though. I shifted awkwardly.

Louise licked her lips and wiggled her butt in the chair.

"Oh. My. God," she whispered, unashamedly happy as she uncrossed and crossed her legs. "These are something else."

Was the brownie living up to its reputation? Damned if I could sit and watch her finish it. I hastily excused myself and marched off in search of the bathroom—hoping no one would notice I had a raging erection.

Some of the guests were still in the kitchen and some had spilled through to the sitting room. I ignored them all, hauled the bathroom door open and locked it behind me. I yanked the zip on my jeans down, and with one hand gripping the hand basin, I released the pressure in my jeans. How the hell had I let things get this bad? I closed my eyes, took the Big Guy in my hand and leaned my head back. All I could see were images of Louise writhing in my bed completely naked as she moaned her way through an orgasm.

"Yes, yes," I hissed and inched closer to the hand basin. I needed serious help.

I took a minute, leaning over the basin, then cleaned up and zipped up, ran the cold water and splashed some over my face, stopping to take in the picture in the mirror. *Jesus.* I had to leave.

There was a knock on the bathroom door.

"Reid, you all right?" my brother asked from the other side.

"Fuck off, Connor."

"I know what you're doing."

"You don't know shit." *Jesus.* Trust him to notice the wood I'd been sporting.

"Don't think you can hide in there all night and avoid people."

I dried my face, tucked myself in, and thought about Liam hitting on Louise. It worked. My anger was back, and my dick had returned to resting position. I unlocked the door and yanked it open. Connor was leaning against the wall, waiting for me. "What?"

"Thought you might like to rescue your girl from Liam. She's just eaten two of those brownies."

"Ah, shit." I stormed off outside to look for her.

At nine o'clock, Hannah declared to the stragglers that she had to be up early. Will got to his feet and said he was leaving too, and he'd drop her off.

"Louise, do you want a lift home?" he asked.

"It's okay, I'll take her," I told him.

"Thank you, Reid, but I'll go with Will and Hannah."

It made total sense for Will to take them both home, so why was I disappointed? Louise could go home with whoever she damn well wanted to. Except Liam. "Fine," I muttered.

Everyone said their goodnights and gradually followed Hannah, Louise and Will out to their respective vehicles. I headed out the back to help Connor pack up chairs and bottles.

"Got to get rid of him, bro," Connor said, striding alongside me, picking up a stray plate and a fork.

"What are you on about?" I snapped.

"The ugly green monster on your shoulder."

"You don't know what you're talking about." I wasn't in the mood for his games.

"Liam's not a threat."

"Why the hell would I be threatened by him?"

"Oh, I don't know." He scooped up a bottle from the lawn. "You tell me." The bastard grinned like a crazed man on meth—not that I'd ever met any—and wandered off.

9

LOU

By the following Monday I was beyond bored, and never more excited about going to work. I'd exhausted my book-reading attention span after finishing my fourth novel. I'd binge-watched two series on Netflix and done as much as I could on the new website and Facebook page. My ankle was back to normal size, but it was still a little sore if I spent too much time on it. I could lead somewhat of a normal life, although going for a walk was out of the question for a while longer.

"Welcome back," Tyler called as I walked through the garage towards the main offices.

"Thanks, Tyler. I got you donuts for morning tea."

"That settles it, you're my favourite girl."

I got clear across the floor before I realised I was smiling. I put it down to the smell of engine oil, and the smell of engine oil reminded me of Reid.

Liam came running over and opened the reception door for me. "Hey. How's the ankle?"

"Nearly as good as new."

"I like the tee. Good one."

"Thanks." Today's shirt read: *You can't drive me crazy, I'm close enough to walk.* "Where's the boss?" On scanning the garage, I hadn't seen either Reid or Connor.

"They'll both be in shortly." Liam followed me into the reception and draped himself over the counter. "Think they had an appointment at the bank."

That didn't sound good. It meant they were either going to arrive back in a jolly mood, or it was going to be a long day. But on a brighter note, someone had replaced the flowers I'd put on my desk a week ago. I took my laptop out of my bag and set it up on the desk beside the computer monitor.

"Better get busy," I told him. I was feeling a little guilty that I'd spent my first week at work on sick leave.

"Me too." He hesitated. "You want to go out tonight?"

"Maybe."

"What about a movie?"

"Okay. What's on?"

"I'll check and let you know what time I'll pick you up."

I nodded my approval and dragged my chair in behind my desk.

Thirty minutes later, I had coffee brewed, donuts on a plate in the kitchen, and had started going through the filing cabinet in my office. It was going to be a big job. I had emptied out the first drawer and was on hands and knees forming piles all over the floor when I heard the reception door open.

"Should you be here?" Reid's gruff voice asked. I jumped at the sound of it and hit my head on my desk.

"Ow! Why? Am I no longer employed?" I asked, rubbing the sore spot.

He ignored my question and I carried on with my task, although it wasn't easy while he was lingering in the doorway. I could feel him watching me. It was starting to creep me out. I climbed to my feet. "Do you want something?" I asked, hands on hips.

He stared at my T-shirt. "I'll take a rain check," he muttered and stomped off towards the kitchen.

Obviously, the bank visit didn't go well.

On Wednesday I cleaned out the second drawer and put the contents in order. Connor worked on the restoration project most of the day, and I never saw Reid at all. I took a few photos to load to the website and social media.

Thursday was one of my days off, so I helped Hannah in the café until the morning rush had eased, then decided to check out the numerous second-hand stores in town for items I could use in the office. I bought six mugs for three dollars so I could throw out the stained, chipped and cracked ones. I found a vase for flowers so I could throw out the ugly pasta sauce jar, two terracotta plant pots for a dollar that needed plants. I was sure Hannah had told me that her waitress, Grace, had a big garden which she occasionally opened to the public; I made a mental note to ask her if she had anything I could take cuttings from.

I found a six-cup coffee plunger for a dollar and a large, old sepia photo of cars parked on the beach someplace, plus a set of three matching frames with hideous prints in them that I could recycle and hang in the reception. I also picked up a couple of novels for myself.

But the most exciting find was a ten-dollar office chair with wheels, which the friendly staff said they'd drop off for me. With everything except the chair in my car, I headed back to Hannah's.

Friday, I arrived at the garage late. I'd had an early appointment with the doctor who told me everything appeared to be repairing nicely, and that although I mustn't be tempted to over-exercise, I was officially free to resume normal life.

"Morning, Louise," Connor greeted, giving me a comforting Hamilton-brothers smile, before he broke into a hearty laugh. "Is that aimed at anyone in particular?" he asked, looking up from my tee.

"Nope." Today it read: *I didn't mean to push all your buttons; I was looking for* mute.

"I like what you've been doing around here," he said, resting an elbow on the reception counter. He was in his overalls and, for a fleeting moment, I wondered why he wasn't married with a bunch of kids either. Although Reid beat him to sex-god status, Connor had the edge over his brother on charm and personality. What the hell was wrong with him and Annie? Perhaps there was something wrong with the Hamilton brothers that I didn't know about. Maybe they both had some inherited deformity, like a third nipple. Or an ultra-small penis.

Smiling to myself, I got up and put my laptop on the counter and spun it around so he could see the screen. "I've finished the homepage and I'm working through the others—do you want to take a look?"

"That looks great," he said, taking in the home screen image. "I'm impressed."

"So, if we click on this menu button," I leaned in next to him, "the dropdown offers an About page, with information about you, Reid and your staff, along with reviews; then I'm setting up a Services page, an Image Gallery and a Contact page—plus any others you want to add."

"Where did you get the reviews from?"

"I rang some of your most recent customers and asked them how they found your service and workmanship."

"Clever. What's that all about?" he asked, pointing to an image of a kid in a go-kart on a page labelled Events.

"That's a link to the kart derby Hamilton's Automotive is running." I grinned at him.

"Are we?"

"You should. It would lift your profile in the community and bring in more business."

"What the hell?" Our heads were in a scrum over the screen, and I popped up to see Reid judging the scene from the door, his eyes dark and accusing. I felt heat shoot up my body to my face, which was stupid, because I had nothing to be guilty about.

"Check this website out, bro," Connor said, without taking his eyes off the screen.

I stepped back from the laptop and the sudden over-abundance of Hamilton testosterone, happy to let Connor show Reid the pages.

Reid glanced at my tee and scowled before reaching out to put a hand on the counter and lean into the head-space I'd vacated. My eyes fell to his hand, travelled across his fingers, took in the ink on his forearm and followed the ample curves of his biceps to his wide shoulders. I wondered what it would be like to peel his shirt off and run my hands over his warm naked skin. Or what damage those hands could do to me in a moment of—

He chose that exact moment to look up, his eyes locking on mine, one brow arching as if he'd just read my mind.

"Are we really that professional?" he asked.

"If you're not, you should be," I challenged, from the safe space behind my desk. "I need to take a few photos of you both, plus Tyler and Liam, for the website and social media."

"You don't need my photo. Use the others," Reid grunted.

"You're both owners. It's been proven that photos help to engage clients, because it lets them form an attachment to the people behind the business."

"Whatever you need to do, you have our approval," Connor replied. "I think we owe you a drink. How about McCarthy's after work tonight? We can sit down and talk about this kart derby we're running."

"No can do, sorry. I already have a date for tonight."

"What derby?" Reid asked, looking from Connor to me.

"A date?" Connor asked.

So many questions.

"I'm going to the movies with Liam. What about another night?" I moved back to the counter to get my laptop.

"Done."

"What kart derby?!" Reid bellowed, and both Connor and I stepped back.

"Louise has suggested we run a derby as a means of creating some positive vibes for our business. It's a fantastic idea."

"For kids? How's that going to help business?"

"We could have two categories," I explained. "One for adults—anything goes—and a pedal-power one for kids. It puts our name out there so that, when the attendees want some work done on their vehicles, they think of us."

"Yeah, right," Reid growled.

"And I suggest you guys make a kart too. One with a great Hamilton's paint job. Perhaps we could even run an auction and sell it after."

"Won't it cost a lot?"

"If we get as much sponsorship as possible, it should keep costs to a minimum; advertising, printing posters. The cost of making a kart."

"I fucking love that idea!" Connor said, then apologised for swearing in front of me. I grinned with pleasure.

"What do we have to do?" Reid asked.

"I'll put together a list of things we need to work through, and we can go over it next Friday. We'll need a prize for both categories."

"What about a free service to the winner of the adult category?"

"That's a great idea," I said, pleased at least Connor was onboard.

Connor stepped back from the counter. "Why don't we meet up at Reid's place on Sunday afternoon?"

"Why my place?"

"Why not?" Connor grinned at his brother as I closed my laptop. "Louise, are you coming to watch the team play tomorrow?"

"What's this?"

"It's the Stallions first match of the season and it's a home game."

"Are you playing?"

"Yep."

"Sounds fun. When?"

"Two-thirty kick-off, down at the sports ground."

"I look forward to it."

"Hey, Louise," Liam said on the other end of the phone. "Something's come up. Can we do the movie night another time?"

"Sure. Everything okay?"

"Yeah. Got a call from my cousin—he has a small removals business and he needs an extra pair of hands for a couple of days."

"Sounds like hard work."

"Bit of lifting, but I go for the free feeds," he told me, laughing.

"I'll see you at work on Monday, then." I ended the call and dropped my phone on the sofa next to me. Riverford didn't have a big cinema complex like the one in Greenhill, but it did have a boutique cinema that housed two smaller theatres. I had been looking forward to an ice cream—they served the best in town: chocolate coated and sprinkled with nuts.

"Who was that?" Hannah asked. She was sitting in her favourite comfy chair with her feet up, scrolling on her phone.

"Liam. We were going to the movies tonight, but something's come up and he's bailed. Do you fancy going in his place? Or to McCarthy's for a quick drink?"

"I'm really tired tonight. I was thinking of turning in early. But don't let that stop you. Why don't you go? Try and talk Annie into spending more time with Connor.

We've got to get those two hitched before they drive us all mad."

I sat on that idea for a moment. What would a strong, confident woman do? "Okay. I think I'll pop down to McCarthy's." I stood and checked my bag for my phone. "I won't be home late."

McCarthy's was full with all the usual people. Annie was working the bar and waved me over.

"Hey, Lou. Nice to see you in here. What'll it be?"

I took a seat and ordered a drink.

"How's it going at the garage? They looking after you?"

"I haven't been told to leave yet."

"Good sign."

"I know."

"I heard the place has never been cleaner."

"Well, I've made good progress, but still a way to go."

"Julie-Ann and Tyler were in for dinner last night. He said the place wasn't recognisable thanks to you." She placed my drink in front of me.

"Just some thorough cleaning, and I added a few bits and pieces I found at op shops."

"I hope you've got rid of those horrendous mugs they've been drinking out of for the last fifty years. It's a miracle they haven't caught something fatal."

I laughed. "First to go." I liked Annie. She had dark hair cropped short, with a face that told you she didn't mess about. Her black winged eyeliner reminded me of Amy Winehouse, and the only colour on her face was from her intense blue eyes. Large hoop earrings hung from her ears. Short sleeves allowed customers to see the giant tiger that stalked down one arm. She moved down the bar to serve someone else and I sipped on my drink.

"Things must be bad if you're hitting the bar alone," a voice behind me said. I didn't need to turn around to know who it belonged to.

"Reid."

"I thought you had a date?"

He took the stool next to me, and I was acutely aware that his thigh was touching mine.

"I did."

"So..." He looked around the bar. "Where's Liam? Stood you up, did he?"

"No. Something came up."

"Same difference."

I twirled my glass in circles and watched Annie mixing drinks.

"Right. I see Hannah's busy."

"She was having an early night." Why I was sitting here, making small talk with Reid, was beyond me.

"Wonder if Will knows that."

"Knows what?"

Matt appeared in front of Reid.

"Steinlager thanks, Matt."

"Should you be drinking before the big game?" Matt asked.

"Just give me the damn beer and stop with the coaching advice."

I stared at Reid like my brain had been short-circuited. He was playing in the game tomorrow? I had thought it was just Connor. My mind skipped straight to the image of Reid in rugby gear. My toes curled.

Then I remembered we were talking about Hannah.

"Why do you say that about Will?" My brain was still trying to stabilise with all the heat coming off his thigh. It was far too close to my V.J. and it was disrupting my ability to think straight. I wanted to slap myself at the realisation that my body was still crushing on him. No way would I let that happen. I needed some serious aversion therapy. I also needed more alcohol. I drained the glass and pushed it across the bar to catch Matt's eye.

"I saw him going in the door as I drove past," Reid stated. "He was carrying pizza boxes."

"Really?" I leaned in a little closer for the rest of the story.

"Looked like he was in a hurry to get inside."

"What's wrong with that? They've known each other since before his wife died, and he works for her."

"Absolutely nothing," he answered, lifting his chin at Matt when his drink arrived. "It's about time Hannah let herself fall in love again after that waste of a husband left."

My eyes widened and I lowered my voice. "You think they're definitely an item?" Why didn't I know this? She was keeping it very quiet. I'm sure she would have said something if she was interested in starting a relationship with him. I snapped my mouth shut. I just hadn't connected any of the dots. My brain was working at warp speed.

"They're being very discrete about it," Reid said.

"I probably dismissed all the signs," I said, taking another long swallow of my new rum and Coke. It was hard to concentrate with the amount of heat being generated between us. "Why do they need to be discrete? They're adults. Both unattached. With the hots for each other."

"Han's just being cautious. And avoiding the gossip."

I snickered. "Well that's not working."

Reid seemed much calmer tonight, dressed in jeans and a sweatshirt with his sleeves pushed up. I decided the relaxed look suited him. I soaked up the sex appeal that he radiated. Apparently so did my lady parts, and I squeezed my thighs together in an attempt to stop the quivering sensation. His eyes, locked on mine, dropped to my lap. Did he feel the clenching? He could ask me to do anything right now and I would agree to all of it. Every goddamn request. Why the heck had I put on such a short slip dress? I tugged on the hem, trying to make it a couple of inches longer.

"What?" I finally asked, unable to take the pressure of his gaze any longer.

He lifted his eyes back to my face. "I was thinking about how much you've changed."

"I didn't want to wear jeans—"

"That's not what I meant."

The gravelled tone of his voice was undoing my resolutions to be strong and confident and resilient when it came to the opposite sex. "I like blue," I blurted out, automatically running fingers through my hair where I'd chalked in some blue highlights.

He lowered his voice. "You know what I'm referring to."

"No. What do you mean?" I knew I was courting danger, but I couldn't help myself, the words were out of my mouth before I could stop them.

"You're much stronger than you used to be." He suddenly broke thigh contact and swivelled on his stool to face the bar and his drink. My thigh iced over from lack of him. "It suits you."

"All this time, you've been imagining what I looked like?"

"I tried not to." His eyes were back on mine, although his body still faced the bar. "But we left things unfinished."

"We didn't start anything, Reid," I hissed, hoping no one was listening to our conversation. "You were dating my cousin."

"Yeah, well, I'm not proud of how I handled the situation, but I'd—"

Someone stepped in between us, shook Reid's hand and turned his attention to me with his hand outstretched.

"If you're trying to buy bad stuff, he hasn't got any." The guy sported a cheerful but ruddy complexion, and black-framed glasses with thick lenses. He wore corduroy pants anchored with suspenders, and was grinning like a Cheshire cat. I noticed Reid tense.

"What's up, Wayne?" he asked.

Wayne shook my hand vigorously and laughed like I'd expect a child to laugh, with an added snort or two.

"I'm Louise," I said.

"You know Reid is a really great guy. He would never do what they accused him of."

"I know."

Matt handed Wayne a tall glass of what looked like Coke; ice cubes clogged the top of the glass.

"Wayne here makes sure all our water bottles are filled for our games. He's sort of the Stallions' mascot, aren't you, Wayne?"

"That's right," he confirmed. "I bring them good luck. They only lost one match last year, and that's when I was sick and had to stay home."

"A lucky mascot. You must have lots of friends."

"Are you coming to watch tomorrow, Louise?"

"I wouldn't miss it. Especially if our team is going to win."

"They *are* going to win. I know it," he said, with more enthusiasm than I'd seen in a long while. Then Wayne spotted someone else further down the bar. "Okay, I have to go now. I'll see you tomorrow, Reid. Bye, Louise."

"Nice meeting you, Wayne."

Reid turned on his seat and resumed thigh contact. It wasn't just a graze of fabric against my bare skin. There was pressure in the connection. I gulped my drink and slid off my bar stool. It was time to leave before I suggested something I'd regret.

10

LOU

FOR SOME UNKNOWN REASON, I was looking forward
to the game where grown men in tight-fitting shorts
sprinted around a field with a ball, trying to outrun other
grown men. Not that I was a huge fan of rugby, but
the chance to see Reid and Connor running around, all
bulging thighs and rugged sex appeal, kind of did things
to me. I shivered and pulled my jacket a little tighter
around my shoulders.

The Riverford Valley Stallions were playing the Western Colts in the opening match of the season. Apparently both teams had only lost one game each last year, so
the clash was receiving lots of attention. I noticed there
were several photographers milling around on the side
lines.

I made myself comfortable in a seat on the third row
of the sports ground's only grandstand. A few minutes
later I was joined by Hannah, and then Will—surprise,
surprise. Slowly, the seating filled as we all waited for the
schoolboy teams to run off the field and the senior teams

to replace them. It looked like the whole town was out to support the locals.

"How are you, Will?" I asked, bumping shoulders with Hannah.

"I'm right as rain," he replied.

"I hear the Colts are going to make it hard for our guys," I said, trying to sound knowledgeable on the subject.

He laughed. "They're all a bunch of old men trying to relive their youth and massage their egos—including our side."

Hannah's eyes widened. "Don't let the Hamilton brothers hear you say that."

"Well, whichever team's the fittest will win," he continued.

I nodded and thought about the Hamilton brothers. A lot. It was hard not to. At least one of them was permanently etched in my mind.

It was well worth the donation I'd paid on entry, which apparently would go towards renovating the clubrooms—even if both brothers made complete fools of themselves.

Thirty minutes and a punnet of hot chips later, the two teams ran out onto the field to cheering and clapping from the crowd. Someone a few seats away wolf-whistled as I kept my eyes peeled for Reid. I spotted him wearing the number six shirt. Connor, who was number seven, tossed the ball to Reid, who then passed it to someone else as the team continued to jump up and down and run across the field. I couldn't take my eyes off

Reid. His hair was messed, and he gave the impression he was a powerhouse. My heart fluttered and I think I sighed.

"Hey," said Annie, inching past and dropping into an empty seat on the other side of me.

"They just ran out," I told her.

"Is Connor on form today?" Hannah leaned across me to ask Annie.

"We'll have to wait and see," she said with a wink. "I think after the last time these teams played each other, they'll be keeping an eye on him. He did a bit of damage in the scrums."

"What about Reid?" I asked, wondering if Annie knew more about Connor's physical condition than she was letting on.

"He's going into this game as an unknown," she explained.

"Right." I had no idea what she was talking about.

"He was inside last season," she explained, "so they don't know what he's capable of."

I nodded. "Makes sense." I'd thought these games were just for fun, but the Western Colts looked big and mean—except for the little lean guy in the number fourteen shirt. I was suddenly worried that Reid might get injured.

Finally, the whistle blew, and all eyes were focused on the Stallions in blue and black as they jogged into their positions. I fixed my attention on Reid as if my life depended on it. I tensed when he was tackled, and cheered when he ran the ball and out-manoeuvred one of his opponents. I held my breath as the ball was thrown to him and sat on the edge of my seat when he sprinted for the try line.

Surely, he was going to come out of this game battered and bruised, because the opposition were no pushovers. I jumped up and yelled when one of our players, a wiry guy with the speed of a racehorse, ran the ball over the line and scored their first try, and again when it was converted. I clapped when Reid tackled one of the Colts and the ball passed into Connor's hands. And then it was half-time, and I felt exhausted from nervous energy.

"I'm going for coffee. Any orders?" Annie asked, standing up, stretching and rubbing her hands together. The wind was coming right into the stands and I was starting to wish I'd worn at least a dozen more layers.

"Yes, please," I answered, keeping my eyes on Reid as he jogged towards the far end of the field to group with the rest of his team. It looked like it was pep talk time, although they were up by thirteen to eight. At the end closest to us, it looked like the opposition team was getting a grilling, by the way the coach was waving his hands around. I saw Wayne with two crates of water bottles offering them to our guys, and then Annie and Will returned with three coffees and more cartons of hot chips, which she handed out to everyone.

The teams changed ends for the second half, and I found every time I diverted my attention to another player, I had to quickly locate Reid again. And then the Colts intercepted a pass and got a clean break, their man making a run for their touchline. From nowhere,

Reid was there. I could feel the crowd surge and the sportsground erupted into yelling as Reid dived at the player, tackling him to the ground. The ball bounced free and Connor was right there to scoop it up. I'd never heard so much noise. Everyone was up out of their seats as the ball was passed out to the wing, and our team ran in another try.

It was not until the final whistle blew that I could relax. As the Stallions left the field victorious, I felt a sense of pride grow in my chest.

"Right," Hannah said, standing and adjusting her scarf. "I think it's back to McCarthy's for a celebratory drink after that win."

We were three drinks in when the teams filed through the doors of McCarthy's. It was now standing room only as players from both sides laughed and discussed elements of the game. I found myself scanning the crowd for Reid and located him laughing with a fellow team member. He was freshly showered, his hair not quite dry; wearing jeans that moulded his butt and thighs to perfection.

I tried to swallow, my tongue sticking to the roof of my mouth like I'd been in the desert for the last year and Reid was a long cool drink. A navy sweatshirt made his eyes look the colour of blueberries at the end of summer; the top buttons were undone and his collar stood upright. A white T-shirt skimmed the open neckline, and my lecherous heart skipped a beat as I thirstily emptied my glass.

Without warning, he swung his head in my direction and his eyes found mine. He excused himself and made his way towards our table, with Connor not far behind him.

"Congratulations on the win, boys." Will reached out and shook Connor's, then Reid's hand.

There were congratulations and hugs as everyone gathered around. It seemed the Hamilton brothers were local heroes. One by one Annie hugged them, then Hannah, followed by Grace. I hugged Connor and congratulated him too.

And then I was facing a freshly showered, pine-scented Reid.

I wanted to reach my arms around his neck and pull his mouth down to mine. My eyes dropped to his lips and back to his eyes. I stepped towards him—and then I panicked.

"Excuse me," I stuttered and fled towards the bathroom. What the hell was wrong with me? I wanted to be like all the others who could hug him and offer my congratulations and think nothing of it. But I wasn't. I couldn't do it and not feel anything.

The corridor to the bathrooms was long, with offices and storerooms opening off it. I blindly pushed through the toilet door and rushed to the hand basins, leaning against them, dragging in air. When I looked up, my reflection showed a flushed face. *Nope. This is not hap-*

pening. I do not need to fall for another guy, especially Reid.

"Honestly, you need serious help." I told myself. Had I not learned my lesson? I ran the cold tap and held my hands under the water, and as I lifted them to my face, I realised that Reid could never feel anything more for me than pity. In his eyes I had to be that scrawny teenager with the braids that followed him and Hannah around everywhere. There could be no chance of a relationship, because I'd fall right back into the trap that I'd just climbed out of, because I'd... Now I was talking to myself. Great. I vigorously splashed water onto my face and pulled a paper towel from the dispenser.

I dried my face and hands before the tears started. I couldn't stay in Riverford Valley. It had been a stupid mistake even coming here. I'd finish the website and get all their accounts up to date, then leave. I didn't need the complications in my new life.

Collecting myself, I dabbed my eyes, put my shoulders back, pushed my boobs out and tossed the paper towel in the bin. Yes, I could damn well do it.

Unfortunately, right at that moment, two things happened. The first was that a young man burst out of one of the toilet cubicles and made a run for the door. The second was that the bathroom door swung open and Reid stepped inside.

What the heck was going on? Was everyone drunk? Couldn't anyone read the sign on the door?

"Reid, what are you doing in here?" I hissed.

The man hastily pushed Reid aside and made his escape.

"You didn't wash your hands, you weirdo!" I called after him. *Eww.* Hands on hips, I stared at Reid. "Well?"

"I could ask you the same question," he said, throwing a glance over my shoulder. "You're in the men's."

What? I spun around. "Oh my God." Urinals. Great. My skin flamed with embarrassment. I wouldn't be able to show my face in the pub ever again. I hastily made my exit. No wonder it smelled bad in here.

"Wait a minute," he said, grabbing an arm.

"Now is not the time."

He dropped my arm and I managed to make it out the door and into the hall before he stepped in front of me.

"What are you doing?" I gasped.

"Checking you're okay."

"I'm fine."

"You don't look like you're fine, and obviously your vision is off," he nodded at the bathroom doors. Although the two were side-by-side, the little male and female icons and the words *LADIES* and *GENTS* made it obvious which was which.

"There's nothing wrong with my eyesight."

"I beg to diff—"

"You played a good game today," I cut him off, trying to steer the conversation away from me.

"You came to watch?"

"I said I would."

His eyes softened. *Damn.* I did not want to see a soft side of Reid. Him being a monster made it easy for me to dislike the man.

"I wanted to see if Wayne brought good luck to your team," I told him.

"Really?" He stepped a fraction closer. My breath hitched.

I nodded, unable to speak. My brain and my mouth were not in sync any longer. It was risky trying to join words into a sentence.

"I think I might have a few bruises."

I wondered where and automatically scanned down his body.

His eyes turned a shade of charcoal. I took it as a warning sign; it was time to leave. I stepped around him, but wasn't quick enough. He took my arm and pulled me in against him. The panty-melting heat radiating from his body immediately transferred to mine. I couldn't breathe. His eyes dipped to my lips and back to my eyes. It felt like someone had kicked my kneecaps out, my legs wobbled and I was feeling faint.

"Where?" I squeaked, my eyes firmly fixed on his lips.

"Stop teasing me, Louise. I know you want me as much as I want you."

I started to laugh but it came out a weird croaking sound.

He spun me around, so I was sandwiched between his furnace of a body and the cold block wall. Past me wanted to taste those lips and see if my memories were still valid or outdated. But *present* me wanted more than a snatched kiss in a hallway. I needed the feel of his mouth on my body.

What would a relationship with Reid be like? *Ha.* I'd never know. Because in a few weeks I'd be gone, and I didn't need the distraction. I was on a mission to become an outgoing, confident woman, and falling for Reid wasn't going to help me achieve that.

"I don't want you, Reid," I murmured. Even to my ears, that didn't sound convincing. *Oh shit.* I was practically purring under his hands while I tried to calm myself. "And you don't want me. I'm a curiosity. A challenge. Find someone more suitable." But the promise I'd made to myself only five minutes ago in the men's bathroom was already crumbling. "We should get back to the others." I stumbled over the words.

"The others can wait." His voice was a husky rumble as he leaned into me. I could feel his breath dust my cheek. "Don't tell me what I want, buttercup. Nobody gets to do that."

I closed my eyes. I could feel the solid state of his arousal as his penis strained beneath the fabric of his pants. I let my body momentarily enjoy the nerve tingling sensation.

"Do you really want to repeat the same mistake we made once before?" I challenged, except it came out as more of a sexy purr. *Damn it.*

A moan rose from deep within him, the vibrations arousing every nerve end in me. My nipples stood to attention.

This new, strong, independent me was not doing well at all. I did the only thing I could: I slipped under his arm. But his hand whipped out and he brought me back to his confines.

"I'm warning you," his whisper silky, "this time there won't be any mistakes."

"There won't be any mistakes, because nothing is going to happen, now or ever."

"Is that what you honestly think?" he ground out, and lifted my chin with his index finger.

"I don't think; I know—"

But I had no chance to finish my sentence as his lips crushed down hard against mine. Raw and possessive, they battered mine into submission. Stealing my breath. All my resolutions to ignore Reid disintegrated with the feel of his mouth plundering mine. His hand cradled the back of my head as his tongue danced and teased mine, proving nothing at all had been extinguished. This was no longer a crush—it was full-on sizzling lust, and it was scorching parts of my body that had been neglected for months, maybe years. I had never felt this way about any of my previous boyfriends.

I couldn't stop myself. I wanted to kiss this man—*needed* to kiss this man. Damn it. I needed to be kissed by him.

He lifted his head as suddenly as he'd lowered it, his eyes steeling into mine as I gasped for air.

"I knew it." He stepped back from me, a cocky grin on his face.

I pushed free. "You don't know anything," I murmured, shoving him in the chest and fleeing back to the others.

Annie had brought more drinks to our table, where our group had swelled from four to twelve in my absence. She was starting her shift in thirty minutes and was drinking cola. She dropped onto Connor's lap and he wrapped an arm around her waist, pulling her tightly against him. I felt happy for them, but there was something else I felt: jealousy. Pure and simple.

"Those Colts have big egos," someone said, "to think they even stood a chance of winning."

A round of jokes followed, I nodded and smiled, but in my head, I was still outside the bathrooms; at the table I was trying to control my heart rate. I shoved my hands under my thighs, if I was sitting on them, no one would see them shaking.

That kiss.

It was everything I had ever dreamed of and more. Much more. *Damn him.*

My gaze lifted to Reid's as he pulled out a seat opposite me and picked up his drink. He sent a look across the table, and something warm and fuzzy bloomed in my chest, which terrified me. I squinted at him in warning; he grinned in response and left me to fight the emotions fizzing in my stomach.

"Everything all right?" Hannah asked, looking from Reid to me.

I nodded. "Sure." My hand was still shaking as I lifted my glass to my lips. So much for convincing her that everything was totally fine in my world.

"Reid." Hannah flagged his attention. "We're all coming to your place tonight for pizzas, beers and more rugby."

"I don't—" he started, before Hannah interrupted.

"Everything's already organised. You don't need to do anything except turn on that big screen of yours. Louise, you're coming, aren't you?"

Spending the evening at Reid's place was the last thing I should be doing, but Hannah was looking at me like she was waiting for me to give her the winning numbers for the lotto draw. I avoided looking at Reid. I could feel the anger radiating off him at having his sanctuary invaded.

"I guess," I heard myself answer.

"Great." Reid stood and stalked off without a backwards glance.

11

REID

I UNLOCKED THE FRONT door and stormed into the house, rattling the front windows with the force of it slamming behind me. I wanted a house crammed with people right now as much as I wanted to throw a tea party for a bunch of five-year-olds. I loved Hannah like a sister, but sometimes she crossed the fucking line.

All I could think about was Lou's face. The cinnamon tint of her eyes stained with dark reflections of something unobtainable. I wanted to shake those emotions free, tell her it was okay. Let her know that all men weren't arsewipes.

I threw my keys at the bench in the kitchen, where they skidded its length and fell to the floor at the other end. I took my gear bag through to the laundry, dumping it on the washing machine.

Before I had a chance to check if the sitting room was tidy, someone knocked, the door swung open and Hannah led the charge. People flooded in and peeled off in all directions.

Really? Had they all followed me home?

"Beers are in the fridge!" Connor yelled across the heads of others. Will followed him, carrying more beer.

Hannah started emptying bags of the potato chips she'd brought into bowls as Grace tried to wedge a bottle of wine between a block of cheese, a bag of apples and a six-pack of beer already in the fridge. Tyler detoured to the sitting room with Julie-Anne and turned the TV on. Voices of retired All Blacks being interviewed about their predictions around the impending game against France filtered through the house. Cans of premixes were being passed out along with glasses of wine. Everywhere I looked, people were making themselves comfortable. It seemed there was nowhere to hide from the hustle and noise as everyone settled in.

"Someone's at the door," a voice called.

"I'll get it," I grumped and stomped off to answer the door. It was Sully from Frank's Pizza with a stack of boxes, and behind him, Marg was walking up the path with a large paper-wrapped parcel, a couple of bottles of cola and a large bottle of rum. Was the whole fucking town coming?

I stood back and let them in, pointing in the general direction of the lounge. Hannah opened the top box and placed it at one end of the table, then opened the second box and handed it around. I noticed there was no sign of Louise. Perhaps she'd changed her mind after all. Good. The last thing I wanted was to have to spend the next three hours in the same room without being able to reach out and grasp a handful of her hair, pull her mouth to mine and taste her...

I took a deep breath.

Cheers rang out from the lounge as a play sequence was shown on the TV. It sounded like the French team were being profiled one by one.

"Meatlovers pizza?" Hannah asked, handing me a box. The large parcel had been unwrapped too, and was filling the house with the smell of battered fish, oysters, mussels, hot dogs, pineapple fritters and chips.

"I have shit to do," I muttered, taking the offered box and heading through to the kitchen. It was empty, thank goodness, but only slightly quieter. The counter, which had been empty just a few minutes ago, was now covered in boxes, glasses, bottles, slices of lemon, loaves of bread and empty chip packets. I took a glass from the cupboard and filled it with cold water, then carried it outside with my pizza.

The evening was mild. The cooling wind from earlier had now dropped off. I sat on the steps of the back deck, put my glass and pizza box down and massaged my temples.

My head ached. Did I really have a morbid fascination with Louise, or was it something real? I couldn't explain why I felt like I did. All I knew was these feelings *felt* real. My mind replayed the kiss at McCarthy's. I wanted more. More than just a kiss. And she did too. I could feel it in the way she responded. She'd definitely kissed me back before she'd suddenly pulled away.

I took a long swallow of water and gazed blindly out into the darkness of my backyard.

The lawn was spacious enough for impromptu rugby games. Beyond the back fence, the trees I'd spent years planting were above head height now, nowhere near as tall as the pines growing in the paddocks behind them, but tall enough that they made a great backdrop for the shrubs and fruit trees I'd planted haphazardly inside the yard.

I lifted a slice of pizza to my lips and paused. Something moved in the shadows, down by the gate that led to the pine plantation. A figure. Who the fuck was snooping around on my property? I rose, stepped down and made my way across the lawn. As I got closer, I knew exactly who it was. I closed the gap and leaned on the gate beside her.

She jumped as the gate creaked under my weight. "Reid!" she hissed. "What are you doing out here?"

"It's my place."

"That's not what I meant."

"The house is full. What's your excuse?" There was no reply. I turned to study her face, but I couldn't see much in the darkness. "Avoiding me?"

"Something like that." She sounded as if she'd been miles away and I'd intruded on her private thoughts.

"I can run you home if you want. No one will mind."

She turned to look at me, and I sensed the fight had seeped out of her.

"I'm fine," she said. "It's lovely out here. You have a nice place."

"Thanks. I like it."

"It would be the perfect place to raise a family."

"If I ever have one." There were four bedrooms, an office and a sprawling country-style kitchen, along with a dining room where I could seat twelve people with ease. The sitting room doubled as a family room, with a pool table at one end and the large screen TV at the other. On the left side of the house, I'd built a large car shed with a man cave at the back, complete with dartboard, sofas and bar.

"Ironic, really," I admitted.

I felt her study me.

"Why?"

"Because who wants their daughter settling down with a convicted criminal?"

"Anyone who knows you, knows you didn't do it. Look at all the good things you and your family have done for the community. Who's always there at fundraising events? Who stepped up and helped paint the primary school after it was vandalised with graffiti that time?"

"How did you know about that?"

"Hannah told me."

I leaned my elbows on the gate. "That's the best part of belonging to a small town like Riverford. Everyone pitches in. You don't ask what's needed, you just *do* what's needed."

She shifted her gaze back to the silhouettes of trees just visible in the darkness, and I took the opportunity to inch closer to her. She had the cutest button nose. Her lips, slightly open, taunted me while the air between us crackled with unspent energy.

We stood in silence for what seemed an eternity before I had to speak. "I'm sorry about how I treated you, Lou. I should never have kissed you—either time. Back then, I was confused to hell. I couldn't understand the emotion I was feeling. You made me question everything I thought was right, and what I wanted: the way I felt about Han, why I felt about you like I did. Even my future. Now, seeing you again has awakened all those feelings I'd packed neatly away. Only now, they're so much stronger."

"It was a long time ago, Reid."

"If we'd got together, you wouldn't have had to deal with scumbags like—"

"I don't want to talk about my choice of partners, and nothing happened between us. Nothing ever will." She turned to leave, and I caught her arm, pulling her against me.

"But it could. I know when I kissed you all those years ago, you felt what I felt. Neither of us might have known what it meant, but there was a connection. Whatever this is between us, isn't one-sided. You can't deny that."

"I'm not good enough for you, Reid. Don't you understand that? I'm damaged goods, and I need to rebuild myself. Walk away while you can."

"Ha. Who's calling who damaged? Besides, there's no way I can walk away from you."

"You're hanging onto a dream. Stop living in the past."

I tipped her chin up. "Lou, you have occupied my damn head all these years. I know what I want, and I want you."

"You just *think* you do."

"Why do you think I've never got into a serious relationship since Hannah?"

She shrugged. "I don't know. Tell me." Her voice was a whisper that feathered across my skin.

As I inched closer, our breath mingled, bodies almost touching in so many places. I edged so close that there was only the fabric of our clothes that separated us, and then her mouth lifted towards mine and lingered in that space; no man's land. I couldn't take it any longer. We both wanted the same thing.

Each other.

"I'll show you," I whispered back, remembering to breathe; wanting to steal hers. Running a thumb across her lips, dragging her bottom lip down, I gasped when she took my thumb into her mouth, circling her tongue around it. Sucking it. Lower down my body, the Big Guy was taking notice and wanting in on the action. A moan rumbled up from somewhere deep within me and I pulled my thumb free and replaced it with my lips.

We became the shadows, embracing our invisibility, oblivious to the party happening in front of my TV. Louise nipped at my lower lip, little whimpers escaping from her into the night air. A growl escaped from my chest.

"Fuck," I uttered, and lost myself to her kiss. I snaked an arm around her waist, securing her body against mine. She felt so good—exceeding anything my imagination had ever dreamed up. My other hand found a breast and cupped it. "Jesus, Lou, you're perfect. I want you so damn much."

"Reid." Her breaths were coming in ragged gasps. She arched her neck back, exposing it to my lips, and I kissed my way down to the vee in her jumper.

Her hand swept through my hair, taking hold and pulling my mouth back up to meet hers. Her other hand was feeling its way down and over my rigid cock.

"Reid." She moaned with that maple-syrup voice. I wondered if she had any idea what the hell she was doing to me.

I groaned my pleasure when I felt her palm finally reach its target. The heat from her hand scaring my skin.

Then her hand moved higher up, pushing under the layers of my clothing to find bare skin. This woman had the potential to crush my self-control, and right now I was powerless to do anything about it. How many times had the thought of her hands on me kept me sane while I lay on my back in my prison cell? And now my wildest dreams were playing out.

I unzipped my jacket and desperately dragged it off, dropping it to the ground. She took that as an invitation and slid both hands under my shirt to push it over my head, so I lost that too. Suddenly her hands were all over me. Discovering me. Delving into the fine curls that spread across my chest. Her lips found my nipples and my body ached for more of her. This was moving at the speed of a freight train.

"Wait." I took a step back, holding her face in my hands. "Are you okay with where this is going?"

"Reid," she groaned into my left palm, radiating warmth up my arm. Her voice tingled right through my body down to my toes. "I want more."

She sounded breathless.

"Are you sure?"

"Damn it, Reid, shut up."

I took the chance to rip her shirt free from the waistband and slid my hand up over all that soft, warm flesh, to the thin lace that protected her breasts. She tipped her head back and moaned. I hissed at the throbbing pain she was inflicting on me. I was going to lose it.

I drove kisses across her scented skin below the lace. I wanted more. So much more.

She gasped and whispered my name, her arm sliding around the back of my neck, fingers threading through my hair as I reached behind and got rid of her bra.

"Have you got a condom?" she rasped. She was ruining me. God damn it if she wasn't stoking this fire that was raging between us.

"You sure about this?"

"Stop talking." Her lips were all over me.

"We're not doing this out here," I stated, "when there's a perfectly good bed inside."

"You're killing the mood. Get your pants off."

She was throwing directions at me as she tore at her own clothes.

I pulled her down with me, and the grass smashed cold against my back as she fell against me, struggling to get her pants off from around her ankles.

I swung an arm out, searching for my jeans.

"What the fuck are you doing? Making grass angels?"

"Jeans! Wallet!"

"This isn't a transaction," she snapped, but I could hear the smirk in her voice.

I was kissing pathways down her neck and over one breast while I worked at removing my wallet from my jeans pocket.

"Condom!" she demanded with a sense of urgency.

Holding her body to mine, I scrambled to find the foiled package in my wallet, fumbling as I tried to multitask. Why the fuck were my hands shaking? I handed it over to her.

"Be gentle with me."

I'm sure she rolled her eyes before she gave a husky laugh and snatched the packet out of my hands, bit into it with her teeth and loosened the condom. I felt her hand grip my shaft and I damn near lost it. Louise Adair was more than I could ever hope for. She was a caged tiger waiting to be set free. I would be a lucky man if I didn't die out here tonight.

"Do you want some cold pizza? I have some on the back step," I offered, helping her pull her jumper over her head and brushing it free of grass.

"Sure," she answered, running her fingers through her hair.

"I think it was over way too fast. I'm sorry. Next time it's going to be much, much slower."

"Next time?" She laughed my promise off.

"Every time." I dropped a kiss to her lips as if to seal my promise, and threaded my fingers through hers as we walked slowly back towards the house. This woman was everything that was missing in my life. As we got closer, I could hear a combination of shouting and laughter coming from the family room. I guessed the game was well underway, but I had no idea how long we'd been out here.

I put my free hand out in front of her. "Pinch me."

"Why?"

"I want to know I didn't really die back there, and that this is all a dream."

She snickered and I felt my cock throb, as though it was ready for the main event.

We dropped down onto the step and helped ourselves to cold pizza.

"You okay?" I took her face in my hand and lifted it to mine. I wanted to see her eyes now we were sitting in the light from the back door; make sure I hadn't hurt her.

"I'm fine. That was amazing."

"Never done it on the grass in the middle of the night before?" I was grinning like an alley cat who'd just got lucky with a sweet Burmese.

"Never."

"I don't think I'll ever be able to forget what we just did. Ever."

"Good, because there's not going to be a next time."

Her comment caught me off guard and my breath hitched like I'd taken a punch to the gut.

"Is that what you really want?"

"Yes." She nibbled on the corner of her pizza slice. "You know I'm leaving in a few weeks—that me staying here was only ever temporary?"

"Yes, but things have changed now."

"Nothing's changed, Reid. I've just made things worse. We can't do this again."

"Why the hell not? You're all I'll ever want." I hated that even to me, my voice sounded needy. Surely tonight proved that there was something between us?

I caught the glint of moisture in her eyes and guilt washed over me. I should have kept my fucking dick in my pants. She was still healing from her last relationship, and I'd just abused every ounce of her self-respect. *Shit*. I'd taken what I wanted. Satisfied my needs. Had she been playing along because she knew that I wanted this? Did she think I'd be able to move on now that we'd had the most incredible sex? *Fuck*.

"You guys okay out here?" Connor asked, dropping down onto the steps next to Louise.

"I'm not feeling the best, Connor. Could you ring a taxi for me?"

Connor glanced over her head at me. I shrugged and shook my head.

"Sure." He stood up again and offered his hand to help Louise up.

"I'll see you at work on Monday," Lou said to me.

I nodded and watched her walk away—with my brother.

It was almost one in the morning by the time the last of the house-wrecking over-stayers had left. I tossed all the empty pizza boxes out, stacked the dishwasher with whatever dirty tableware I could find, and was making myself a sandwich before I headed for bed.

Someone knocked on the door.

"Who the fuck is it now?" I grumbled as I headed to unlock it. "Connor? What the hell?"

He shouldered past me and stormed through to the kitchen, huffing and puffing like a bull ready to mow down a matador.

"Come on in," I muttered, although my sarcasm was lost. I followed him in and resumed making my sandwich.

"Reid!" he yelled.

"I'm right here."

"What did you say to Louise?" he demanded.

I stopped slicing a tomato and put the knife down. Getting mad with a knife in my hand was not a good idea. "What the hell are you talking about?"

"I ran her home and by the time we got there, she was sobbing her eyes out."

I slapped one slice of bread on top of the other. "Yeah, well, your driving will have that effect on people." I carefully picked up my sandwich.

Connor strutted around the kitchen counter and shoved my shoulder. The fillings in my sandwich dropped to the floor.

"I'm fucking sick of your constant sarcasm and black moods."

"Why don't you fuck right off home and leave me alone?" I snarled, slapping the pieces of bread back on the counter.

"What the hell did you do?"

"Mind your own fucking business." I pushed him back, but he was braced against the counter and didn't move.

"It's my business when she's crying on my shoulder." He stomped over to the back door and yanked it open. "Outside."

"Really?" I asked, slightly bewildered. "You want to fight?" This used to be a regular occurrence as teens, but we hadn't sparred for a few years now.

I rounded the counter and marched outside. "Come on then. Put your money where your fucking big mouth is." I had just stepped down onto the bottom step when Connor pushed me from behind. Not expecting it, I flew off the deck, landed flat on my stomach, rolled and scrambled to my feet. An excellent recovery, I thought.

My brother was waiting. Taunting me. "Come on. This is your chance to pick on someone your own size."

"Fine," I roared, rushing at Connor and missing him as he sidestepped me.

Bastard.

I rolled to the ground again and sprung to my feet. I could feel the anger build and surge through me.

"Come on," Connor urged. "You're fighting like a toddler."

"*Grrr.*" I charged again; this time we connected, like in a rugby scrum. My shoulder wedged against his chest until Connor threw his arm around my neck and punched me in the gut. I wheezed and staggered but came back swinging, landing a solid hit to the side of Connor's chin.

"Fuck!" he bellowed, stumbling backwards.

The success at hitting my brother square in the jaw was short-lived. Connor drew his hand back, and a second later, I felt his fist smash against my eyebrow. *Damn it.* I wrestled my brother to the ground—there wasn't a clear winner yet, and I was determined I could pull one off against him. I took another blow to the mouth and then managed to punch him with force in the stomach.

Connor moaned, spluttered and rolled away, cursing. I paused, staggering to my feet as I prepared for the next assault.

"Okay! You win," I bellowed, as freezing cold water rained down on me.

"It's about time you two grew up!" Hannah yelled at us. I hadn't noticed her arrive but she was standing to one side of my house, with the garden hose on us.

"Jesus, Hannah," Connor grumbled, climbing to his feet, slipping and taking another dive.

She turned the hose off and dropped it on the ground. "Look at yourselves. Two grown men acting like five-year olds."

"I was just helping this idiot out," Connor muttered.

"Out of what? Any brain cells he may have left?"

"It's okay, Han, I asked for it," I said, shaking the water out of my hair and resting my hands on my knees while I caught my breath.

Hannah moved across the deck and met Connor and me on the steps. "How about shaking hands?"

"With this arsehole?" Connor glanced at her before turning his attention back to me.

I groaned, put a hand out and shook my head, keeping an eye on him in case he decided to throw a sneaky undercut. "Sorry, man. Now go the hell home."

Connor reluctantly shook it.

"Don't apologise to me," Connor muttered. "Go see Lou and get it sorted."

I grumbled something about him minding his own damn business and watched him leave.

12

LOU

SUNDAY MORNING, I WOKE feeling emotionally wrung out. I hadn't slept for thinking about what I'd done with Reid. Someone I'd crushed over since I was a kid. The reality was, now I'd had a taste of the forbidden fruit, I wanted more.

I rolled over and thumped the pillow into submission. One minute I was disgusted at myself for caving in, then I felt liberated about having casual sex with someone who wasn't a boyfriend. I realised I was free to do that now. I didn't need to be in a relationship. Didn't need someone to follow or hide behind. At least that part felt okay.

The problem was, I was still attracted to Reid, and I was worried that having earth-shattering sex with the man once definitely wasn't enough. Why couldn't I sleep with Reid if I wanted?

"You awake?" Hannah whispered, as she quietly made her way into the sitting room and my temporary bed-room.

"Morning," I greeted, hauling myself up until I was sitting against the pillows on the corner of the sofa. I'd heard her come in late last night and had pretended to be asleep.

"Rough night?" She walked through to the kitchen, where she filled the jug with water and spooned coffee into a plunger, her thick chenille dressing gown was pulled tight around her and tied at the waist.

"I'll survive."

"Are you okay?"

I pressed my palms to my face, then ran them through my hair and came up smiling. "I think so." For all the sleep I'd missed, I couldn't help the warm fuzzy feeling that lingered in my stomach when I thought of Reid Hamilton. She handed me a mug of coffee and took a seat on the other end of the sofa.

"You know I'm always here if you want to talk."

"Thanks."

"I don't know what happened last night, and I know it's none of my business, so tell me to butt out, but Reid is a really good guy. He's loyal and caring and he wouldn't take advantage of you. Ever."

"I know."

"And he likes you." A smile played on the corner of her mouth. "A lot."

"How do you know that?" The coffee, thick and hot, was just what I needed. I could feel it cruising through my body.

"I know him better than almost anyone in this town, including his own brother, and he's got it bad for you.

You're the first person I've ever seen him this crazy about."

"Well, I'm not sure what I can do about that. I don't want him to think he's a rebound, and I'm not even sure I want to get involved with another guy right now."

"But you feel something for him, don't you?"

Damn it, I couldn't hide anything from Hannah. "Maybe."

She nodded. "I'll take that as a yes. You don't need to rush it. See how it goes."

I sipped on my coffee and looked at her over the rim. "It might be a little late for the *slow* part." I screwed my face up and cringed.

"Is that why you left early last night?"

I nodded. "Partly."

Hannah laughed some more.

The door buzzer sounded and she got to her feet. "Don't be embarrassed about your feelings. Own them." The door buzzed again. She gave me a reassuring smile and went to answer it, and I pondered over my goal to be a confident woman in charge of my own destiny. At the top of my list was making my own choices, and rolling about on the grass with Reid and a condom had totally been my own choice.

When I looked up from my coffee, Reid was standing at the top of the stairs. He looked like he'd come straight from a boxing ring. Hannah bustled past him and disappeared into her bedroom and closed the door.

Conscious of the fact I was in a loose-fitting *No Ordinary Body* T-shirt and my hair was probably standing at all angles, I put my coffee down and pulled the covers slightly higher, as he dropped into one of Hannah's chairs.

He studied his feet, while I took in his battered face.

"Are you—?"

"I didn't expect—" we both said.

"You go," we offered together.

I pointed at him. "You, first." I sensed he was nervous.

With his elbows on his knees, he twisted a braided cord on his wrist then lifted his eyes to mine. "I'm sorry about last night."

I started to say something, and he held his hand up.

"I should have shown some self-restraint. I acted purely out of this... this hunger I have for you. I can't seem to help myself. You were in my head for years before I allowed myself to think you would never come back. And now, here you are, a hundred times more beautiful than I could have ever imagined."

He paused, and I sensed there was more.

"I know what you've been through, and I don't want to push you into anything you're not ready for. But hell, it's hard seeing you all the time." He ran a hand through his hair, and it fell in a just-got-out-of-bed kind of way. My Stud-Finder-Meter dial swung from tempted to hold-me-back.

"What happened to your face?" I asked, once I could form words again. He had a puffy, mean-looking bruise around one eye and a small cut above one eyebrow.

"Connor tried to give me some brotherly advice."

"Oh my God, Reid." I sprung off the sofa and moved closer to him, automatically taking his face in my hands to inspect the damage. He looked down at the flash of black lace and my bare legs, and I yanked at the hem of the T-shirt to try and make it stretch it further.

A groan escaped Reid's throat, and it was a hot minute before he could speak. "It looks worse than it is," he mumbled, gesturing to his face.

I hastily retreated to the security of the duvet and covered myself. "Last night was as much my fault as yours. I knew exactly what I was doing. I should have walked away."

"But you didn't, and we both know if that scene was to play out again, we'd both do the same thing."

I nodded and dropped my head, so he couldn't see it was full of all the things I'd like to do with him if I was given a second chance.

"Can we be friends?" He reached over to me and tipped my chin up with his finger. "Start again? No expectations. Just two old pals spending time together."

I thought about it. What harm could come from hanging out with Reid? My body desperately wanted to hang out with the man.

Naked.

On any surface. But I'd take whatever I could get. "Okay," I agreed, trying not to sound too excited about it.

"Good. Because we're going to a dinner party tonight."

"Tonight?" I hadn't been expecting that. I didn't know if I could spend a whole evening with Reid after yesterday. It was too soon. It wouldn't give me time to adjust to our new *just old pals* status.

"Connor and Annie are hosting. They've invited us both."

"Your brother isn't going to try and give you more advice, is he?"

"Probably. That's how we roll. Don't worry, we sorted that particular grievance."

Reid knocked on Connor's door and turned to face me. I got the feeling he wanted to say something, but before he had a chance, the door swung open and Connor welcomed us in. I noticed he had a split lip and I couldn't hide the grin, knowing Reid had given his brother some *advice* of his own.

"Hope you're hungry," Annie greeted, giving both Reid and me a hug.

"Starving," Reid replied, shrugging out of his jacket.

"Something smells delicious. Can I help with anything?" I offered.

"No, thanks. It's all done and in the oven. Connor, get them a drink—Louise?"

"Beer is fine, thanks." I followed Annie through to the sitting room, surprised to see a fire burning in the grate. Out of habit, I walked over and stood in front of it.

"Second fire of the season," Connor said, handing me a beer. Reid had disappeared somewhere. "Things good between you?" Connor asked, keeping his voice low.

"Yes. Thank you."

He nodded. "Good."

"How about the two of you?" I returned the question and touched my lip in reference.

"Yeah. Not the first time we've slogged it out of our systems."

"You really love your cars, don't you?" I said, glancing at the framed images of hot rods and classics that seemed to hang on every inch of wall space.

"Yeah, you could say that," he joked.

I wondered if that was the reason he and Annie hadn't made things official yet. Maybe Annie felt she was second best in the relationship.

"Dinner will be ready in ten minutes," Annie said, heading back towards the kitchen. "Connor, why don't you show Louise your pet project?"

"Don't tell me you haven't finished it yet?" Reid said, joining us. He walked over to me and took my hand. My fingers buzzed with his touch. He looked at me and narrowed his eyes like I'd done it on purpose.

We'd agreed to a friendship, one without the sex—sensational as it had been. If he was going to touch me like this, I didn't know how long I could keep my end of the agreement. It was best for both of us if we kept what we had to pleasant conversation at work and the odd coffee date at Hannah's Café. There hadn't been any discussion around touching, and I was realising too late, it was a huge oversight on my behalf.

Reid gripped my hand tighter. The warmth glided up my arm like a yellow-bellied sea snake and bit me.

"It's almost ready for its paint job," Connor said, as we followed him out to his large garage behind his house and waited while he pressed a series of numbers into the keypad, then flicked a switch. The space was suddenly swamped with light. I felt like I was standing in an aircraft hangar.

Connor crossed the room and pulled a fabric cover from a form exposing a shiny, sleek black car. "What do you think of this?"

"Is that a Ferrari?" I gasped and let out a low whistle as I bathed in the beauty of the panther-like car in front of me. Even I knew a sexy-looking vehicle when I saw one.

"Sure is. A '72 365 GT4." He produced a cloth from his pocket and rubbed at a spot on the side panel. Beside me, I knew Reid was rolling his eyes with impatience. I was learning that Connor was meticulous with everything he did. Every little detail was covered. Reid, on the other hand, was more of a *let's get the job done* kind of guy.

"*This* is your project?"

"One of them. But the one Annie was talking about is over there," Reid answered, and sauntered towards another cloth-covered vehicle on the far side of the garage.

Connor pushed the cloth back into his pocket. "I picked the Ferrari up after the owner wrote it off. Worked on it until I got it looking good as new."

"Muppet won't let me touch it," Reid called from across the vast space.

"No one gets to touch it."

"Anal jerk."

"Wow, I'm impressed," I said, reluctantly moving back from the Ferrari in case I accidently tripped and fell against it. God knew what it was worth, but I certainly couldn't afford to be paying to get any scratches taken out.

Connor beckoned me towards Reid. On the way, we rounded an old military Jeep and a vintage-looking Volkswagen Beetle sitting on blocks, missing its tyres. I noticed a work bench ran the length of the garage, and heavy chains hung from rafters in one corner. It smelled like the workshop in town, but everything here was polished and shone in the overhead lights. When we got to Connor's current project, Reid was sitting in the driver's seat, checking out the dash.

"What is it?" I asked.

"This beauty is a 1947 Ford V8 sedan," Connor said, with pride. In its current state, it was in desperate need of a paint job and doors. It had definitely seen better days.

"I think I'd prefer the Ferrari," I told him.

"Fair enough. But these old beauties are really something special. Wait till you see it completely restored and hear the motor rumble."

"Have you turned it over?" Reid asked.

"No. I plan to next weekend."

"I have to be here for that."

I left the men to carry on with their car-related talk and headed back to help Annie in the comfort of a warm kitchen.

13

LOU

THE FOLLOWING FRIDAY, I arrived in the office to the smell of coffee brewing. It added to my good mood. After I'd accepted that earth-shattering sex had occurred, and that I'd enjoyed it more than I'd enjoyed anything in a long time, my week had been wonderful. I felt as if in some small way, I was taking my life back; adulting with someone who I was sure wasn't going to exploit my fragile confidence. Reid was a good man. He was caring and attentive. And thoughtful. I was beginning to feel at ease around him, even though my body wasn't. And it was empowering.

I dropped my things on the desk and took the bag of strawberry and white chocolate muffins through to the kitchen. Bringing morning tea for everyone had become a habit now.

It wasn't until I walked past Connor's office and noticed the door was closed that I realised he had someone in there with him. I could hear a voice that didn't belong to either of the Hamilton brothers. I wondered who it was. They never closed their office doors.

I poured myself a cup of coffee and stole a glance through the office windows as I walked back to reception. Connor and his visitor were seated, while Reid paced the floor with his back to me.

We had a meeting scheduled for ten o'clock to talk over the details of the go-kart derby. I peeled off my jacket, switched the heater on low and noticed my ten-dollar wheelie chair had been delivered and was tucked neatly under my desk. I pulled it out, spun it around and sat on it, completing a three-sixty. It was just what I needed. I propelled myself out from behind my desk, and pushed myself around the waiting room, channelling my inner child and circumnavigating the coffee table like a pro.

I was scooting back behind the desk when Reid steamed out of the office, cutting through the reception.

"Stop playing and do some damn work," he snapped at me.

He disappeared without further comment while I sat, staring after him. He was followed a minute later by the visitor—a middle-aged man dressed in corduroy pants, a sports jacket and a thinning comb-over. He nodded at me with friendly eyes, and I gave him a smile before quietly putting my head down.

Reid had put me in my place, and it had been a sharp reminder that I was his employee, and I didn't need to be told twice.

Five minutes later, Connor stepped into the room.

"Morning. We good for the meeting at ten?" he asked.

I nodded. At least one of the brothers was speaking to me. "Is Reid okay?"

"Yeah, don't mind him. It'll take him a few minutes to calm down. He's not keen on being reminded about his stint inside."

"Was that what the office huddle was about?" It was none of my business, but I was worried about Reid.

"Yeah. Prisoners' Aid and Rehabilitation. Just checking in to see that he's okay."

"Surely that's a positive thing?"

"Not where Reid is concerned. For him, it dredges up something he's trying to forget."

I nodded and continued on with my sorting and filing. I was almost up to date with everything—all I had left to do was sort through a stack of old receipts and invoices from pre-Hamilton-brothers days, and a dozen or so invoices that didn't relate to anything I could find, but my mind kept drifting back to Reid and the thunderous look on his face.

At five to ten, everyone filed inside for their coffee fix. I thought Tyler looked a little tired as he followed at the end of the procession.

"Morning, Lou," Liam greeted, and grinned at the *Women do it better* T-shirt I was wearing over a long-sleeved thermal. "Love it—but how do you know?"

"Trust me, Liam, we do."

He laughed as he headed for the kitchen, shaking his head.

"Morning, Tyler."

"What goodies did you bring us today, lass?"

"You've got strawberry and white chocolate muffins today," I advised.

"You're my favourite girl, you know that?" he said.

I grinned and turned back to my laptop screen as Reid stepped into the reception area, followed closely behind by Connor.

Reid had his overalls on, and despite his foul mood, I wanted to ease that zip down and slide my hand inside to check if he was wearing a shirt today. I hadn't had time to explore every inch of his body last weekend while we'd been rolling around on the grass like a couple of dogs on heat. I'd willingly refresh my memory any time he was up for it—not that I'd share that snippet with him. I kept telling myself I would be walking away in a few weeks. No looking back. No ties. I glanced up and his eyes met mine and widened a fraction at the shirt. I quickly looked away, heat flooding my cheeks. Damn the man if he didn't know what I was thinking.

Connor and Reid wandered back into reception with their drinks and pulled chairs up to my desk. I got a pad and pen out.

"So, do we have a date for the event?" Connor asked.

"I thought a month from now. Do either of you have any problems with that? You'll need the time to organise sponsors, marketing, and get officials on board. Plus, we have to allow time for entrants to make their karts."

They both nodded. I looked up the date and jotted it down. I could give myself another month in town.

"Rules?" My eyes moved to Reid, who was peeling the paper case from around his muffin.

Connor put his coffee down. "I agree with your idea that children's karts should be propelled by pedal power. We need to keep safety our first priority."

"Agreed. Why not make all karts pedal?" I suggested, glancing up at Reid and finding I couldn't look away. "Make it... um... more of a challenge for the adults."

Reid bit into his muffin and closed his eyes. I shifted in my chair.

Connor and I both watched him devour the muffin, bite by slow bite.

"Fuck, that was good," Reid said, shoving the last of the muffin in his mouth and making me remember which parts of my body had been in his mouth last week.

"Language." His brother glared.

"Sorry. That was delicious." A smile spread across his face and he licked at his lips. It was a vast change from his face an hour ago.

Connor grimaced. "We don't want to know."

I thought it best to change the subject. "What's the age categories?"

"Kids ten to fourteen, and adults fifteen up?" Connor looked from me to Reid, who was now licking his fingers.

"What?"

"Ages!" his brother yelled at him impatiently.

Once Reid had agreed, we moved on to discuss where the event was going to be held. They said there was a smallish hill heading out towards Old Man Matheson's sheep farm, with just enough slope on it to get up a decent downhill speed, without it being too dangerous for the younger kids, then a straight past the berry farm owned by a Becky Adler. The finish line could be at the sports grounds on the edge of town. Ideally, contestants would only need to pedal for the second half of the race.

I made a note to ring Mr Matheson and see if we could use one of his paddocks for a car park and staging area. By the time the meeting had finished, Tyler and Liam were both back out in the workshop and the muffins were gone. But we had all the rules and regulations sorted, and I told them I'd work on a poster and sort out some sponsors and advertising around it.

With lots of notes and lists of people to contact, my bosses headed out to the workshop while I added a couple of ideas and then took the used mugs to the kitchen for washing.

"Hey," a husky voice sounded from the door a few moments later.

I looked up from the dishes I was washing to see Reid standing there, arms crossed over his chest.

"Oh, that's right." I picked up the tea towel and dried my hands, then dropped it on the bench. "I forgot. I'm not paid to wash dishes. I'll go back to my desk and do some actual work." He wasn't back in my good books yet.

Reid shifted his weight from one foot to the other. "Yeah, about that..."

"I don't need an explanation."

"No, but you need an apology. I'm sorry I snapped. I was angry and embarrassed. I had no right to take it out on you."

I folded my arms and stared at him, trying not to notice the flecks of silvered grey at his temple, or the laugh lines that sat dormant at the very corners of his eyes. "No, you didn't, but maybe you're no different from any other guy I've been with. I'm beginning to actually expect shitty behaviour."

"I'm not like those other guys, so don't compare me to them."

"If you'll excuse me, I need to get back to work." I elbowed my way past him and arrived at my desk just as Liam opened the door into the reception.

Liam spotted Reid and made a beeline for him. "Hey, boss."

"Liam," Reid acknowledged, still watching me.

"This go-kart we're making... If no one minds, I'd love to have a crack at building it."

"Yeah, okay. I'll come find you shortly and we'll talk about it."

"Really?"

"Sure."

He waited until Liam had disappeared, then closed the distance between us. "Let me make it up to you."

Now he was leaning way too far over the counter towards me, and I didn't know if I wanted to reach up and kiss those beautiful, generous lips or slap his sexy, gorgeous face out the door. "No need," I mumbled.

"There is a need. I'd like to take you out tonight. To The Greenery, and then somewhere special."

"Nope. Thank you, but I don't think that's such a good idea."

"I can promise you it will be a magical experience."

"Great pick-up line." I couldn't help but laugh at the look on his face. Then his stare darkened, and my overactive imagination went into a frenzy. What *magical* things was he planning to do? "You might be able to make heads spin, and okay, I'll agree the sex was pretty spectacular, but do you know how corny that sounded?"

He straightened up in a defensive pose.

"I'll take that as a yes."

I went back to the pile of papers on my desk. "Do you do business with a company called Kennedy's Engineering very often?"

"No. Never. They're in the city and they're dodgy as hell. Got a reputation for shady deals."

"And who normally orders stuff for your business?"

"Connor or me. Sometimes Tyler might—if it's urgent and we're not around. Why?"

"No reason." I'd found a couple of invoices with *paid* scribbled across them, filed in odd places, and I couldn't find any record of corresponding payments going back through the bank records. I needed to recheck the dates on them and dig a bit deeper.

"Louise?"

I sighed and looked up at Reid. Tousled strands of his hair fell loosely as though he'd repeatedly run his fingers through them. The intensity in his eyes hid a well of feelings that plummeted to depths I'd never be able to reach, and yet I felt a desire to know what they were and fix them. I licked my lips, wanting to reach out and cradle his face in the palm of my hand. Feel the stubble that darkened his jaw.

"Earth to Louise?" He waved a hand across my vision.

"What? Oh, God, you were talking to me, weren't you?" I said, hoping he hadn't been able to read my thoughts.

He nodded and gave me a sexy smile that made me want to act like my Aunt Caroline's dog. She would have rolled onto her back, legs in the air, for belly rubs as soon as Reid looked at her.

"I was trying to persuade you to come out for dinner with me tonight."

I really had no will power to say no when it came to Reid Hamilton.

That was my problem.

It had also been my problem with Jayden and my previous boyfriend Aaron, but not in a sexual way. When I think back, the sex with them had been infrequent, and even then, nothing to rave about. And way back when I was eighteen, a fresh face at university and didn't know any better, Michael Blenkstrop had manipulated me into sleeping with him. He'd told me I was the most attractive girl in the computer sciences class, and we'd started dating. I'd been foolish enough to think he loved me, and meanwhile, he was getting his leg over some English major with a chin full of pimples. Turned out she gave him private tuition, and he gave her a romp in the back seat of my car while I was at work. I used to wonder why he needed to borrow it so much.

"Okay," I agreed absently, before I realised I'd forgotten what I'd agreed to.

"Good. I'll pick you up at seven. Wear something warm."

Blast.

He beamed at me, and my heart sank in the knowledge that, as much as I shouldn't want to, I was definitely going to have whatever magical experience he wanted to give me.

I watched his sexy-as-sin butt retreat through the door, checked off the calls to Mr Matheson about using his land, and to the secretary of the sports club about using their car park. I typed up a list of potential sponsors for prizes, then spent the remainder of the day ringing them to pitch our go-kart race. By the time I was ready to head home, I'd been promised two thousand dollars' worth of prizes. I was feeling very pleased with myself indeed.

And very nervous.

14

REID

I TOOK CORBETT STREET, then right onto Middle Street and turned at the only set of lights onto Richmond Road. It would take me straight out of town towards Greenhill and the restaurant I'd made a reservation at. It was hard to concentrate when my head was full of honeysuckle.

"Are you playing this weekend?" Louise asked.

She was wearing a figure-hugging white Aran-knit jumper with dress jeans and boots. Her hair looked like it would if she'd spent a marathon night in a bed with me, but bare of bright colours. She wore a slick of black that winged at the corner of each eye and her lips were a pearlescent dark red that I wanted to smudge the hell out of. She looked incredible. It was going to take a shit load of restraint to keep my hands off her.

"Yeah," I said, suddenly remembering she'd asked me a question. "Coach thinks I made enough difference to the outcome of the last match to let me play again."

"Is it a home game?"

"No. We're playing in Ashford against their A team."

"Do you think you have a chance of winning?"

"I don't know. I haven't played against them for a couple of years. They've got a reputation for playing smart on the field compared to the Colts, who are all thugs."

She laughed and the sound gripped my heart and squeezed. I wanted to hear her laughter more often.

"Have we made another rugby fan?" I asked, stealing a glance at her.

"Maybe, although Dad always watched the All Blacks matches; I wasn't so interested."

"And you feel different now?"

"It's different when you personally know some of the team."

I nodded.

The restaurant was quiet when we arrived; only a handful of diners were dotted around the room. I was relieved not to recognise anyone. I didn't need to give Riverford residents any more reason to gossip.

"So, how are you finding work?"

She looked up from her menu. "I'm enjoying the challenge."

"Creating order from chaos?"

Another laugh bubbled up from her throat and I felt the immediate warmth embrace me.

"I guess," she said. "Although I'm enjoying the other things, too."

"Such as?"

"I'm enjoying the challenge of cleaning up your business. Literally, and figuratively."

"You enjoy cleaning?" That just sounded weird to me, but hell, it was to be admired. "And here I was thinking you enjoyed our scintillating conversations over morning tea."

"I don't *mind* cleaning." She fiddled with the cutlery. "The website's going live on Wednesday, along with the social media pages. And I'd like to get an article into one or more of the national magazines."

"But what's the point advertising nationally? We want local business."

"Well..." She rolled her eyes like I was missing the obvious. "If Connor wanted to get his car painted, and there was nowhere in town that could do the job, wouldn't he look in other towns or cities?"

"I guess." I could see her point.

"So, it won't hurt to let people out there know that if they're looking, Hamilton's Automotive is the best place to get the work done.

"Fair enough." She wasn't just gorgeous; she had a logical brain too.

"You know you could attend shows and meets too—hand out flyers, take a car along and let potential customers see your restoration work first hand. Or you could organise trips to America for hot rod fans."

"Whoa!" This time it was my turn to laugh. "Let's just get the kart race done first, before we plan to take over the world." I had to love her enthusiasm.

She ordered chicken, while I opted for the steak. We sat and talked about families, and if Connor and Annie would ever get hitched, or Hannah and Will. Although I was constantly aware of the sexual tension that hung in a fine balance between us, we both did our best to keep it light.

"Want to get out of here?" I asked, needing to have her to myself, rather than share her with everyone in the now busy restaurant.

She nodded. I paid the bill and reached for her hand. She hesitated before threading her fingers through mine as we walked outside.

I needed to take things slowly. There was no hurry. But her hand in mine sure felt nice.

"I really want to kiss you right now," I admitted.

She lowered her head, and I thought she was going to remind me this was a friendship, not a relationship. But when she lifted her face, her eyes were warm and her lips dangerously sexy.

"I think I'd like—"

Before she could finish, my mouth was closing over hers. I felt her hesitate momentarily before her arms circled around my neck, fingers grabbing at my hair.

Damn, that felt good. I was being swallowed up by so many fucking emotions. She gave me all the feels. Her lips were marshmallow-soft under mine as our tongues danced together. My dick wanted in on the action. I held her closer so she could feel what she did to me, before I remembered we were standing on the street.

"Hey," I said, coming up for air. "Sorry about the Big Guy. He gets excited every time he gets anywhere near you."

"Big Guy?" The flush of colour on her cheeks disappeared and she screwed her face up with laughter.

My cock decided not only was kissing Louise one of the biggest turn-ons it had experienced, but that her syrupy voice laughing was the sound of the whole fucking cheerleading squad before the big game.

"What's so funny?" I asked her.

"You." She shoulder-bumped me and I wrapped my arm around her waist and led her across the parking lot to the truck. I buried my face in her hair and dropped a kiss to her forehead before opening the truck door.

Although the Big Guy was left dejected, I drove back towards Riverford feeling lighter than I had in the last two years. I'd been living in a world of stress-induced anxiety and anger since the moment the police had first set foot in the garage with a search warrant. Right here, sitting next to Lou, I felt I'd found what was missing in my life. The one thing that balanced everything else out and made all the bad shit null and void.

"Where are we going?" she asked, as I turned the truck back onto an almost deserted Corbet Street.

"Someplace special."

"You're taking me somewhere special, this late at night?" Louise asked as I drove past the café.

Grace's husband, Charlie, gave me a wave as he drove past. He was on his bread delivery run to the stores before morning, and Cam Donald, a guy I went to school with who played fullback for the Stallions, was starting his shift at the fire station. His wife, Claire, who owned the hair and beauty salon in town, knew everything there was to know about the residents of Riverford. I could see him now, whipping his phone out and texting Claire that he'd seen me drive through town at ten-thirty with Louise in the passenger seat. I'd bet a dozen brownies it would be all round town before the stores opened in the morning.

"It's better at this time." I followed the road out to my place and, instead of pulling into my drive, drove on and pulled into a gated entrance two hundred metres past that ran into my pine plantation.

"Are we here?"

"Almost. Sit tight." I jumped out and opened the gate, climbed back in and drove through. "I made this track, and my bulldozing skills aren't the best." The headlights picked the track and then I reduced my speed to a crawl, pulled up, carefully reversed into the centre of a stand of trees, turned the lights off and cut the engine. Everything went silent.

"Why are we stopping here?"

"Wait and see."

I climbed out of the truck and opened the passenger door for her. While she stood looking around for the reason I'd brought her here, I peeled the cover back on one side of the tray. Then jumped up onto the back deck of the truck and held a hand out to her, pulling her up to join me.

"What—"

"Make yourself comfy." I'd loaded a mattress along with cushions and blankets onto the deck of the truck. While Louise got comfy, I made my way to a power box attached to a nearby tree. "Ready?"

"I think so."

I flicked the switch and heard Louise gasp as the trees became a fairy grotto. Tiny specks of light glittered and flickered above our heads at three-sixty degrees around the truck.

"This is beautiful!"

I rejoined her on the truck, plumped the pillows and sat back, pulling her to me. With one arm around her, I used the other to gather the blankets up around us.

"When did you do all this?"

"A week after I was released."

"Why?"

"Let's say, I developed a healthy respect for open spaces. I love the strength and smell of pine. The lights were my first project when I needed to be kept busy." She nestled against my shoulder and I felt a fuzzy warmth spread through me. The Big Guy approved.

I needed a distraction.

Stat.

I desperately packed my head with images of my Great Aunt Edna, who had one of the most impressively hairy chins in the country. The distraction lasted about sixty seconds. This was not the time to jump Louise's bones. *Remember*. I needed to take it slow. Prove to her I had some self-control. *Jesus*, that was a joke.

I forced myself to revisit my aunt and had a sudden flush of guilt at not having spent more time with her—or that I hadn't called her more. The Big Guy deflated a little.

"I would never have thought you—"

"What? Could string up a few fairy lights?"

"I was going to say, I didn't realise you had such a romantic side."

"It's something I keep to myself." I angled myself towards Louise. A smile made her face even more beautiful. She hugged her knees to her chest and stared up through the circle of trees to the universe beyond. She had to be the most wonderful person on the planet. A work of art.

As if she sensed me watching her, she turned to look at me.

"It's very romantic."

"I used to bring the truck out here and sleep under the trees at least twice a week. I've even had plans drawn up to build a small cabin out here."

"Do you still come out here to sleep?"

"Now and again. It's relaxing in summer, when the crickets are singing. And on winter nights like this when it's clear, mild night, I lie here in the darkness watching the stars and the occasional sky train, and it makes me realise just how lucky I am."

"You are lucky."

I thought I detected a hint of sadness in her voice.

"Does Connor know you sleep out here?"

"I've never told anyone."

We sat quietly, both of us lost in our thoughts.

"Thank you," she eventually said, breaking the silence.

Her hand reached out to cup my face and her lips grazed mine. My heart pounded, skipped a beat and exploded in my chest.

"What for?" I told myself it was just a kiss. Nothing more.

She was staring at me with eyes that melted any remnants of my ruptured heart.

"Sharing this with me."

"Sleep out here with me tonight," I whispered against her face, wanting her to be part of this so that every time I came out here, it would remind me of her. This would be our place now.

"I'd love to," she whispered.

Nestling snugly into my side, she surprised me by sliding a hand around my waist. It felt so fucking natural to be out here with her. To be like this. I didn't want to rush things with Louise if it meant I had a second chance at forming a relationship. I needed to prove I was serious about doing this right.

I'd let her take the lead.

Her hand moved to my belt buckle and she worked on removing my pants, stopping to peel off her jacket and kick off her boots. I hauled my jeans down my legs in record time and started on hers. She lifted her jumper over her head and I nearly passed out at the thought of what she was giving me. Touching her bare skin ignited raging fires all over my body, as I kissed her neck, slowly working my way down to one beautiful breast.

She whispered my name in a breathless sigh as I took her nipple in my mouth. A fire surged through me and licked its way from one end of my body to the other. I nipped and sucked, and she arched in pleasure as I rolled and lifted myself above her. I switched to the other breast and showered it with attention, Lou moaned under me and drove her hands to cup my butt cheeks, snaking one around to find my cock.

Sweet baby Jesus.

There was only the here and now, and it was destroying me. I seriously doubted I'd live to see the morning.

"Sweetheart, I need to get a condom."

"It's okay," she panted, "I'm on birth control."

"You sure? I'm clean."

"Reid... I don't think I'm... able to hold, *aah*... a conversation right... now."

I inched my mouth down her spectacular body with a sense of urgency. She wrapped her legs around my waist and held on as I buried myself in her. For every one of my actions, she gave me the perfect reaction.

If I was struck dead right at this moment, I would die a happy man indeed.

15

LOU

I WAS SITTING IN the café, about to enjoy a latte and risk an orgasmic brownie, when the door swung open and Connor sauntered in. He strode straight to the counter, placed an order and joined me at my table. So far, it had been one of the best weekends I'd had in ages, and I was determined nothing was going to spoil the new week and my good mood.

"Morning, Lou," he said.

"I'm on my way to work, I promise." I sipped the coffee and relished the smooth, satisfying calmness it instilled in me.

"No hurry," Connor said, sitting back and folding his arms over his chest. "Actually, I'm after a favour."

I raised my eyebrows. "Sure."

"We've got the tax inspector coming in on Thursday to go over our books. You wouldn't be able to swap days and come in while he was here, would you? Take him through things?"

"Happy to help."

"Thanks. That would take a load of pressure off. I see you and my brother have worked out your differences."

"I think we've finally become friends." A mouthful of the brownie was making me feel warm and compliant.

"I think he sees you as more than just a friend."

"Whatever works for him." I paused, trying to sound nonchalant about it. I didn't really want to discuss my relationship, or the fact we'd spent most of the weekend screwing each other senseless. Our friendship had morphed into something far more enjoyable, and although I knew I shouldn't have crossed that particular line, I couldn't resist the temptation. "Actually, I've been meaning to talk to you about something."

"Something to do with Reid?"

"No."

"Work?"

"Mmm." I took a bite out of the brownie and closed my eyes as I basked in the chocolate, caramel gooey goodness. "Oh. My. God." The after-effects trickled all the way down to my toes and I decided they were definitely an excellent runner-up to having sex. I closed my eyes and finally licked my lips.

"Louise, perhaps you should think about eating those in private."

I spluttered, choked and put the remaining brownie down. "Sorry." They should be declared illegal.

"Anyway, what were you saying about work?" he asked.

"Morning, Connor. Louise," Tyler's wife, Julie-Anne, greeted as she walked past our table.

"Morning," we both said in unison.

She hesitated.

"Join us for coffee?" Connor invited.

"Thanks." Julie-Anne pulled out a chair and sat down next to us. "You're not eating one of Hannah's brownies, are you?" She looked at me like I was just about to commit some deadly sin.

I nodded guiltily, stuffing the last of the brownie in my mouth before anyone could talk me out of it. All that was left on the plate were a few crumbs which I'd hoover up before I left.

"Oh dear." She looked from me to Connor.

"It's okay, Julie-Anne, I didn't have one. I'm going for the lamb, kumara and rosemary pie this morning. Breakfast," he added.

Julie-Anne nodded her approval and threw me a sideways glance, like she didn't trust my ability to control my food-provoked emotions.

"What's up?" Connor asked her.

"Did Tyler tell you he's got a specialist appointment next week in Greenhill?"

"Nope. Is he okay? Nothing serious, I hope?"

Again, she hesitated, and I got the feeling she was trying to decide what was the right thing to do.

"I shouldn't really say, but... he's got cancer." She had a look of complete sadness about her, as if the fight had already been fought and lost.

I choked and spluttered for a second time and hurriedly set my coffee down. "Have they got it in time? Does he need to take time off for treatments? I'm so sorry. Is there anything I can do?" The questions spewed out of me before I had time to formulate them properly. I backed up. "I'm sorry, I didn't mean to sound nosey."

"Thanks, love. He's okay. I'm not sure he'd like me telling you—you know what he's like; stubborn old coot. Doesn't want it turned into a big thing."

"Can I ask what type of cancer?" Concern was etched on Connor's face.

"Prostate."

Connor grimaced.

"It looks like he might have to fly down to Wellington for specialist treatment, maybe even an operation. I don't know what I'll do if something happens to him."

"Nothing's going to happen, except they'll get him treated. Everything's going to be fine," Connor tried to reassure her.

"I'm worried that he'll get worse, it'll spread, and he won't be able to work any longer. We rely on his pay each fortnight to bump up our pensions."

"Don't worry, Julie-Anne. He can take as much time as he needs on paid sick leave."

"Thank you, Connor. You're a good man." Her voice waivered and her eyes glistened. "It means a lot."

"Keep me up to date with what's happening, and if there is anything at all any of us can do, don't hesitate to let me know. Doesn't matter if it's something simple like mowing your lawn." He reached across and took her hand as a gesture of comfort. "Or running him to appointments. We've got it covered. Okay?"

"Okay." She claimed her hand back and took off her glasses, dabbed at her eyes with a tissue and replaced them.

Grace appeared at our table and deposited takeout coffees in a tray in front of Connor and a bag of donuts in front of me.

"All good?"

"Thanks, Grace," Connor answered. "We're good. Although not sure about Louise—she looks strange ever since she ate that brownie."

Everyone looked at me, but I was elsewhere, with a new idea blossoming in my head.

"Connor, I've got an idea," I told him as we walked back to the workshop.

"What might that be?"

"Well, you know how we were going to donate any profits of the derby to a charity?"

He nodded.

"What if we were to give it to the Prostate Society?"

"Okay."

"Help boost their funds."

"That's a great idea."

I could see he was giving it some thought.

"What about we make it more personalised to our community? Set up a trust and monies are used for any-one in Riverford who is sick or needs treatments and doesn't have the money to pay for them or the transport to get them."

"Like Tyler?"

"Exactly."

"I think it's a great idea," I said excitedly. "You could turn the race into an annual event!"

"Let's see how this one goes first. Do you think you can you pull it off without letting Tyler know he would be the first recipient?" We reached the workshop, and he stalled on the footpath outside, waiting for my answer.

"I think so." I grinned at him. "Leave it with me."

When I reached reception, there was a box sitting on my desk. I looked at the postage address label and knew exactly where it had come from and what it contained. I immediately cut at the tape with my new scissors and peeled back each flap to reveal T-shirts. Twelve of them. Six of them big enough to fit Connor and Reid, and the remainder should fit Liam, Tyler or me.

I read the note Eddie had included for me, smiled and pulled an extra-large out of its wrapping and held it up to admire the artwork. Perfect.

"What's that?" Reid shouted at me through the window of his office.

I jumped. In my excitement, I hadn't even noticed he was there.

"Please God, don't tell me it's a T-shirt," I heard him mumble.

"It's a T-shirt!" I yelled and jiggled it in front of his window.

"Dear God in heaven, save me."

He pushed back from his desk and joined me in reception. I thrust it at him.

"All yours. There's one for Connor too. And the guys out there."

"The things I do for you," he grumbled, pulling his sweatshirt off, followed by his tee. So much exposed skin was not good for my heart so early in the morning—especially after that brownie. I swallowed—just in case I was salivating—and hastily grabbed a tissue off my desk and dabbed at the corners of my mouth. But I had to look—a half-naked Reid was too good to miss.

He pulled the new shirt on over his ruffle of dark blond hair and tugged it down to his waist, until it sat around his hips. It clung to his body like it had been painted on. I had to admit he made the shirt look mighty good.

He hunted through the box of shirts until he found what he was looking for. "Now your turn," he said, dangling the shirt in front of me.

I unzipped my jacket and slipped out of the sleeves, revealing my T-shirt with *Just here for the perks* written across it. I glanced up at Reid in time to see his eyes widen and a smile form on his mouth.

"Give me the shirt." I snatched it from him. "You don't think I'm going to get undressed out here, do you?"

When I returned from the bathroom, Connor had joined Reid and he now sported one too.

"You made a great job of these," Connor said, looking impressed. "Thanks."

They had a small Hamilton's Automotive logo over the front left pectoral and on the back, there was a souped-up classic car with the words: *Hamilton's: making cars better since 1968.*

"I'll give one to Tyler and Liam," I told them and hurried out to the workshop floor.

When I returned the reception was empty. I unpacked the remaining shirts and fired up the computer. I had posters to design.

16

LOU

FROM MY OUTSTRETCHED POSITION on Han's sofa, I could see the rain steadily washing against the window. Great. And I'd promised Reid I'd go watch his rugby game.

I'd celebrated a productive week last night at McCarthy's with more rum and cola than I should have consumed, but it felt like things were going right for once in my life. Reid was being nice and I'd told him I'd be at the game today.

The Stallions were playing at the sports ground at three-thirty, this time against the Invaders. Eighty minutes of sitting in the rain didn't sound tempting—no matter how delicious the eye candy was.

I wondered about Reid. I hated to admit that I was enjoying our 'friendship', but I suspected nice Reid was far more dangerous than moody Reid.

I dragged myself up and headed for the shower. I'd hosted the tax department inspector's visit on Thursday because both brothers were intimidated by the guy. It was pathetic, but had gone well in my opinion, although the brownie he'd been given for his morning tea might have had something to do with it. I was proud of how I'd whipped everything into shape, and I'd readily accepted a couple of suggestions the inspector had given me and had added them to my list of things to implement before I eventually left Riverford.

Friday, I collected the posters and smaller flyers from the printers and spent several hours distributing them around town. I'd placed posters in as many shop windows as I could and some of the stores had flyers on their counters. I had the form loaded on the website and we were ready to take entries.

Next week I had a reporter from the Riverford Valley News coming to interview us about the race. It was already generating a great deal of competition around town. Matt had told Reid his grandson wanted to make a kart, and Will's next-door neighbour was building one in his garden shed with *his* grandson. The town was buzzing with excitement and kart designs were being kept top secret.

Liam had started building the Hamilton's entry and Connor and Reid were happy to leave him to it. They'd told him he could use the workshop when it was quiet, or on the weekends, when it wasn't normally open.

I dressed in my thermal long-sleeved top and rifled through my selection of tees until I found one that made me smile. Standing back to evaluate it, I nodded, pulled on a clean pair of jeans and finger-combed my hair. The café was already open and I'd go down and help out, even if it was only doing dishes. Then it would be time to head out to watch the rugby.

"Hi, Louise," Zoe Ford greeted. "I'm pleased you're here. I wanted to ask you something." The teen worked Saturdays and some weekdays after school, cleaning while she saved for a car. She deposited a stack of plates beside the sink next to the dishwasher and removed the top one with the food scraps on it.

"Sure. Ask away." I pushed my sleeves up. "I'll load these up for you."

"Thanks. You know how we have our school ball next Saturday," she said, scraping the leftovers into a bin.

I nodded. I'd heard about it when I'd taken a bunch of flyers to the high school for the metalwork department.

"Well, I wondered if you'd be able to do the makeup for me and a couple of my friends."

I stopped, mug in hand, and looked at her as if she'd just suggested Spider-Man was really the Easter Bunny. "I don't know. That's a big responsibility. What if I mess up?"

"Your makeup always looks amazing. We'd love you to do it, and we've saved up for our hair, makeup and nails, so we could pay you."

"You wouldn't need to pay me."

"Does that mean you'll do it?" She was looking at me like a puppy looks at its owner when there's food and cuddles involved.

I nodded. "Okay. I need an address and a time."

"Thanks! I'll write it down and give it to you before I leave." She rushed out of the kitchen to clear more tables.

"That was a nice thing to do," Hannah said, dropping a piping bag into the sink.

"I hope I can pull it off."

"I'm sure they'll love whatever you do. And they'll all have photos for reference."

"Are you and Will going to watch the game this afternoon?" I asked.

"I hope to. But we'll wait and see what the weather's doing first."

I finished loading the dishwasher and turned it on, then started on the dirty pots piled high in the sink.

"So, what's with you and Will?" I asked. "I think you've been keeping secrets from me." Will wasn't here this morning, so we had the kitchen to ourselves while Zoe was serving customers.

"What do you mean?" Hannah asked, sounding far too innocent for someone who had been sneaking a man into her apartment while I was at the pub drinking.

"Well, it's just that you seem like you've got a"—I trawled for the right word—"*connection* with Will."

She stopped mid-step with a tray of custard squares in her hand. "A connection?" And then she laughed.

I shrugged. "Yeah. Like you two have a thing happening."

"Well, thanks. I'll pass that news on to Will."

I felt embarrassment sweep up my face. "What I meant was, you two should definitely get together. You're perfect for each other."

"Maybe we are. But I'm not looking for a replacement husband right now." She carried on out to the café floor and slid the tray into one of the cabinets, before coming back to the kitchen.

"Anyway, you could live together without having to be married," I suggested, following her out to the café and then back again, wiping my hands on the apron I was wearing.

She looked at me and raised her eyebrows.

"Just saying." I quickly returned my attention to the sink and the dishes I was supposed to be washing.

By the time the café closed, the rain had eased up and was now a steady drizzle.

"Do you want a ride?" I asked Hannah as I hung up my apron.

"No, thanks. Will's picking me up."

I raised my eyebrows.

"Don't read anything into that. I've got a couple of apple crumbles to drop off to two elderly ladies who are housebound at the moment. You go on. I'll meet you there."

"Okay," I called over my shoulder as I headed upstairs to grab my coat, hat and scarf. "I'll save you a seat."

I felt like the Michelin man with so many layers on, but I knew it was going to be cold— worse than cold if I got wet. I grabbed my car keys and decided I'd just take my wallet so my bag wouldn't get soaked.

No bag. I always left it on the coffee table next to the sofa and then I spotted it on the floor. I rummaged inside. No wallet. Puzzled, I rechecked the floor. On top of various pieces of furniture. Behind cushions on the sofa. Pockets. Kitchen counter. It was nowhere.

"What's wrong?" Hannah asked, walking in and finding me crawling around on my hands and knees.

"I can't find my wallet. I thought it was in my bag, but it's not and I've searched everywhere."

"Did you check your car?"

"Not yet."

"Where did you have it last?"

I stood in the middle of the room, scratching my head. "I had it at work yesterday. I slipped it into my drawer. It's probably still there." So much great friends-with-benefits sex with Reid was addling my brain.

"Will you be able to go without it until Monday morning?"

"I'll stop off on my way to the game. Liam was supposed to be working on the kart, so the workshop should be open." I did have a key to the garage if I needed it, but I didn't like to use it if I was on my own.

"I'll see you shortly." She waved me off and I ran down to my car. I didn't know for certain Liam would be at the workshop, but it was worth a try.

As luck would have it, his vehicle was parked outside next to two other runabouts. One had a Kennedy Engineering logo on the door. As there was an empty shop on one side of the garage and small car parking lot on the other side, I wondered where the owners of the cars were.

I climbed out of my car and locked the door. The large garage door was closed, but the smaller side door was partially open. I pushed it further and, hearing voices, stepped inside. The large space fell deathly quiet, as though I might not notice the three men huddled together.

"Hi Liam," I called. "I'm just collecting something from the office." I pointed in the direction of the reception.

When they turned in my direction, although I couldn't see them all clearly, I felt awkward, like I was interrupting something top secret. Maybe they were talking race-day strategies.

Liam nodded at me and went back to talking with the other two men in a hushed voice. I wondered what they were discussing. I felt them watch me as I hurriedly walked through the workshop and unlocked the office door. Had Liam looked nervous, or was that just my imagination? I noticed there was no sign of the kart, and four small tyres sat stacked one on top of the other on the floor between them. I did notice Liam was dressed in faded jeans and a sweatshirt and didn't look like he'd been working.

Thankful to get to my desk, I found my wallet exactly where I'd left it. I shoved it in my coat pocket and when I turned to leave, Liam was standing behind me.

I gasped in fright. "Geez, Liam. I didn't hear you come in."

He glanced over his shoulder and turned back to me. "I remembered I still owe you a movie. How about tonight?"

He was standing close enough that I could smell his aftershave. I sidestepped him and moved towards the reception door. I really liked Liam—he was always fun—but right now, he was creeping me out.

"I totally forgot about that rain check."

"So, are you up for it?"

I was hoping there would be a few drinks at the pub after the game this afternoon, and I'd get to perve on Reid some more—maybe even have dinner with him. I knew the more time I spent with him, the bigger the wrench would be when it came time to leave Riverford, but I couldn't help myself. It was like he was this humongous magnet, and I was a clusterfuck of iron filings. With every move he made, I was uncontrollably drawn closer to him, and after a glimpse at his romantic side, I was being pulled to him even faster. And I realised I'd far sooner spend time with Reid than Liam. There was no hope for me.

"Louise?"

"Sure." *Damn.* Why didn't I suggest a drink out at McCarthy's? "But could we go tomorrow night?"

"Great. Seven-thirty. I'll meet you outside the theatre." He glanced out at the garage and looked relieved.

"Deal. How's the kart coming?" I asked, locking the office door behind me and making my way back across the workshop.

"I'm making good progress with the kart. Reckon she'll leave the other entries in the dust."

I nodded. The two men had disappeared. I did a quick scan of the workshop floor and couldn't see them. I still couldn't see any sign of the kart or the tyres. "Who were the men?"

"Just a couple of mates."

"Wait—it's a *she*?" I asked.

"Who?"

"The kart."

"Yeah. Motors always are."

He gave me a corny smile and I laughed. "Sexist much?"

"Not me."

"Yeah, right. You men are all the same. I'll see you tomorrow night." I edged my way out the door and onto the street, thankful to get into my car. I noticed the two vehicles had gone.

The rain had settled in and the stand at the sports ground was almost full when I arrived. I stood at the bottom and scanned the rows, looking for Will or Annie. I caught Hannah waving and climbed the steps, easing myself along the row of knees until I got to her. She and Will had saved a seat for both me and Annie. What the heck were they wearing?

"Find it?" she asked.

"Oh. Yes! It was exactly where I'd left it. Hi, Will," I added, leaning around Hannah.

"Here." He unfurled a couple of rubbish bags from a roll and reached across Hannah to hand them to me.

"Thanks. What should I do with them?" It was then I noticed *that* was what both Will and Hannah had on over their clothes. I laughed. "Uh-uh. I'm not climbing into one of those."

"Laugh if you want," Will said, giving me a smug look. "But if you want to stay reasonably warm and dry, make a hole in the sealed end and stick it over your head, and likewise with the other one for your feet."

I scrutinised Hannah's outfit. Apart from her feet and head, the rest of her body was sheathed in black plastic. I looked further along the row and noticed this attire was a trend. I tore a hole in the end and pulled it down over my head.

"Hi all," Annie greeted, dropping into the empty seat on the other side me. "Damn, I forgot to bring my bags. Got any spares, Will?"

He rolled off a couple more and we passed them along to Annie. She wiggled her way into each one and I smirked.

"What's so funny?"

"Us."

"Laugh now, but at the end of eighty minutes when you're dry and warm, you'll thank Will."

"I look like a bedraggled homeless lady."

Annie grinned. "Actually, you're now a fully certified Stallions supporter."

"Dry, homeless and fully certified." What more could I want?

Although my hair was plastered to my face like I'd fallen in a vat of hair gel, the rest of me, as predicted, was reasonably warm and for the most part dry, unlike many of the visiting crowd who were dressed only in raincoats and had soaked pants.

Reid had played another good game, but the coach had substituted him and two others at half-time. I sat disappointed during the second half with only Connor to watch, until they took him off the field too. The Stallions won the game by an overwhelming margin and we all headed for McCarthy's to celebrate another triumph.

"What will it be, ladies?" Matt asked, as we barrelled up to the bar and grabbed a seat.

"Rum and Coke for me, thanks, Matt, and can I have a large serving of fries?" I wanted the instant gratification only deep-fried potatoes would give me.

"House white," Hannah ordered. "And a beer for Will."

"How'd the boys do?"

"It was an all-too-easy victory to the Stallions," Annie filled him in. She rounded the bar and shrugged out of her coat and disappeared to hang it up. "Here they are," she announced, tying her apron on.

I spun on my seat as an arm of muscle wrapped around my waist.

"Hi, sexy," Reid's voice sounded in my ear. He gave Will a friendly slap on the back and squeezed his way between us. "So, you came to the game."

I automatically ran my fingers through my damp hair. "What gave it away?" I grinned up at him. Thank God he hadn't been able to see me looking so glamourous.

He stepped back and turned to Will. "Did she look good in uniform?"

"Uniform?" I had no idea what he was rambling about.

Will winked at me. He pulled out his phone and tapped out his PIN before showing the screen to Reid. "Next level, mate. You've got a keeper there." He gave me a wink.

Reid studied the screen and erupted in laughter. Will angled the screen in my direction.

O.M.F.G.! "I look like a giant lubed condom! Delete that at once," I ordered Will.

"You know I can't unsee that, don't you?" Reid smirked.

Great. Now I was going to be the laughing stock of the town. I took a long swallow of my rum to try and quell some of the embarrassment and changed the subject. "Why did you get sent off?"

Matt slid a beer across the bar to Reid followed by a large bowl of fries for me. Reid reached around me and helped himself to some of the hot crispy potatoes.

"If it's obvious we're going to win the game, the coach will pull the best players off the field so there's no chance they'll get hurt. It gives the reserves a good run and saves the slightly better players for the tough games."

"So, you're saying you're one of the best players?"

"I'm not saying anything. I just do what the coach tells me to do," he said, helping himself to more fries.

I finished the last of my drink, stepped down from my seat and grabbed my wallet.

"Leaving so soon?" Reid asked.

"I'm leaving before the whole bar sees me dressed as a huge prophylactic." Will was showing Ellie on the other side of the bar. "I'm going to head home, take a hot shower, then veg in front of the TV and watch a movie."

"What's for dinner?"

"Don't know."

"Why don't you come back with me? We can call in at yours and you can pick up what you need and head back to mine. I'm making my famous lasagne and there'll be plenty. You can shower and change while I make dinner, then we can watch a movie together." He gave me a panty-melting smile that hoisted every red flag in my body, before reaching across to the bar to deposit his empty glass. His arm brushed against mine and I felt a familiar warmth spread down my spine. The flags waved harder for attention.

"I don't know," I started, not wanting to sound over-eager, but he did have a large screen and a fireplace. It was an offer too good to turn down. "I guess I wouldn't mind spending some time with your fireplace and your enormous TV screen."

He placed a hand on my back and allowed it to slide up over my shoulder to my neck and bury his fingers in my hair. "Don't forget my cooking," he murmured against my ear.

"I love lasagne!" I said in a voice a little too loud.

Everyone turned in my direction. I felt my face flood with heat as I realised I'd sounded far too excited about what we'd be eating.

"Well, it's my favourite," I muttered and shrugged back into my coat.

17

REID

AFTER WHAT I CONSIDERED was a wasted day at the rugby, most of it spent sitting on the bench, I reasoned that Louise accepting my invitation to dinner and a movie meant that our blossoming relationship was heading in the right direction. I knew how to make a handful of recipes well, and lasagne was one of them.

"Got everything?" I asked as she dumped her overnight bag on the back seat and climbed into the passenger seat next to me.

"Thanks," she said, clicking her seatbelt into place as I reversed out of the parking space. "I hope all this talk of lasagne isn't just a ploy to get me naked in your shower?"

I spun my head to her and inadvertently crunched the truck's gears. Since I stepped out of McCarthy's it was all I could fucking think about: Lou, naked in my shower. I turned back to the road.

"I'm sorry you think so little of me." I turned away to look out the side window where she couldn't see my grin.

"It's not that. I do trust you—"

"Don't worry. I promise the pasta is seriously good."

She sang along to the Lorde song playing on the radio until I pulled the truck into my drive. "Hey," I said, turning the ignition off. "Thanks for today."

"For what?"

"Coming to the game. Dressing the part. Sacrificing your reputation. It's really nice to know you're there in the crowd shouting my name."

"How do you know I wasn't cheering for Connor?" She dipped her head hiding her eyes.

She was fidgeting with a fingernail, and I reached across and lifted her chin. "Were you?"

She looked up and stared at me for what seemed an age before she spoke. Her answer came out as a murmur, but I heard the *no* as if she'd yelled it at me. Her eyes held promises of pleasure. My heart somersaulted in my chest.

"I want to kiss you so much right now." I reached out a hand and cupped her cheek in my palm. She didn't flinch. "I told myself I wouldn't do this, that I need to take it slow, but damn, you make it so fucking hard."

Her eyes widened and sparkled as she leaned across the console. "I want you to kiss me."

I also wanted to drag her into my lap and steam up the windows, but if I did that, the lasagne wouldn't get made. We had the whole night ahead of us.

I pulled her closer. With her breath warm against my skin, I slid my hand around her neck and up into her hair, easing her face to mine. I paused, our eyes lost in each other's, and then my lips met hers. The softness of them made me want to nestle into them and stay there. She gently nipped at my lower lip and all the blood drained from the top half of my body. I knew what she was capable of. What lay locked away inside her. Protected from anyone who might hurt her.

"Let's go," I croaked, then coughed to cover my inability to control my voice. I climbed out, rearranged my package and grabbed her bag from the back seat. She followed me to the doorstep and waited while I unlocked and pushed the door open.

She shrugged out of her coat and hung it on the hook by the door.

"I'll grab a towel and leave you to take a shower if you want one, while I make a start on dinner."

She nodded and silently followed me through the house. I wanted to take her hand and lead her straight to my room, but I settled for fetching her a towel and left her to it.

While I worked in the kitchen, I could hear the shower running and my mind kicked into overdrive as I sliced, diced and sautéed celery, onion, garlic and carrots. Thinking of what was happening in that bathroom made my hands shake. I had to put my knife down. Twice. As if my feelings for Lou weren't dangerous enough.

I lit the fire and was busy layering the lasagne sheets with the filling and cheese sauce when a movement at the door made me glance up.

"Hi."

"Hi." She was leaning against the doorframe, watching me, dressed in a floor-length full skirt and a tank that said: *I'm not here to talk*. Fine by me. She pushed off and moved to the other side of the counter. "That smells delicious."

"I told you it would be good. Do you want something to drink? I have rum and I have Coke. Or would you like a beer? Water?"

"Rum, please. Can I help with anything?"

"No. The fire is on, if you want to go through." I liked how much skin she was showing and my hands were shaking again. I wasn't even this nervous when I was behind bars. What the hell was wrong with me? "I'll be through in a minute." I finished assembling dinner and shoved it in the oven and organised the drinks. I needed to keep busy to take my mind off the scent of honeysuckle that was drifting through the house.

I found her curled up on the sofa. "Shower okay?"

"It was. Thank you." She took her drink from me, looking up abruptly when our fingers touched, then quickly sampling it before placing it on the side table. "I've got a question for you," she said, standing up and crossing to stand in front of the fire.

"Okay."

"What's wrong with you, Reid Hamilton?"

I spluttered and put my drink down before I spilled it. "What do you mean, what's wrong with me?"

"Well," she paced away from the fire, then turned back to stare at me. I could see the challenge in her eyes, but there was also a vulnerability that took my breath away.

"Why aren't you married with a beautiful wife and a bunch of kids?"

Her directness caught me off guard and I stumbled around the words. "I've never found anyone who interested me that much." She sized me up and I narrowed my eyes at her, waiting for her next question.

She did the same back to me, though with a slight grin pulling at one corner of those full lips. "There's something else, isn't there?"

Damn this honesty shit. I crossed my arms over my chest in a defensive move. "There's no secret. I like my privacy. I don't like the limelight. It's bad enough playing rugby and running out on the field knowing there are several hundred people watching."

"But they aren't all watching you."

"It doesn't matter. That's why I'd be happy if Connor took centre stage with the website and all the marketing shit. I'm in my element working in the background." I ran my hand over the stubble on my chin and sighed. "Being locked up didn't help that. Why are you asking me so many questions, when you're not here to talk?" I nodded at her shirt.

"Don't know." She shrugged and I noticed the way her breasts moved and realised she wasn't wearing a bra.

"It's fun asking you questions and watching you squirm. Maybe we need to talk more?"

I crossed to stand in front of her. "I think I'm done talking."

"Are you?" Her voice was quiet, then she stepped into me and slid a hand up over my chest and grabbed the collar of my shirt. Tonight, I wasn't waiting for instructions. I took her head in my hands and let my mouth crush against hers. Our tongues tangoed and explored each other's depths. I held my breath.

"Fuck, where did you learn to kiss like this?" I asked when I could breathe again. Then she was back stealing my soul, her tongue moving with mine, drawing me deeper until I'd be nothing but a pool of liquid lust with a raging hard-on.

My body was in sensory overload as Lou's hands pushed my jumper over my head and worked on the buttons of my shirt. I liked where this was going. The whispered moans escaping from her lips didn't help me tame my desire for her. My hands searched under her tank and found the curves of her breasts while I inhaled the scent of her.

Her skin was satin-soft and my lips wanted to cover every inch of it. I lifted her tank and started with a nipple. She moaned her pleasure out loud.

I reached down and ran my hands up under the floaty floor-length fabric of her skirt until I found her thighs. My heart stopped and I pulled back to glance at her. There was an evil, sultry grin plastered across her face. She wasn't wearing any fucking panties.

Hoisting her up off the floor, she wrapped her legs around my waist and kissed the life out of me as I strode back to the kitchen counter and sat her on it, sliding the skirt up over her hips.

Sweet Jesus. I gulped, nearly swallowing my tongue. Her fingers were lost in my hair and her mouth was fucking with the skin on my shoulder. She was one hell of a package, and I was damned if she was leaving this town any time soon. Possibly never.

I patted my jeans pocket.

"We don't need a condom," she reminded me. I could withstand the force of a rugby team, but when this woman breathed in my ear and told me to go in naked, my knees almost buckled and I had to hold on in case I blacked out.

I pushed her back against the cool surface of the marble until she was exposed to me. Her beautiful soft body with its perfectly proportioned curves. My lips danced over the inside of her thigh; she groaned and arched her back as I moved towards my target. My head was spinning. I licked like she was coated in fucking maple syrup.

"Reid?"

I reached the apex of her thighs.

"Oh... God... Reid. Your... phone."

"Ignore it," I growled. I had multiple orgasms on my mind that didn't involve me speaking to another living person right now, except the one lying on my counter.

She pushed herself up, grabbed my hair and yanked me upright. "Answer your phone. It might be important."

I blinked. "Really?"

She nodded.

I'd be lucky if I could get the damn phone out of my back pocket, my pants were now so fucking tight, thanks to her. I sighed, struggled with the phone and finally dug it free. "Hello? Julie-Ann? Slow down and start from the beginning."

I paced the kitchen and looked up to see Lou pull her skirt back down and jump off the counter. I swore the Big Guy was trying to gnaw his way out of my boxer briefs and it was extremely difficult to concentrate on what Julie-Ann was saying, but something in my brain caught at the word ambulance. I turned away from the kitchen and Lou so I could think. It sounded like Tyler had collapsed.

"Slow down and breathe. You need to be calm for Tyler, okay? I'll jump in the truck and be right there. I'm only five minutes away. He's going to be fine. Just sit tight, I'm on my way."

"What's wrong?" Lou asked, pulling her top back on and following me out into the hall. I pulled both my T-shirt and my jumper back over my head and tucked myself in.

"Tyler collapsed and it sounds like he's unresponsive. Julie-Ann has rung for an ambulance but she's scared and panicked about what's going on and couldn't get hold of Connor." I pulled my jacket off the hook by the front door and slipped my arms into it.

"I'm coming with you."

"You're definitely coming with me, but not to Julie-Ann's." I leaned into her face, kissed her pillowy lips and offered her a lame apology for not being able to fulfil her wildest dreams—just yet. "Can you watch the dinner? It has another ten minutes in the oven. If I'm not back in half an hour, eat and make yourself at home." I patted my jacket pockets for truck keys and gave Lou a quick kiss on her lips, wrenched the door open and ran for my truck.

18

REID

IT WAS JUST MY luck that Connor hadn't answered his phone. The bastard. But I wasn't one to shirk my responsibilities, and Tyler was like a father to me. He was the last of our father's friends still alive. He probably should have retired years ago. Guilt squeezed my gut as I drove.

I got to their home—a modest two-bedroom town house set back from the road—as two officers were unloading a gurney from the back of their ambulance. I jumped out of my truck and ran up the drive and through the open front door. I could hear Julie-Ann sobbing and uttering the same *you'll be okay* mantra over and over.

"Reid!" She rushed to my side, and I wrapped an arm around her in support.

"How's he doing?" I asked.

"He's still not responsive. They're taking him to the hospital."

"What happened? Did he take a fall?"

"I don't know. I went out to the kitchen to make a cup of tea and when I came back in, he was on the floor."

"Julie-Ann, would you like to come with us?" Jake, the young ambulance officer asked.

She turned to me, and I nodded.

"If he wakes, it would be reassuring for him to see you there by his side," Jake added.

"But—"

I took her hand. It was shaking. "I'll follow behind the ambulance and meet you there. Julie-Ann?"

She dabbed at her eyes.

"He's going to be okay. Now, grab your purse, find a warm jacket and go with your husband."

She nodded and returned a minute later, following her husband outside. She handed me her door key.

"I'll turn things off, lock up and meet you there."

I watched them leave, then walked through the house, turned off the small fan heater in the sitting room and made sure everything was secure before I jumped in my truck and started it up. I got to the hospital as they were unloading Tyler from the ambulance into the emergency department. Since my brother still wasn't picking up, I left him a voice message, then rang Louise as I walked across the car park and into the ED.

"Hey," she answered, concern telling in the strain of her voice. "How's Tyler? Is he going to be all right? Where are you?"

"I don't know anything yet, it's too soon. I'm at the hospital with Julie-Ann. She's pretty upset, so I'll stay with her and wait for an update."

"Give her my love and if there's anything I can do, let me know."

"Thanks, sweetheart, I will."

I sat in the waiting room with an arm around Julie-Ann's shoulders, thinking about what it must feel like to lose your partner of fifty years or more. The grief, I imagined, would be unbearable. My thoughts drifted to Louise with a warm fuzzy feeling in my gut like it was full of velveteen rabbits. She got up to use the bathroom. With elbows on my knees, head in my hands, I massaged the worry throbbing in my temples. I didn't want to lose Louise again. She was the best medicine for what ailed me. But there was another ache that was growing in intensity that I'd probably need a crash cart for, and that was love. I was falling—no, I *had* fallen in love with Louise. Head over fucking heels. What we had wasn't a fling, wasn't some *fun* while she was in town. It was the forever kind, and it scared me batshit crazy. We needed to talk when I got back home. I needed to tell her how I felt, even though I wasn't the best at offloading any touchy-feely thoughts.

"Reid?"

I looked up and found Kerri Allworth standing in front of me. She was the ED doctor who I'd been on a couple of dates with after Hannah and I had split. She'd been too career-focused for me. Training to be a doctor, she took her studies seriously, unlike me, who'd been a general dick and didn't take anything seriously. In all honesty, she was way out of my league.

"Kerri. How's Tyler doing?" I got to my feet and sat back down again when she took the seat next to mine.

"It doesn't look good. We suspect the cancer has spread and it's much worse than Julie-Ann is aware. It's going to be hard on her, but I think he's going to end up in palliative care."

"I didn't realise he was so bad."

"I think Tyler has kept working in order to keep things as normal as possible for her. You know what that generation is like. They'll turn up at work no matter how sick they are."

"I feel like a total shit. I should have paid more attention."

"To be fair, you've had your hands full the last year or so."

She was right. I had only seen Tyler twice during my incarceration when he'd come in to visit, and I'd told him I didn't want a man like him setting foot inside a joint like the one I was in. He'd complained, but I'd told him he was helping me by keeping an eye on Connor and the garage.

"We're getting him prepped to fly down to Wellington. They'll run all the tests and if it's feasible, they'll start treatment, but if it's as bad as I think, they'll fly him back and he'll go into care here in town so he's close to Julie-Ann."

I got to my feet and paced. "How long do you think he has?"

"Without seeing any test results, it's only a guess. But I'd say, maybe a month. Two, tops."

Shit. "Does Julie-Ann know?"

"No. I don't want to share any guesses I have, because at the moment, that's all they are. The doctors in Wellington will tell her once they have the results." She ran a quick glance over me and placed a hand on my shoulder. "How are you doing, Reid? I haven't seen you since you got out."

I was surprised at her touch. It felt healing.

"I'm fine, but I keep to myself when I can."

"I hear you're quite the hero on the rugby field."

"I doubt that. I heard you got married to Owen Hayes while I was away. I hope he's taking good care of you." Owen Hayes owned a helicopter charter business that often took him away from home. He was also rostered on as a rescue helicopter pilot. Kerri worked long, odd hours and by luck, they seemed to be able to make their marriage work.

"He is." She smiled at me, and I wondered if she was comparing her husband with me and thanking her lucky stars she escaped the clutches of Reid Hamilton.

I eventually drove Julie-Ann home, where she packed a few clothes and toiletries together before I took her back to the hospital. When we arrived, Connor was sitting in the waiting room.

"Julie-Ann, how are you holding up?"

I narrowed my eyes at him, but let her talk.

"They are flying Tyler down to Wellington. I'm going with him."

A nurse appeared. "Mrs Ramsden?"

We all turned to face her.

"Mr Ramsden is comfortable and ready to go now, if you'd like to come with me."

Julie-Ann nodded and turned to me. I wrapped her in my arms and hugged her. Then Connor took his turn. For once in my life, I couldn't say everything was going to be okay, because I knew it wouldn't be.

19

LOU

I OPENED MY EYES and immediately noticed two things: one, I didn't recognise the ceiling I was staring at, and two, I could smell bacon. I didn't care about the ceiling, but the bacon was a whole different ball game.

Propping myself up on an elbow, I remembered I'd climbed into Reid's bed at midnight when he hadn't returned. Dinner had been delicious and when he was a no show by nine, I covered it and shoved it in the fridge. Making myself comfy, I settled in and watched two full-length movies on Netflix, then decided that if *he* wasn't using his bed, I might as well enjoy it.

I swung my legs over the side and remembered I only had my underwear on. I noticed Reid's T-shirt where he'd dropped it on the floor and pulled it on. I loved that it smelt like old cars and pine trees. From the kitchen door, I was rewarded with the sight every woman dreams of: a topless god cooking breakfast. His hair was tousled and the muscles across his shoulders moved in waves as he worked. He was turning the art of cracking eggs into a sexual fantasy. His chest still held a tan leftover from summer and his nipples begged to be licked.

This man made me drool.

I swallowed and ran my tongue across my lips. His grey pyjama pants rode dangerously low on his hips; the funnelling V lines forced my eyes down over his resting penis to his uncovered feet. Strong, perfectly manicured toenails... I took a breath... They bordered on erotic. A man with good feet was a man who took care of the rest of his body. My heart was beating so rapidly I was sure anytime now I'd have a cardiac event.

He looked up and gave me a wicked smile as I ventured further into the kitchen.

"Good morning, gorgeous."

His voice had a saucy tone to it. I lifted a finger in response, beckoned him to me and kissed him like I needed the air he was breathing.

"Thanks," he said, looking down at the massive hard-on he was now sporting. "You've woken the dragon."

I waved him away. "Don't point that thing at me until you've fed me."

He laughed and my body temperature increased, parts of me tingling with anticipation. I felt powerful when I knew I could create this reaction. I stood a little straighter and stuck my boobs out.

He was looking at me like he'd far sooner eat me than the hash browns and bacon he was allocating to plates, and I was beginning to think that would be a better idea.

"How is Tyler—have you heard anything?" I asked, hoping it would take my mind off the orgasm-producing machine he kept in his pyjama bottoms.

"I rang the hospital about an hour ago. He was awake and in a stable condition."

"Julie-Ann must be relieved."

"Unfortunately, the diagnosis isn't good. He's been given a month."

"A month? You mean that's how long he has to spend in hospital?"

"No." His voice dropped, and I could hear the pain in it. "Life expectancy."

He looked down at what he was doing and turned his back to me.

"I'm so sorry." I slipped off the stool I was perched on and put an arm around his waist. "He's like a father to you and Connor, isn't he? It must be so difficult for you both right now."

"Yeah."

I could hear the anguish, and I knew it must have been hard for him at the hospital with Julie-Ann. "If there's anything I can do, please, tell me."

"Thanks. It's not just that he was a father figure, but he's the end of an era, you know? He's kind of the last human link to Dad."

I dropped a kiss on his shoulder blade as I moved past him. A moment later, he slid my plate across to me. I was suddenly starving, and dug into a fried tomato and layered it with some hash brown and mushroom.

"You're pretty good in a kitchen. You'll make some-one a good wife one day," I said, trying to lighten the sombre mood that had descended.

He lifted an eyebrow. "You have no idea."

I had a fair idea, but I was far too hungry to discuss it. "I checked the number of entrants in the kart race last night," I informed him, shovelling bacon and hash brown into my mouth. "We've got ten in the children's category and six in adults so far."

"That's more than I expected we'd get."

"It's just the start, O ye of little faith. I'm going to take some posters over to Greenhill today and see if we can't get a ton more entries."

He nodded and we ate in silence for a while, each of us deep in our own thoughts, until Reid put his knife and fork down and stared up at me.

"What? Do I have something on my face?" I wiped my mouth with the back of my hand.

"No, you don't. I was just thinking how nice it was to come home last night and find you asleep in my bed. I could get to like that. A lot."

"To be honest, it was sheer luxury not to be sleeping on Han's couch."

"Oh, I see." He lifted his chin and dipped it. "You're using me to get to my Egyptian cotton sheets."

"Maybe. That and the fact you've got a fully stocked fridge that would drive any woman crazy, and your rain shower head is total bliss."

Laughter rumbled from some place deep in him, which triggered that tingly buzz between my thighs.

When we'd finished eating, I gathered the dishes, rinsed them in the sink and stacked them in the dishwasher.

"Leave those. You have a second course to finish."

"Second course?" I pictured a stack of pancakes with raspberries and banana with maple syrup drizzled over them. And a scoop of vanilla ice cream...

"Interested?"

"What is it? Pancakes? I love them."

He met me at the counter and scooped me up in his arms. "Nope," he said, kissing my lips and faintly tasting of bacon. "An orgasm."

"What? Only one?"

"I don't want to break you, sweetheart."

"You wanna try?"

I made an embarrassing high-pitched squealy type of noise as he carried me back towards his bedroom and threw me on the mattress, impatiently dragging his tee over my head like a toddler rips into a birthday present. He knelt at the end of the bed, his hands smoothing up my legs. Inching closer to my—

With one swift movement, he flipped me and I was on my stomach. He grabbed my ankles and pulled me closer towards him. My heart palpitated and my vision blurred. I gripped a handful of bedding. Orgasms, here I come.

It was raining again when I ran across the road to meet Liam outside the movie theatre. He wasn't here yet, so I moved back from the kerb and huddled in the doorway to keep dry. I hadn't wanted to come tonight. I hadn't wanted to leave Reid, but I'd made a promise and I'd keep it, because that's what I did.

I hated conflict. I avoided it at any cost. And that had been my biggest downfall. I'd let both Jayden and Aaron walk all over me instead of standing up to them. I didn't know why I couldn't say no to Liam, when I had no trouble at all saying no to Reid.

He hadn't been happy when he found out I was meeting Liam at the movies, and refused to let me drive there on my own. But I'd promised it was just the movies, nothing was going to happen, and I wouldn't be repeating the date.

"Hey!" Liam shouted, slamming his car door and locking it as he stepped onto the pavement. I waved and waited for him to join me from a couple of parking spots away.

"What's with all this rain?" he asked, shaking himself. I stepped back out of the way. Liam opened the theatre door for me and I entered the bright buzz of the cinema's foyer. I hadn't been inside since my last visit, when I'd gone one night with Hannah and Reid. The place had been repainted, but it had the same appealing old-fashioned vibe.

"What are we watching?"

We stood and looked at the offerings and I let Liam pick one. When we got to the ticket booth I stood back. It was the first time I had done that. Normally I would rush to pay for both of us. Pay for the chocolate covered ice cream cone with the nuts, and pay for anything else either of us might want.

But tonight, I hesitated.

"You first," Liam put his hand on the small of my back and pushed me forwards.

I handed over my card and paid for both of us. *Damn.* I couldn't help it. It was a habit that was obviously going to take a while to break. I handed him his ticket and then fumed silently to myself as we found our seats in the dimly lit theatre. My job at the garage meant I was starting to accumulate some savings, but after paying board to Hannah and keeping my car in petrol, there wasn't a lot to set aside. A night out at the movies was a luxury I couldn't really afford.

I sat through car chases and loud, sudden explosions while Liam hooted and cheered and kept nudging me in the shoulder, as though he needed my approval to enjoy it. And when the movie finally ended and he suggested we head to McCarthy's for a drink, I was so pleased to be leaving, I readily jumped at the idea.

It was almost nine p.m. and there were a few couples chatting over a quiet drink. I noticed local cops Gaylene Dewinter and Johnny Martin at one of the tables, and wiggled my fingers at them. Gaylene waved back. I didn't know either of them well enough to know if they were an item, but they looked like they'd been having an intimate conversation about something.

"Well, this is a surprise," Rachel, Annie's younger sister, greeted us. She always worked the slower shifts,

Sundays to Wednesdays, and other days only if Matt was short-staffed.

"Hi, Rachel," I said, walking straight to the bar and sliding onto a stool.

She looked from me to Liam. "Don't usually see you in here on a Sunday evening. What will it be?"

Liam was grinning like he'd just scored the winning lotto ticket. "Heineken, thanks Rach."

Rachel glared at him. "Louise?"

"Orange juice, thanks."

She busied herself with our orders and then wandered off to clear a table. The pub would be closing in an hour, and the kitchen was already in darkness. When Liam hustled off to use the bathroom, Gaylene appeared at my side.

"Hey, Louise," she greeted casually.

"Hi. Off duty?"

"Yep. What's going on between you and Liam?"

"Nothing. Why?"

"Just curious."

I eyeballed her, but before I could get any more out of her, Rachel appeared at my side.

"Are you going out with Liam?" she whispered, leaning against the counter.

"What? No! How can you even think that?"

"Does he know that?"

"I don't really care what he thinks he knows."

"How's Reid taking this?"

"What do you mean?"

"I thought you and Reid had a thing?"

"Are you and Reid officially a couple?" Gaylene asked.

I nodded and shook my head all at once. I suddenly felt like I was being interrogated.

"Does he know you're out with Liam?" Rachel continued.

I heaved a sigh. "Reid and I are... just good friends. And yes, he knows."

She rolled her eyes and gathered up the empty glasses on the nearest table. "Like friends with benefits."

"Who's getting the benefits?" Liam asked as he returned from the bathroom and skulled his beer.

Gaylene went back to her table and Rachel loaded glasses into the washer.

"What did they want?" Liam asked.

"No idea. I need to be getting home," I said. I had a busy day planned at work tomorrow and I didn't want Liam getting the wrong idea.

"I gotta take a run over to Greenhill after work tomorrow night to pick up some tyres for the kart. You wanna come?"

"I thought you had tyres?"

"I got some special ones made, but they didn't fit. We could grab some McD's on the way home."

"I don't think so. I promised Hannah I'd cook dinner tomorrow night for her and Will." I hadn't, but it was the only excuse I could come up with at such short notice.

"Fair enough. See you tomorrow." And with that, he turned for the door and left.

I turned and found Rachel leaning on the bar, watching. I couldn't help but laugh. "I think I've just been dumped."

"I don't think so." She nodded towards the door, and I turned to see Reid walking towards me.

20

LOU

APART FROM TYLER STILL being in hospital in Wellington, there was an unusual buzz in the workshop. I guessed it was over the impending race. The phone rang constantly with enquiries, I'd got a couple more sponsors onboard and three new jobs were booked in. Both Connor and Reid were helping Liam on the workshop floor, and if Liam wasn't working on someone's car, he was working on the kart. It was only a month away now and we had just hit fifty-one entries from around the region. With a list of things to do, I was happy that everything was progressing well.

"Excuse me!"

I'd just stepped out of Hannah's with everyone's lunch orders and turned to see a woman striding towards me. She looked to be about Hannah's age and was dressed in a silk shirt with a tailored jacket and matching pants that allowed the toes of her black shoes to poke out at me. I disliked her on sight, with her perfectly coiffured hair and carefully sculptured nails.

"Louise Adair?"

"That's me," I answered, feeling underdressed and wishing I'd made more effort with my hair and makeup.

"Ah, Louise. It's finally lovely to meet you. I've been meaning to track you down." She held her hand out and I juggled the assortment of brown paper bags to free up a hand. I remembered where I'd seen her face before.

"I'm Jeanette Monroe—"

"Mayor of Riverford," I finished, noting her perfect application of strawberry-red lipstick. "I was going to call and ask if you'd do the honours and present the winners of the charity kart race with their prizes. If you're available that day."

"Perfect," she said. "I saw your posters around town and I'd love to support the event. I wanted to know how I could help Connor and Reid."

The breeze caught strands of long, straightened, blonde hair and curtained them across her face, but not before I noticed the far-off look in her eyes at the mention of Reid. She casually guided the strands back behind one ear, and as I wondered how well she knew either of the brothers, one of the bags in my hand slipped and splatted on the pavement. Damn. I scooped it up, hoping the contents still resembled food.

"That's great," I stuttered. Why couldn't I have at least half the confidence our honourable mayor radiated?

"Did you know that three empty stores on the main street have been hired for pop-up businesses over that weekend? This charity race is certainly attracting visitors to our wee town. I must call in and see Reid and Connor and tell them."

"I'm just heading back to work. I'll tell them for you. Actually, I'd better get back there now. They'll be waiting for their lunches."

"How's Reid doing these days? I must catch up with him."

"He's busy with work." I lifted my hands, clutching the bags of rapidly cooling food, and smiled pleasantly at her. "And waiting for lunch."

"Right. Ring my office and confirm the time you'd like me at the finish line."

I nodded. She flashed me a row of gleaming white teeth, with not one trace of lip colour on any of them, before pushing through the door and disappearing into the café.

I was stopped twice more before I made it back to the garage. The race was on everyone's lips and I was happy to chat about it. It was for a cause that would benefit all Riverford residents—I was just sorry we couldn't do more for Tyler.

"Geez, Louise, what took you so long?" Liam called, when he spotted me enter the workshop floor. The guys were standing around one of the analytic machines and all three of them stopped and followed me, although I suspected it was the food they were after.

I picked up the pace and made it to reception before they swamped me. I put the bags down and took cover behind my desk to let them find their now-cold, half-mutilated lunches. A minute later, I heard Reid's familiar growl and looked up to see him staring at what used to be a lamb, sweet potato and rosemary pie, before it had been dropped on the ground. He was not happy.

"Blame the mayor!" I yelled, as I got up and rushed along the hall to the bathroom and locked myself in.

The week passed quickly, and I spent most of my days organising an assortment of food trucks for the sports club, arranging to collect prizes and writing press releases. The local paper had done a full-page spread on the event, including interviews with a couple of kids. Everything was coming together nicely.

On Friday, I was tidying up before I left for the day when Reid strode into reception with a customer. He'd been working on Chelsea Richards Swift since before lunch, and hopefully was finished.

"Take a seat, Ms Richards, and we'll get your account finalised for you." He was pulling his overalls down around his waist and exposing the contoured surfaces of hardened muscle under the Hamilton's T-shirt. I leaned back in my chair and admired his form. By the way Chelsea's eyes were bulging from their sockets, we were about to start up a team event.

He rounded the reception and disappeared into his office. I swung back to the job in hand and discovered Chelsea leaning over the reception counter, watching him through the window that divided our spaces.

This was not good. Regaining my common sense, I stood up straight and blocked her view. If anyone was going to be fluttering eyelashes and salivating, it would be me.

"Take a seat, Chelsea, I won't be long," I told her, pointing at the seats behind her.

Chelsea Richards was four years older than me, and had trained as a teacher, worked at the local school, and then decided she wanted to live in London for a while. Apparently, she'd got married while she was over there to a personal fitness guru and then, after two years of marriage, he'd taken too much interest in a client and Chelsea had left him and returned home.

"How do you cope, you know... working with Reid all day?" she asked in hushed tones, her head on an awkward angle as she tried to look around me and catch another eyeful of sculptured body.

"It's tough," I told her, checking my computer screen, waiting for Reid to update the invoice. A moment later, he stood and disappeared down the corridor, and a long minute after that, with Chelsea leaning over the reception counter, the printer hummed to life and spat out the piece of paper. I whipped it out of the tray and thrust it at her.

"EFTPOS, is it?"

She took her fat time paying while I patiently tapped my fingers against the varnished wooden counter. It seemed that now news had spread around town that Reid and I were an item, most of the female population of Riverford thought he was fair game. So much for the hardened criminal no one wanted to associate with.

Five minutes after she'd left, Reid ambled out of his office.

"You know Chelsea is looking for another husband, don't you?" I told Reid as I closed my computer and pushed my chair under my desk.

"Not my business," Reid said, coming to sit on the corner of it.

"I'm beginning to feel the women in this town have been trying not to notice you since you got out of the slammer"—I was not allowed to use the word *jail* in Reid's hearing, for fear of a grumpy tantrum—"but now, suddenly, you're the chocolate-coated nut every female wants to eat."

"Nut?"

"Chocolate-coated, don't forget."

"And what about you?" One corner of his mouth lifted in a cocky smirk. "Do you like chocolate-coated... nuts?"

My face heated like a radiator. "I... um... I suck the chocolate off the almond, then crush it between my teeth."

A low moan rumbled from Reid's chest and I felt my lady parts give an involuntary quiver. I needed to get out of here before I was rendered unable to walk.

"How about we grab a beer and a bite at McCarthy's after I finish up here?" he suggested.

"I'd love it, but don't you have a big game tomorrow?" This past week had been busy, and it would be a nice way to start the weekend. I'd spent two nights at Reid's place enjoying knee-buckling sex, and it seemed our friends-with-benefits relationship was easier than I thought, as long as I shut out all thoughts of leaving for the time being. I smiled at him. "I mean, aren't top rugby players supposed to be on strict diets or training regimes, abstaining from sex—or something?"

"Not this one," he winked at me as he slipped off the desk, caught my hand and pulled me to him, placing a brief but wholly satisfying kiss on my lips. I staggered backwards when he released me, briefly forgetting where I was.

"This body has had plenty of high intensity workouts this week. It's in peak physical condition."

I nodded. I could certainly vouch for the condition of every inch of his body—if anyone wanted to know.

"Right. I'll meet you there," I told him, as I scooped up my bag and made a beeline for the door.

"You off?" Connor called as I walked through the workshop.

"I am. Oh, and I need to talk to you at some stage about a couple of invoices I can't figure out, but everything is up to date. Monday we'll be running the new accounting program, and I'll talk you both through it."

"Thanks, Louise. Did you know Tyler is back tonight?"

"No. Will he be at home or in the hospital?"

"As far as I know, he's being transferred to our hospital, then if he's stable, he'll go home in a day or two."

"That's fantastic news."

Connor looked down at his boots. "Not if he's coming home to die."

"I didn't think—I'm so sorry, Connor. I know what he means to you and Reid. I'll pop around and see him tomorrow once he's settled in."

"I'm sure he'd like to see you."

"So," Annie said, arriving at the bar to offload a tray of empty glasses. "You waiting for anyone special?"

"Nope."

Matt slid a rum and Coke across the counter to me. It looked heavenly and I was eager to it.

"Cheers." I lifted my glass in appreciation, ditched the straw, and guzzled half the contents, then burped rather loudly. I slapped my hand over my mouth. "Sorry."

Annie looked me over and tutted. "Reid?"

I glanced down. "Too much cleavage?"

Annie laughed and leaned on the bar, watching me.

Inspired by our mayor, I'd made a conscious effort to look half-presentable. I'd dug out some of my job interview clothes: a white silk shirt and blue blazer, which I'd teamed with my jeans and boots. I'd spent extra time on my makeup and my lips were a sexy shiraz-red.

I turned my attention back to my drink, knowing full well everyone in town probably knew Reid and I were an item.

Annie nodded in an *I knew it* way and loaded fresh drinks onto her tray.

"So, what's happening with you and Connor?" I asked, shifting the attention back to her.

"What have you been told?"

I raised my eyebrows. Did she answer that a little too fast? "Nothing. Just curious." I took a leisurely sip from my glass. "You seem quite loved up. I thought perhaps you might be taking things a little more seriously? Or moving in together?"

The laughter in her face disappeared.

"You two looked pretty domesticated the other night at dinner."

"He's loved up alright, but it ain't with me."

Oh my God. Had I missed a vital update on the Annie/Connor situation? "Don't tell me he's found someone else?" Why didn't I know about this?

"There's always been another love. Until that changes, Connor won't be getting all the benefits of this particular pleasure without some commitment." She swept a hand up and down her body.

I sniggered, but she had me now. "Who is it? He's not seeing a prostitute, is he? Do you want me to run them over?"

Annie laughed. "It's his damn cars! He loves them more than he'll ever love me."

"No! Well, it is a relief, though." I shook my head. "I know which one I'd sooner snuggle up with on a frosty night—not that I'm suggesting we, you know, snuggle."

"You'd be surprised. I doubt he'll ever marry." She looked like she was about to burst into tears and my heart went out to her. I could tell she was in love with Connor. It was just a shame he couldn't see that.

"You know what?" I said, a sense of responsibility for Annie's love life overcoming me. "I reckon you need to make him jealous."

"Ha, you must be kidding. Connor is so goodhearted, he'd never be jealous of anyone or anything."

"Yes, but would he be happy you were out with another guy, and you were in a short black dress with your hair done up and your lipstick smeared?"

Annie laughed. "Like *that* would happen."

"Well, perhaps it should."

"First up, I don't know anyone in this town I'd like to go out with. Second, I don't own a little black dress. And thirdly, I don't even own any—wait—does a tinted ChapStick count?" Annie slid the tray off the counter and disappeared to deliver the drinks.

I sat my glass back on the counter, my brain whirring with ideas as I waited for her to return.

"What time do you finish tomorrow night?"

"I could ask Rachel to swap a shift and get away at eight."

"Excellent. I have an idea. Come to Hannah's as soon as you finish. Do you have any heels?"

"I do. But I haven't worn them in years."

"Bring them with you. We're going to kick the shit out of Connor's inability to get jealous. He won't know what hit him." I gave her an evil smile and she laughed.

"I have no idea what you're planning, but I'm willing to give it a shot."

"Excellent." I drained the remainder of my drink and wondered what was keeping Reid. "Same again, thanks, Matt."

He glanced at someone over my shoulder, flicked his chin like men do, and scooped my glass up. The man of my many dreams and desires was in the house. I puffed my chest out and spun in my chair.

But the man standing in front of me wasn't Reid.

21

LOU

JAYDEN CARTER GRINNED AT me like we were an old married couple catching up after a long day at work. Then, stepped into me, dropped a kiss square on my lips and swung an arm around my shoulder. I shrugged it off like it was a venomous tiger snake and scrubbed at my mouth.

"What in the name of God are you doing here?" I was mortified someone, namely Reid, might see him. I looked over his shoulder and scanned the room to see if anyone else had witnessed his fake act of affection. Heads spun in other directions. Great.

"Louie, babe. Is that any way to greet an old friend?"

"*Friend?* After what you did to me? You've got to be kidding."

He lifted his hand and signalled for service.

Ellie, who was working the bar, sidestepped Matt and appeared in front of us. Smile on her face. I rolled my eyes at her enthusiasm.

"What will it be?" Ellie asked.

"Lager, thanks."

"Haven't seen you here before. Are you a friend of Louise's?"

Jayden smiled delightedly and held his hand out. "I'm so much more than an old friend. And it's nice to make new ones."

Ellie shook his hand while I tried to stop myself from throwing up. Did he wink at her? "No, Ellie," I butted in, horrified that Jayden was flirting with her. "No old friend. No new friend. In fact, don't bother with the beer, he's about to leave."

"Whoa, hold on there, Louie. I went to a lot of trouble to find you, I'm not leaving yet."

What did I do to deserve this? Nervously I scanned the room again. No sign of Reid. Or Connor. Where were they when you needed them? "What do you want, Jayden?" He was a slimy, weasel of a human being. I must have been out of my mind to think I loved this man.

"What makes you think I want something?" He looked hurt.

"Oh, I don't know. Maybe it's because you stole everything I owned? Or maybe it's because you were using me. Making me believe you loved me, that we had a life together, until I found you out."

"Okay, okay, keep your voice down." He draped his arm over my shoulder again. "I'm sorry, Louie, babe. Honest. It was all just a temporary measure."

"And don't call me fucking Louie. I hate that nickname. Christ." I tried to drown my frustration with my drink and get rid of his arm. Someone stepped up to the bar on my other side and pressed against my body. I knew instantly by the way my nipples tightened it was my knight in shining armour.

"Sorry I'm late, sweetheart." He looked over my head at my ex. "Is there a problem here?"

"Reid," I said. Jayden slid his arm off my shoulder and I inched closer to Reid. The man made me feel like a million dollars—his million dollars—and I knew he'd protect what was his. A warm, fuzzy feeling began to bloom in me. "This is Jayden Carter." Jayden put his hand out. Reid ignored it and motioned to Ellie to bring him his usual.

"So, this is the lying, scheming, low life who stole from you?"

"I'm right here," Jayden sneered.

"Unfortunately," Reid muttered, loud enough for Jayden to hear.

"And it was just a loan. A temporary thing. I was always going to pay Louie back."

"Louie?" Reid queried. His brows dipped.

I emptied my glass and ordered another. A double. "Jayden, this is Reid Hamilton. My boss."

"So, you're sleeping with the boss, now. Very cosy."

"I'd watch your fucking mouth if I was you," Reid growled.

"Okay. That's enough," I snapped, jumping up and placing a hand on Reid's lovely chest. He made my ex look like the cartoon character Wile E. Coyote... a stick-thin loser, and jumpy as hell. I didn't want any fighting because one of them would end up beaten to a pulp.

"I can deal with Jayden," I stated, hoping I sounded calmer than I felt. I faced the coyote. I hadn't noticed before just how old he looked around his eyes. I wondered if he was finding life hard without all my financial assistance. "Tell me what you want and then you can leave."

Jayden glared at Reid. "It's a private matter."

"I've got no secrets from Reid." I found Reid's hand for moral support and threaded my fingers through his.

"Well, my business is with you, not him. I'm staying at The Riverford Motel—why don't you come and see me tomorrow... say, ten? We can have coffee for old times' sake."

"I won't be doing anything for anyone's sake. If you want to see me, I'll be at Hannah's Café. It's two blocks from here. Tomorrow... say, ten," I said, mimicking him.

He sculled the remainder of his beer, turned and walked out.

"Sorry about that," I said to Reid.

He had his hand on my back, doing wonderful things with his fingers. "How'd the scumbag find you?"

I shrugged.

"And you've no idea what he wants?"

"No. But he won't be getting anything because I've got nothing left to give. Except the car, and I'm keeping that," I said, defiantly.

"Well, you're not going on your own."

"I don't need you to come with me. I can handle this. Now, are we eating or not?"

I slept over at Reid's after he'd told me how much my silk shirt turned him on. I had my suspicions it was more the eyeful of cleavage that did it. Somehow, he had the ability to make me feel like a goddess. He'd spent his evening giving me multiple orgasms and I'd finally fallen asleep in his arms, oblivious to anything or anyone else in the universe.

"Hey sweetheart, do you really have to get up? I'm sure we could make it to eight," Reid said, as I dragged my weary body away from his.

Seven. Seven times I'd been on the brink of dying from sexual pleasure. I didn't think I could take much more.

"I need a rain check. I don't know if I can still walk."

Reid laughed. "Rain check accepted." He slid out of bed, magnificent to look at—especially that disgustingly erect appendage that had me calling out his name so much last night. He scooped me up and carried me through to the shower.

I made myself a latte, took it to a table at the back of the café and waited for Jayden to show up. I needed the coffee because no matter how much Reid had tried his calm-inducing strategies on me—and he'd done an excellent job, no complaints there—I was still a bundle of nerves. I had no idea what Jayden wanted, but whatever it was, it couldn't be good.

"Morning, Louise." Kate from the florist pulled out a chair and made herself comfortable.

"Huh? Oh, hi, Kate. How are all those beautiful blooms this morning?"

"Gorgeous. I'm finishing the buttonholes for the Jellico/Wilson wedding this afternoon, and I've got a dozen corsages to make for the school ball tonight, then things will calm down a bit. How are the kart derby plans?"

"We've got so many entries; it's going to be a great race." I looked around her at the sound of the café door opening and saw Jayden step inside. My stomach dropped. He scanned the room until he found me.

"And Reid? How's he these days? I hear you tamed the Stallions' star stud."

"He's a star all right," I answered, distracted by the figure of my ex making his way towards me. I wished Kate would leave. I didn't want to be introducing Jayden to any more locals than was absolutely necessary. It was as though he'd taint this town for me if he knew too many people.

"Hey, Louie. How are you this morning? You're looking tired—guessing you didn't sleep last night?"

He smirked and I seethed. So help me if I jumped up and tried to drag his head through the meat mincer out in Han's kitchen. It made me cringe to think I'd actually slept with him. I didn't realise my Man-o-Meter had been stuck on the *abysmal* setting for so long. I had to admit, it was a relief to know that Reid was knocking that baby right back up to *megatastic*.

"And who's this picture of beauty?" he asked, switching his attention to Kate.

"Kate," I interrupted, "this is my lying, cheating ex, who is here for no more than five minutes, so he needs to cut the small talk and get right to the point of his visit. The clock's ticking." I made a point of looking at my wrist, even though I wasn't wearing a watch.

Just then, Hannah called out to Kate from the counter, and I sighed with relief as she went to retrieve her coffee. She wasn't married and the last thing I wanted was to be responsible for another disastrous relationship with Jayden.

Good luck, she mouthed at me as she made her way around tables to the door.

Jayden dropped into Kate's empty chair, closer to me. "Such pretty friends."

"Spit it out, Jayden?"

I folded my arms over my chest like a boss. If he thought he could intimidate me, he was out of luck. He was dealing with the new me now.

He shifted nervously in his chair. "I need a favour."

I laughed like a crazy woman, momentarily forgetting where I was. Heads at various tables turned in our direction. "I don't think you're in a position to be asking for any—"

"Come on, Louie. I just need to borrow a thousand bucks. I'm desper—"

"A thousand dollars?!" I hissed, this time keeping my voice low.

"You know I wouldn't have asked you if I could have got it elsewhere. I'll do anything, Louie. Come on," he pleaded, "loan me the money." He looked as though his life was hanging on my answer.

"What do you want the money for?" I demanded. The balance of power had taken a gigantic swing in my direction, and it suddenly felt really satisfying.

He shifted again. "Okay, I'm not going to spin you a story. I owe a guy and if I don't pay up by next weekend, he's going to break both my arms. And probably my legs."

"And tell me, why I should care?" I casually took a sip of my rapidly cooling coffee.

"Well, we were close once. We were engaged. That should mean something."

I spit my coffee out and grabbed my serviette to mop up the mess.

"Please Louie, I'm begging you. You're my last hope."

"And suddenly you forget how you bled my bank account dry."

"I'm really sorry. I'll pay you back. Every cent. I promise."

"Actually, there might be something you can do for me." He might just be able to help me out.

"Anything, Louie. Just name it."

"Well, stop calling me Louie for a start. My name is Louise."

He nodded vigorously, waiting on my next request.

"I want you to meet me at The Lazy Biker tonight at nine-thirty."

"What's The Lazy Biker?"

"It's a pub. In Greenhill." I finished my coffee and stood.

So as not to be left out, Jayden stood, too. "Why?"

"Don't ask any questions. Just be there. I'll need you for about an hour. Then I'll give you five hundred dollars and you'll be free to go."

"*Five hundred?* But that's not enough."

"Take it or leave it. My one and only offer." Now it was my turn to gloat. Jayden looked miserable. I almost felt sorry for him. I had no idea if he was telling me the truth and he was about to get all his limbs broken, or if it was all another sob story. Either way, it might have worked once, but not any longer.

"I'll take it," he muttered.

"Oh, and there's one more thing."

"What?"

"You're never to contact me again after tonight. Understood?" I was on a roll now and he was screwed. And he knew it.

"Sure."

"Sure? Or did you mean, *understood—I will never come near you again, Louise*?"

"That's what I meant." He almost spat the words at me.

"Good. I'll see you tonight. Don't be late." I picked up my coffee cup, walked out into the kitchen and collapsed in a chair. I was shaking all over. But I'd stood up to him.

Face to face. I'd agreed to give him money, but oddly enough, it felt great. This time, he was going to work for it.

I stayed and helped Hannah in the kitchen until one p.m. I cleared and cleaned tables and washed dishes. Visiting Tyler at the hospital helped take my mind off what a sad person Jayden had become. I also needed the time to go over the plan for tonight.

When I found Tyler's room at the hospital, despite the network of tubes feeding into him, he was propped up in bed chatting to Connor, with Julie-Anne seated in the recliner chair beside him.

"Hello," I greeted, making my way to Tyler's side. He lifted a hand to me, and I leaned down to kiss his cheek and hug him.

"Well, if it isn't my favourite girl." His voice was shaky, and the hand holding mine was bony but warm.

"You look far too healthy to be in here," I told him, with all the courage I could muster. It wouldn't look good to start crying in front of him. "I miss you at the garage, you know. It's hard to keep these guys under control without you there."

"I wish I could come back, but I don't think I'm up to it yet." He smiled a tired smile. I looked up at Connor, his gaze fixed on something out the window, but I could see the strain etched on his face and wondered if Tyler knew how bad his diagnosis really was.

I chatted with Julie-Anne and made small talk with Connor and Tyler, and promised I'd come back tomorrow.

An hour later, I walked back to Hannah's apartment with my coat zipped up and pulled tight around my neck. A southerly wind had turned the air bitterly cold, but I needed to walk. Seeing Tyler had been sobering.

I thought about losing my own parents, and in a way I had. My mother's heritage was stronger than her need to be close to me, and I understood that, but it would be nice to see them more often. My father had met mum on a sports trip to the United Kingdom and they'd married and set up home in a leafy suburb in Auckland, but seven years ago, they'd shifted back to England and I missed them. I pushed my hands deeper into my pockets and made a mental note to ring them and catch up.

It was almost four o'clock when I arrived at Zoe's house and wondered what was going down. Cars were parked on the lawn and in a line that stretched down the street. I pulled into the drive, which was the only space available. Loud music penetrated the walls of the bungalow and bombarded me as soon as I stepped out of the car.

Zoe's mum answered the door, looking slightly frazzled.

"Hi, Mrs Ford," I yelled. "I'm Louise. Zoe asked me to come and do her makeup."

She shook her head and pointed to her ear. "What?" she screeched back.

I mimed the act of putting lipstick on. She nodded, glanced up and down the street and ushered me inside. I hoped I'd make it out again without needing a hearing aid.

I followed her into the sitting room. It looked like a bomb had exploded at a jumble sale in a bordello. Girls lounged everywhere in robes, some singing and practising their dance moves exuberantly to the music, while others scrolled on their phones or painted their toenails. One girl was trying to style her friend's hair in front of a large mirror. Cans of energy drinks littered the floor. Pizza boxes and potato chip bags were stacked under the coffee table. Clothes were draped over the backs of chairs, and fashion magazines lay open at pages displaying styles they were obviously trying to emulate. This was going to be a challenge, but I'd enjoyed my fair share of social events in my school-age years, and I reckoned I could nail it.

I pushed aside a pair of jeans, a push-up bra and several magazines, and dumped my meagre supply of makeup on the sofa. Zoe jumped up, turned the music down and introduced me to the room. Someone handed me a Mother energy drink. I took a swallow, more for courage than anything else. It was horribly sweet and I set it aside.

The music changed. "I love this song!" one of the girls squealed, and the volume went back up.

One by one, I worked through their makeup, trying to get the look each girl wanted while answering question after question about Reid. They were on a mission to find out if I'd slept with him yet, and what he looked like completely naked. By the time I'd finished the last face, the first girls were already dressed in their ball gowns, and I was two cans of energy drink down and giggling like a hyena on speed.

"We got you these," Zoe said as I packed my things. She handed me a bouquet of flowers and an envelope.

"Thank you, Zoe. You didn't have to, but they're lovely. I hope you all have a fun night tonight." For some obscure reason, I found that funny too, and laughed my way to the front door.

Mrs Ford appeared and walked me to my car.

"Thanks, Louise. That was a kind thing to do for the girls. They all look twice their age, but absolutely gorgeous. Here's something little from me to say thanks." She handed me another envelope.

"I can't take that."

"It's just a wee voucher. You deserve a lot more."

"Thank you." I tried to sound gracious. "To be honest, it was fun. It brought back lots of memories from my days at school. Are you sure I can't help tidy up?"

"No. It's the one day a year that I let Zoe take over the house. It's her night and I happily run around after her and pick up. The boys will be here soon, and some of the parents will be arriving for pre-ball nibbles and drinks. You're welcome to stay."

"No, thank you. I feel old enough already. I'll look forward to the photos next week when I see her at the café." With a wave, I rushed to my car and drove back to Hannah's. I was shattered, but the energy drink was flowing through my veins at breakneck speed, and I had Annie arriving in half an hour. Connor wouldn't know what hit him.

22

REID

I SAT ON THE team's bus staring blankly out the window, not seeing a damn thing. It had been a fucking shitty day. I'd wanted to go with Louise to the café to meet this Jayden tosser, but she threatened to withhold sexual favours if I did. So, I'd dropped in to see Tyler at the hospital and left there feeling miserable and helpless at not being able to do anything to help him, either. I promised Julie-Ann I'd mow their lawns tomorrow, which wasn't much, but it was the least I could do.

Then today we'd played an away game and lost by one point after the Southern Stags delivered a drop goal in the last minute of the game.

In this mood, it would have been the perfect night to sleep out on the back of the truck among the pines, but the wind had picked up and it was icy cold.

We filed off the bus and I strode over to my truck, unlocked it and threw my bag on the back seat.

"Are you seeing Louise tonight?" Connor asked, stopping at my door.

"Apparently, she's busy." I felt a wave of depression sweep over me.

"I was going to pick up Chinese. Why don't you come around and join me? Put your feet up, have a beer. There's some snowboarding on TV tonight. We'll have a boys' night in."

"Yeah, okay," I said, with as much enthusiasm as I could muster.

I started up the truck and drove towards Connor's place. I knew exactly why I was feeling a puce shade of shitty.

Louise.

Or more to the point, her ex. He had to be bad news. I missed her, as stupid as that sounded. I loved knowing she was cheering me on at the rugby. I loved seeing her at work, watching her run her hand through her hair in frustration, or the way she practically skipped up the hall to make coffee in the morning; her cheerful voice when she answered the phone; the way she said my name. And I fucking adored the shit out of her when she walked out of my shower naked, and let me worship her body. I hated the thought that she was seeing him again.

A figure on the darkened street caught my attention. They were huddled in a storefront doorway, peering through the window. I slowed down to get a better look. The residents of Riverford were vigilant about protecting their own, and shops didn't often get broken into. I glanced at the road and back at the figure, suddenly recognising them. I spontaneously pulled the truck to the kerb, braked and jumped out. "Hey!" It was Louise's scumbag ex, Jayden.

"What do you want?" he muttered in a surly voice.

"I'll tell you what I want," I said, inching closer until I was right up in his face. I was in the mood for a good fight. "I want you to stay the hell away from Louise."

"Right." He took a draw on the cigarette he was holding and expelled the smoke at my face, then turned his attention back to whatever he'd been staring at through the window as if I wasn't there.

I was rapidly getting fucked off with his attitude. "And while we're at it, I want you to make it your life's mission to pay back all the money you stole from her."

"Or you're going to do what?" He took another deep suck on his smoke and tossed it towards the gutter. "Punch me in the face? I bet that's your answer to everything, isn't it?"

"I don't need to." He looked at me as though I was something he'd scraped off the bottom of his shoe. I seethed with anger, and did something I had promised myself I would never do. Ever. I played the P card. "You know *why* I don't need to?"

"Nope. And I'm not interested, either."

"Well, you should be. Cause where I've been, it pays to have friends. In prison you meet all sorts, and there are people in there who owe me."

He shrugged.

"I met people who know how to achieve things—they like to get the job done, if you know what I mean. Money extraction is a speciality." We were practically nose-to-nose now. "There'll be nowhere you can hide where they won't find you."

"Are you threatening me?"

"Not at all. Call it broadening your horizons."

He took a step back. "Well, as charming as that sounds, and I'd love to stay and chat longer, I've got to be going. Some of us have hot dates with cute chicks, and don't have to cruise around the streets looking for quick fixes."

I narrowed my eyes at him and felt my nostrils flare. The maggot had a very short life expectancy. I turned and stalked back to the truck, slammed it in gear and took off. He'd only been in town five minutes. Who the fuck did he have a date with? Was he meeting Louise? Had he asked her to move back with him? Was that what his private conversation was all about? I pulled my phone from my pocket and called Lou's number. It went straight to her answer message. My night was getting better and better.

I let myself in to Connor's, switched on the lights and made my way to his fridge. I needed a beer. On second thoughts, I needed something stronger. I helped myself to the bottle of Johnnie Walker I knew he always kept on the top shelf of his pantry. It was three-quarters full and I poured a generous double measure into a tumbler. I was staring at the bottom of the second glass when Connor walked in.

"Jesus, what's wrong?"

"Nothing," I said.

"Bullshit," Connor said, placing an assortment of containers on the counter.

"I just ran into Louise's ex-boyfriend. The animal that fleeced her of all her savings."

"What?"

"Yeah. Short version is he took everything Lou had and when she found out, she took off and that's how she came to be in Riverford." I retrieved two plates from the cupboard and put them on the counter next to the food and refilled my glass.

"Shit. I didn't know."

"Yeah, well, he turned up at McCarthy's last night wanting to talk to her."

"You don't think he wants her back, do you?" He scooped a healthy portion of fried rice onto his plate and pushed the remainder across to me.

"He might. Who knows. He's a first-rate leech and I don't want him hanging around Lou. I don't even want the fucker in the same town as her."

"Do you know what he wanted to talk to her about?"

"Nope. But I saw him on the street as I was driving here, and I stopped and gave him a warning."

Connor dished himself a generous serving of beef, broccoli and cauliflower before moving onto the sweet and sour pork. "You didn't hit him, did you?"

"Nah. He's not worth the energy," I said. Connor didn't need to know every little detail of our conversation, and to be frank, I wasn't proud of myself for using a little blackmail.

We took our meals through to his sitting room and made ourselves comfortable in front of the television, cycling through the sports channels until we found the snowboarding, and arguing about who on our team had let that fucking dropkick happen.

"You know what shits me the most?" I asked my brother. I'd polished off the bottle of whisky and was now making my way through my third beer.

"What?"

"I think I could spend the rest of my life with Lou." I was feeling pretty damn mellow now the alcohol had kicked in. "I wish she'd stay. I'm gonna miss her if she leaves."

"Yeah, I know."

"You don't know shit."

"I know enough."

"You've got a woman who'd do anything for you, and you totally ignore her."

"You're drunk. Let's change the subject."

"Instead, you drool all over those fucking cars of yours."

"Shut the fuck up, Reid."

"You need to face the facts," I ploughed on. "Annie loves you and you just turn a blind eye. And she's a real looker, you know."

"I'm warning you. Change the subject."

But I wasn't going to change the subject, because I felt as though things needed to be said, and the large quantity of alcohol I'd consumed meant I was the one who was going to say them.

"You've been seeing each other for years. Why don't you grow a pair of balls and ask her to marry you? Or are you afraid to commit? That's it, isn't it? You've got commitment issues. That's it," I repeated. "You're scared to commit, aren't you?"

Connor choked on the cola he was drinking and scrambled out of his seat. He was stone-cold sober, which meant his reflexes were much quicker than mine. But as he made a lunge for me, his cell rang.

He pulled up short. "You're fucking lucky, bro," he snarled as he grabbed the phone off the coffee table and answered the call. "Connor."

I relaxed back against the seat. I was feeling rather untouchable in my happy state of inebriation.

"Louise? Where are you? Who? What's wrong?"

I dragged myself upright. I could hear the thump of music through the phone. Why was Louise ringing Connor and not me? I staggered up to search for my coat. I'd go and get her.

Connor grabbed my sleeve. "Whoa, cowboy, you're not driving anywhere. Sit down." He put a hand on my shoulder, pushed me back down and kept talking to Louise. My Louise.

I finished my beer and slapped the can down on the coffee table. "Lou needs me."

"You don't even know where she is."

I shook my head and pointed towards the street. "She's out there."

He disconnected and put his phone in his pocket. "She is. Louise is also fine, although dirt-drunk. So's

Annie. I'm going to get them. You can come for the ride if you want, but I don't want any more wise cracks or life advice, or you'll be walking home."

"Fair enough," I mumbled.

We drove to Greenhill to the dulcet tones of me singing country and western songs with the radio. I thought I was doing a great impression of Carrie Underwood when Connor switched it off and glanced at me in disgust.

"You're pushing it."

I grinned happily from my seat. I was going to see Louise.

He pulled up outside The Lazy Biker on the northern side of Greenhill. In all my years, I'd only been to this place once and it had been full of horny old bikers with the sleeves cut out of their jackets and who stank of leather, weed and beer.

Beer.

"We might as well get a drink while we're here," I suggested.

"Nope. Wait here," Connor directed. "Do not leave this vehicle." He gave me the stink eye again and pocketed his keys.

I waited until he'd crossed the car parking area and disappeared inside before I opened my door and rolled out of it. The ground was hard and cold. The air was bracing as I staggered to my feet and aimed myself in the direction of the bar's entrance. I know Connor didn't drink, but that didn't mean I couldn't enjoy one for the road while he was looking for the girls.

I pushed the door open and a blast of Iron Maiden hit me square in the face, followed closely by a bar stool. Fuck! I put my arms up, but not fast enough. The furniture hit me on the side of my face and sent me flying on my backside. I flung it off and dragged myself to my feet.

I couldn't see my brother anywhere, but I could hear him shouting. As it happened, he was centre stage, in the middle of a fight with—was that Lou's ex? A group of bikers and brawl enthusiasts had formed a ring around them. One beefy biker was peeling his jacket off, ready to join in. Connor was laying into the arsehole. Annie and Louise were screaming for Connor to stop. I was drunk, and I knew the cops would be here sometime really soon. I crawled my way through the protective barrier of black leather-clad legs, grabbed Connor by the neck of his jacket and pulled with everything I had.

"Sorry, gentlemen," I said, "we gotta go. Show's over." I leaned into the ex, who was bent double, clutching his stomach. "Don't forget my warning, you prick," I said to a chorus of boos.

I stumbled away with Connor. Louise and Annie followed us outside. Annie, I noticed, had her lipstick smudged across her face, her top was ripped and it made her look borderline hooker material.

"I could've handled that," my brother growled, rubbing the side of his jaw. "Why did you get out of the car? I distinctly told you to stay there."

"Cops are coming." I grinned as if it was the biggest joke.

Connor shrugged out of my grasp and grabbed hold of Annie and hugged her against his body. I wasn't too drunk to notice that behind Annie, Lou did a fist pump and grinned like a Cheshire cat. Even in my inebriated state, I knew there was something fishy going on here.

"That bastard had his hands all over her," Connor stated. And his mouth, by the look of her face.

I looked from Louise to Annie. Louise looked like she was as sober as Connor was. Glowing, in fact. And Annie did too, despite the attempt to play the part by staggering around on her heels.

"Sorry, Annie," my brother was repeating over and over. "It's my fault this has happened. If I'd paid more attention, you'd be out with me, not some slimy con artist."

As if planned, Annie started crying. My brother held her tighter then opened the door for her.

"I'm getting in the car before I die of exposure." I was feeling a little more sober than I'd been thirty minutes ago. It was amazing what some arctic air and a blow to the head can do.

Connor helped Annie into the front. I climbed in the back beside Louise and put my arm around her. She was busy doing something on her phone, but looked up when her ex staggered out the pub door and shouted: "Where's my fucking money, you whore?"

I nudged her. "Is he yelling at you?" The poor guy was still bent double after the pummelling he'd taken from Connor, but if he didn't shut that mouth of his, he'd get another one from me.

She shook her head and nestled against my shoulder, slipping a cold hand under my jacket. I caught a whiff of honeysuckle, and almost forgot about the ton of questions she was going to have to answer when I sobered up enough to remember what they were.

23

REID

MY BED WAS EMPTY when I woke. I distinctly remembered there had been another body in it when I'd fallen into it the night before. I got up and dragged on a pair of sweatpants and wandered out into the kitchen in bare feet. It was toasty warm and a picture of domestic bliss. The coffee smelled great, the pancakes even better. Lou, dressed in her bra and panties, was humming to herself as she shimmied around my kitchen looking like menu fodder. I was suddenly ravenous. So was the Big Guy.

"Morning," she greeted, when she noticed me. "I made you breakfast."

I groaned. "Morning."

She flittered around the counter and kissed me briefly, then moved on to fill a mug with the strong black elixir of life.

"What a fantastic day. It's not raining, no wind, and the sun's out."

I glanced out the kitchen window and squinted. It was indeed a perfect winter's morning, with the layer of frost that coated the lawn beginning to melt in patches. Except that my tongue was stuck to the roof of my mouth and there was a drum solo on repeat in my head. "Don't think I haven't remembered what happened last night," I warned her, as I filled a glass with water and sculled it.

"Nothing happened last night." She leaned over the counter towards me and her tits plunged forwards, on the brink of falling out of her bra. I lifted my coffee, gulped a mouthful and burnt the inside of my mouth. *Shit!*

"Good try, sweetheart," I said, once the skin stopped blistering. "But it ain't going to work. And I've got the bruises to prove it." I touched a finger to my cheek and winced.

"I have no idea what you're talking about." She stood and dished up breakfast, sliding mine to me before working her way through buttering a stack of toast.

"Are you going to tell me what happened last night, or am I going to have to use devious methods to make you talk? I know neither you nor Annie were drunk."

She gave me a seductive smile. "You don't know shit."

She made those four words sound like the world's thickest maple syrup. I decided my best plan of action was to scarf down the food and then approach the line of questioning another way. A more horizontal way. Louise's phone vibrated on the far end of the counter. She rushed for it and checked the caller, keeping one eye on me.

"Well?" she asked.

I shovelled a healthy portion of pancake and banana into my mouth. It was heaven, even with the coffee burns.

"Yep," she continued. "I'm sitting down."

She wasn't sitting down. She was pacing back and forth in front of me, flaunting way too much bare skin.

Liar, I mouthed, and she accidently-on-purpose brushed a fork off the bench onto the floor and bent over slowly to pick it up. So much bare flesh and so little lace triggered a chain reaction through my body. I didn't know if I should leave the pancakes, rip my sweatpants off and throw her phone away, brace myself for a heart attack, or go take a cold shower.

"No way! Really?" she yelled, laughed and bounced up and down on the spot. The throaty sound of her voice was not helping my predicament. If she was trying to wear my resolve, it was working. I'd almost forgotten about the interrogation.

"Congratulations! That's amazing. I'm so excited for you both. Yes... where? Okay, we'll be there." Her eyes lifted to mine. "No, I won't tell him. Okay. See you tonight." She placed her phone back on the counter and, casually and quietly, helped herself to a piece of toast.

I felt like I should be suspicious. "Well?"

"Your brother just got engaged," she blurted out, and did the bouncing thing again. I spluttered pancake across my plate.

"Engaged? Let me guess. To Annie?"

"Who else? And you're not supposed to know. Connor wants to break the news to you tonight over dinner."

"And you wouldn't have had a hand in that some-how?"

"Nope." She practically skipped around the counter and threw her arms around me. "Well, maybe just a tiny bit." She held up her index finger and thumb to show me just how much constituted tiny. This woman was evil.

The more evil the better.

And I was beginning to thrive on her brand of evil.

The first chore of the day was to do Tyler's gardening. Lou came with me and while I mowed, she weeded the flowerbeds; while I trimmed edges, she tidied the vegetable plot. By the time we'd finished, the place looked neat and ready for Tyler's arrival.

"Look at us," Lou said sitting down beside me.

"What about us?" I was sitting at a small iron-work table on their back porch, drinking cold water and admiring our efforts. But I had to admit, I'd also been admiring her. She was dressed in leggings that seemed to go on forever and her T-shirt today read: *original and unrestored*. I'd never had to try and kill a hard-on while mowing a lawn before. It seemed I was experiencing a range of firsts since Louise had arrived in town.

"Aren't we the domesticated ones? It's kind of nice."

"Thanks for your help. You did a great job today."

"Don't thank me. Thank the weather gods," she said.

"Oh, I'll be thanking the gods all right. Later." Images of a partially naked Louise tangled in my bed sheets flashed through my head. "Now, how about telling me what happened last night."

"You have to promise not to tell Connor. I don't want to lose my job." She held her little finger up. "Pinky promise."

I hooked my finger around hers, pulled her in and smacked a kiss to her lips. "Okay. Talk."

"We set him up."

"No kidding." I grinned. My big brother would not like the thought he'd been had.

"Annie said he never gets jealous, and I wanted to prove her wrong."

"But she's dated other men. What was different last night?" I was sure I was missing something.

"You don't get it, do you?"

I shook my head. "Nope."

"With those other men, Connor knew Annie was just letting off steam, that there was nothing serious happening, because Annie's loyal and would never do that. He knew she'd be back with him in no time. But last night I used Jayden to make it look like she'd picked the wrong man this time, and that she'd put herself in danger."

"So, you were relying on Connor to not only get jealous, but want to protect her from the bottom-feeders who could take advantage of her—for the rest of her life?"

"Something like that."

We sat in silence for a while.

"Reid?"

"What?" I didn't know if I felt angry about her meddling, or if I should congratulate her on what she'd achieved. I knew Annie and Connor loved each other. *Shit*, half the town knew. We were all waiting for them to hook up officially. I grinned. It just took Lou to move things along.

"You're not mad at me, are you?"

"No, sweetheart. I could never be mad at you. But one thing puzzles me. Why did your ex agree to taking the fall for Annie?"

Louise laughed. "He didn't. He didn't know you and Connor were related, and he didn't know Connor was going to come busting in and deal to him."

"He didn't do it for nothing, did he?"

She dropped her eyes to her gloved hands in her lap. "Nope."

"You didn't give him more money, did you? Louise?"

She nodded.

Fuck. "How much?"

"It doesn't matter how much. It was well worth it to see Connor beat the crap out of him."

I growled. "Let's get packed up. I don't know what I'm going to do with you, Ms Adair." The woman could be so damn infuriating.

"You'll think of something," she muttered under her breath.

"So, tell me," I said, as we loaded the tools back into my truck. "What happened—you know, how did you find out your ex had been stringing you along?"

She stalled then looked me in the eye. I could tell she was giving the answer considerable thought. "It makes me feel sick just thinking about it."

"Sometimes, it actually helps if you talk about it."

She sighed and peeled off her gardening gloves. "I feel such a gullible fool. I was hanging some clothes in our wardrobe one weekend and I noticed a wad of papers on the shelf above the hangers. They were partially hidden under a couple of sweatshirts and pushed into the far corner above his shirts. I was alone in the flat so I got them down. They weren't mine and none of my business."

She lifted her tee and wiped at her forehead. "I slipped them down and pulled the rubber band off a stack of envelopes. I knew instinctively I was staring at something that was going to upset me, but I couldn't stop. I had a premonition those envelopes contained something I shouldn't look at. Something that would destroy me. But I didn't know what."

I reached out and took her hand. I wanted her to know I was here, that no one would hurt her again. She gave me a smile that I suspected was bravado.

"Curiosity got the better of me. One by one, I shuffled through the dozen or more envelopes. The top one was a bank statement. I mean, who gets paper statements these days?"

I shrugged.

"I pulled it out of its envelope and unfolded the page. It was dated the month before. I felt so guilty at reading his mail, and it wasn't even addressed to him at our flat. They had all been addressed care of his parents. I couldn't believe what I saw on that page. My hands were shaking that much, I was worried I wouldn't be able to get it back in the envelope."

"What did it say?"

She nodded slowly. "Jayden's bank balance was one hundred and ninety-three thousand dollars. I had been paying for everything we needed—*he* needed. From music to clothes to dinners out to the rent on the flat and a fucking car. Even the odd weekend away. At the end, I had been struggling to cover the bills while all the time, he had been hoarding away a tidy sum."

I let out a low whistle. I wished I'd tag-teamed with Connor at The Lazy Biker and given the guy a good beating.

"I didn't know what to do. I started struggling to meet rent and insurance and things like power and food; I told him he had to get a job. It was then he hooked up with the woman downstairs and disappeared. By complete accident, I found out he'd been *let go* from his job because two women he worked with made sexual harassment claims against him. What a complete idiot I'd been. I stuffed all my clothes in a case, filled my backpack with shoes, grabbed books and photos and my coffee machine, and loaded them into the car. The rest, you know." She looked up at me, and I could see tracks on her cheeks where tears had run through the dust.

"Don't let him upset you. Karma will catch up with him eventually." I gave her a huge bear hug. I'd make it my fucking mission to see it catch up to him—and soon.

I dropped Lou back at Han's apartment. She wanted to clean up and visit Tyler, and I wanted to do some maintenance work on my property while the sun was out. We agreed that I'd collect her later that evening before we joined my brother for a celebration dinner.

Back home, I pulled out my phone, dialled and waited for my call to be answered. It was time to call in a favour.

"Hello?" the gruff voice I remembered from prison answered.

"Hey Muzza, Hamilton here." Murray "Muzza" Stephens had been my cell mate. He'd been put away for repeated traffic offences and causing a pileup of cop cars when a high-speed chase went wrong. They also suspected him of some shady firearms deals, but couldn't pin anything on him for those. He'd got out a month before me.

We'd had a mutual understanding and respect for each other. I'd looked out for him a time or two, and he said he'd repay me some day. Today was that day.

"Hamilton! My brother! How's things? I hear you're on the outside now."

"I am. And things are looking up."

"You found yourself a missus yet?"

We both laughed. "Not quite, but working on it."

"Pleased to hear it, man. I was beginning to wonder about you."

"Actually, that's what I'm calling you about. My intended arrived in town damaged goods. Her ex bled her dry of every cent of her savings. And he's on the hunt for more. I reckon he owes her a hell of a lot. It would be real nice to see her get some of it back, if you know what I mean." I didn't need to spell it out.

"What am I aiming for here?"

"No idea the exact figure, but ten grand would be a great start."

"I'm gonna need some deets, man."

"I'll text them through."

"I owe you brother, so consider it done."

"Thanks, Muzza. I appreciate this."

"Anything for you, brother."

It was a relief to feel that somehow, I could help Louise. Hopefully, whatever money she got back would help her reclaim some independence.

I was making myself a hot drink when someone knocked on my door. I opened it to find Hannah on the doorstop.

"Hi. You're just in time for coffee."

"No, thanks. Water's fine. What on earth have you been doing?"

I looked down at my grass-stained overalls. "Weed-eating around some of the young trees out the back."

She nodded.

"To what do I owe this pleasure?" I asked, filling a glass. "Is Lou with you?"

"No. When I left, she was whipping the bathroom into shape. She insisted she do the cleaning so I could grab some downtime before I start prepping at the café for tomorrow. So, I thought I'd pop over and run something past you."

"Oh. Sounds serious."

She pulled out a bar stool and made herself comfortable. "It is and it isn't."

"Now I'm really intrigued. Spill."

"Well," she hesitated. "Will has asked me to move in with him."

"And?"

"You're not shocked?"

"No. It's about time. I see the way he looks at you every chance he gets. The way you act around him."

"How do I act around him?"

"Like he's your hero." I sipped my coffee. "You don't need my blessing. You've wasted far too much time with the wrong man already. Now go get the right one."

"Thanks." She reached across the counter and slipped her hand in mine. I picked it up and kissed the back of it. "It means a lot that you approve."

"I love you like a sister, and I only want to see you happy. If Will makes you happy, then do it."

"I thought I would ask Louise if she wanted to take over my apartment."

"I think that's a great idea, for purely selfish reasons." I'd sooner Louise moved in with me, but if she had a place of her own, perhaps she might be tempted to stay on in town.

"Reasons I don't want to know about," Hannah said.

"Have you heard she pulled off the miracle of the decade?"

She put her glass down. "No. I knew she and Annie were up to something, but I didn't ask questions and she didn't say anything."

"It's top secret, so you didn't hear it from me, but Connor and Annie got engaged last night. Or this morning."

"Finally. And that was Louise's doing?"

"For the most part."

"Engaged. Wow. Never saw that coming—although we all hoped it would." She got up and put her glass in the sink. "I underestimate that woman. Well, I think I'll go ask Will if he can pencil in some time in the near future to help me shift my things. Maybe having a place of her own might encourage Lou to stay on in Riverford? Anyway, I should be going. Thanks for the water." She leaned in to me and kissed my bruised cheek. I winced, but she was too lost in a world of exciting changes to notice, so I shooed her off and headed for the shower.

Louise looked amazing when she climbed into my truck. Instead of the bright colours she favoured, she was wearing a short black wool coat that exposed long legs covered by black stockings, accompanied by black heels.

"Is everything all right?" she asked when she caught me staring at her.

"It is. I was just thinking about removing those stockings."

"Don't you dare. I had to rush out and buy some especially for tonight."

"They were totally worth it."

She told me she'd been to see Tyler and he was being sent home in three days' time. I'd call in and visit him in the morning and see if there was anything else they needed doing. But she didn't mention that Han was moving in with Will. Perhaps she didn't know yet. When we finally pulled into the parking area in front of The Greenery, Louise pointed at a car.

"That looks just like the one Connor has."

A sleek, black Ferrari was parked near the door.

"That *is* Connor's car," I said, bewildered that my brother's prized possession was sitting outside a restaurant in Greenhill. "The man's had a fucking breakdown. He only takes that out of the shed to get it warranted." We got out of my truck and I made a beeline for the car. "Yeah. He must have taken a bigger blow to the head last night than I realised."

I held the eatery's door open for Louise and inside, the lights were down low and the atmosphere romantic. Someone was playing a set on the piano and every table was occupied. Candles flickered on tables and around the room and I suddenly hoped no one was setting me up too. Beside me Louise squeezed my hand and I squeezed it back.

The server showed us to my brother's table and I felt like we were intruding. My stomach rolled at the sight of the two love birds, hands all over each other, glassy eyes.

Connor stood and hugged Louise then shook my hand. And Annie gave me a quick squeeze but seemed to hug the crap out of Louise, and was there whispering? We all sat down.

"Are you okay, bro?" I asked my brother. "I noticed that car outside."

"I couldn't be happier." He looked from me to Louise and back. "You know, don't you?"

I nodded. "By Lou's excitement levels, I knew something was up. Congratulations, you two. A better match could never be found, and it's about fucking time!" The server arrived, filled our glasses with champagne and we toasted to Annie and Connor. "So, what's with the car?"

"I decided tonight was the perfect time to blow out the cobwebs."

"And guess who drove it?" Annie added, beaming.

Louise and I both turned to Annie.

"You got to drive the Ferrari?" Louise asked, obviously impressed.

"Yes."

"Go on, tell them," Connor winked at her.

"My fiancé gave it to me as an early wedding present. And we're going ring shopping next week."

I let out a low whistle and focused on my brother while Louise and Annie talked like maniacs. "That's some serious shit you've got going on."

"There are a few stipulations, like she can't sell it. When she no longer wants it, it comes back to me."

I couldn't help the laughter that erupted from me. My brother was nailing this relationship business.

"I guess that's one way to show her she comes before the cars."

"Well, I reckon I owe Annie," he said. "You know how many years she's been there for me? Been the person who's always had my back?"

I shook my head. I knew it was a long time, but not an actual figure.

"Twenty-two years." He snaked an arm around Annie's waist and pulled her into his side.

We made several more toasts during the meal and even Connor put aside his alcohol ban and polished off three refills.

Louise stood and motioned to the far corner of the restaurant. "Be back in a hot minute," she said, as Connor portioned the last of the Dom Pérignon into our glasses. Annie got up too, and the women disappeared.

"So," Connor said. "What's with you and Louise?"

"Mind your own fucking business."

"Come on, it's me you're talking to. Have you asked her to stay?" he continued, totally ignoring me like he always did.

"No." Big brothers were annoying.

"And why not?"

"She might not want to stay."

"You won't know unless you ask her."

If he didn't stop with the inquisition right now, I was going to lose my patience. I would wait and see if Lou decided to stay on in Han's apartment; if she said no, then I knew where I stood. "That was a smart thing you did for Annie," I said, changing the subject.

"The car?"

I nodded.

"It hurt, but I was trying to make a point."

I laughed. I could only imagine the huge pain that little gift inflicted. "You're setting the bar pretty fucking high."

"Hey," Louise said, dropping into her seat next to me with fresh lip colour that I immediately wanted to smudge off her mouth. "Don't look now, but who's the guy sitting at the table over there?" She discreetly pointed over past the concierge's desk. Connor, Annie and I turned in unison to get a better look.

"I said *don't look now*," she hissed.

A growl rumbled from me and a fierce anger began to gnaw at my insides. "That's Tony Selgrave, the pig who arrested me." I'd seen him around town from time to time, but he lived and worked out of Palmerston North, a big city fifty-five kilometres the other side of Greenhill. The man—if you could call him that—evoked an immediate response in me. He was as bad as half the men I'd been in the slammer with, except he hadn't been caught. Yet.

Connor put a hand on my shoulder. "I think we're done here. Let it go. He's not worth it."

"Why'd you want to know?" I asked Louise.

"I saw him."

"Where'd you see him? In Riverford?"

She nodded. "At work."

"The garage?" Connor asked.

She nodded.

"What the fuck was that man doing in my garage?" I asked.

"He was talking to Liam and another man in the workshop last weekend."

I pushed my chair back and Connor automatically reached for my arm again. "Don't." His voice was threatening. I stifled the urge to cross the room and confront the man. Instead, I took a deep breath and sat where I was.

"Sorry, that's fucked my night." I tossed my napkin on the table, stood and made a hasty exit before I did something I'd live to regret. *Fucking piece of shit*.

Liam had some questions to answer.

24

LOU

WHILE CONNOR TOOK CARE of the bill, I followed Reid outside. He was leaning against the side of his truck, arms folded. I could feel the rage radiating off him and decided to approach with caution.

"You okay?" I asked, stopping a couple of feet shy.

He ignored my question and went straight for the jugular. "Why the fuck didn't you tell me he'd been sniffing around the garage?"

"So, I'm supposed to know he was a police officer?"

"He's a dirty fucking detective and if he's snooping around, it's got to be for a reason." He pushed off the truck and wrenched his door open. I hurried around to my side and climbed in.

"For all I knew, they were Liam's friends." That's what I'd originally thought, but something had seemed familiar and now I knew who he was, I remembered why. I'd seen images of him on the internet from when Reid had been arrested.

He started the truck and drove out of the car park with more speed than necessary. A few metres up the road, he glanced at me, veered the truck off the road and slammed his foot on the brakes. I jerked forwards and bounced back against the seat.

"They?" he snarled at me.

"There were three of them," I mumbled and fingered my hair back into place.

"What did the third one look like?"

"I didn't pay much attention. Tall. Maybe chubby. Thinning wispy collar-length hair. I don't think he was a cop."

"What makes you think that?" His voice had softened a fraction, but I could still hear the anger beneath the surface.

"There were two vehicles parked outside and one of them had a business logo on the door. But I didn't really take much notice."

"Would you recognise the logo again if you saw it?" He leaned across me to reach the glovebox.

"Maybe. What are you doing?" I was worried about him now. This was the old suspicious Reid, the one who wore a chip on his shoulder like it was a precious jewel.

He retrieved his phone and scrolled the internet. "Here," he said, thrusting it at me.

"That's it." I nodded in affirmation. "I'm sure."

"*Fuck.*" He thumped the steering wheel with the palm of his hand, rested his forehead on it for a moment, then put his phone away.

I sat silently, not knowing how to help. Seconds later, he indicated and pulled back onto the highway.

"Do you know him?" I was intrigued now.

"From your description, I guessed it was Phil Kennedy. That logo proves it."

"Of Kennedy's Engineering?"

"The very same." He lifted his head and narrowed his eyes at me. "How do you know that?"

"Because there are invoices at work from them."

"What?" His words were at least twenty decibels louder.

"I've been meaning to talk to you and Connor about them."

"I want to see them."

"What? Now?"

He didn't answer and sat in stony silence until he pulled the vehicle up in front of the workshop.

"Get out."

"Excuse me?" I didn't like the direction this was going in. And I certainly didn't like his tone. The new confident me sat where I was. Reid got out and crossed the footpath and unlocked the side door to the garage, turned around and saw I was still sitting in the truck. He marched back and opened my door.

"Did you not hear me?"

"Oh, I heard you all right."

"Well?"

"Well, it's late and you can either drive me back to Hannah's or I can get out as you suggested, and I can walk home."

He let out a long sigh and ran his hand through his hair. He now had that *I just got out of bed* look, and my nipples hardened automatically. *Damn it*. Not ideal in an argument. I crossed my arms over my chest.

"Sorry."

I didn't move. "I didn't quite catch that."

"Oh, for—Okay. Look. I'm sorry. I shouldn't have spoken to you like that, but you don't know what it's—"

"No, I don't." I cut him off. "And I hopefully never will. But I have an appreciation for what you went through, and so do your friends. We're not the enemy here."

I could see him relax a little. "I'm sorry, Lou. I let the rage take over." He turned and walked back to the garage door and locked it again, and returned to the truck. Five minutes later, he dropped me outside Hannah's and drove off under a dark cloud of contained anger. I guessed he'd be sleeping out in the pines tonight.

I opened the mail on Monday morning to find the latest issue of the *New Zealand V8* magazine. I flicked through its shiny pages until I got to the article on the Hamilton brothers and their craftmanship.

"What's that?" Connor asked, coming up behind me and peering over my shoulder. "Is that an article on us?"

I nodded. "It's good, too." I handed it over. "Where's Reid? I wanted to get that training done this morning."

We both glanced up as Reid walked through the door.

"Where's Liam?" he asked as he passed through the reception area.

"Good morning to you too," I greeted in my sweetest voice. "How are you? Oh, I'm fine—thanks for asking. And you'll find Liam in the kitchen on his tea break."

Reid scowled at me but didn't say anything. Connor and I watched him go and we both waited for the fallout.

"What were those two scumbags doing in my garage?" we heard him ask.

There was a brief silence before Liam answered and both Connor and I strained to hear.

"Which scumbags are you referring to?"

I sniggered and Connor rolled his eyes.

"Phil Kennedy and his pet pig," Reid replied.

"Not much."

"They didn't just wander in for the hell of it." Reid's voice lifted. I noted Liam's stayed the same.

"Apparently Phil had some guy rip him off for parts, you know, skipped out on the bill. He'd gone to the cops and—"

"Let me guess. The debt was so big they sent a detective to check it out. Yeah, right. They came here because once you've done time, you're always guilty. I fucking knew it."

"They were checking to see if anyone had called in selling parts, or if the same guy had been here to get any work done on a vehicle. They were here for five minutes, max. Ask Louise. She was here. She saw them."

Connor looked at me. I nodded. "I don't know how long they were here before I arrived, though," I whispered to Connor. "Why doesn't Reid like Kennedy?"

"Reid accused Kennedy of stealing a car off him about ten years ago. Remains of the car were found in a chop shop two weeks after it was taken. The chop shop was owned by Kennedy's cousin. Then when Dad died, someone spread rumours all over Greenhill and Riverford that he was a crook running a bad garage. Reid's had a grudge against him ever since."

"And you haven't?"

"Let's just say, if he takes enough rope, he'll eventually hang himself." He shifted his attention back to the magazine. Two minutes later Liam wandered out, his mouth full of a cheese scone, today's morning tea. Reid stormed out behind him.

"Where are those invoices?" Reid demanded.

I looked up at Reid. "Are you speaking to me?"

He flipped his hands palms up and shrugged.

"I thought we had a conversation about using our manners last night." I pushed my chair back, walked over to the filing cabinet, pulled open the top drawer and rifled through the manila folder titled *miscellaneous*. The invoices weren't there. I hunted through more files. Nothing. The drawer below. Nothing. Perhaps I'd left them on my desk? My desk was neat and tidy.

"Louise?"

"They're not here."

Connor looked up from the article he was reading.

"What do you mean they're not here?" Reid asked. He stalked around the desk to my filing cabinet. "Where did you put them?"

"They were just in the front of the top drawer. I was leaving them there until I had talked to you and Connor about them." I slumped down into my chair. "They're not here."

"Who would take them?" Connor wanted to know. "They're of no use to anyone."

"Unless they wanted to hide something." Reid slammed the filing cabinet drawer shut. "We've never bought anything off Kennedy's." He paced back and forth across the reception floor while Connor sat quietly on the corner of my desk.

"There's no record on the computer?"

"Not with the system you've been using," I told them.

Reid butted his hand against the door frame and swore under his breath. "There's something dodgy going on, and it stinks."

"Perhaps now's a good time to do some training with this new filing system?" I ventured, and braced myself for the fallout.

25

REID

THE FEELING I WAS being set up again stuck with me all morning. I couldn't pinpoint anything specific—all I knew was that somehow, Liam was involved. Hell, maybe even Louise was mixed up in this as well. It was annoying the hell out of me.

I left work early, changed into my sweats and hit the road. It was the quickest way of ridding my head of the anger I was feeling at everyone and every damn thing.

The clouds were turning an ominous shade of gunmetal as I jogged Falls Road. There was rain coming too, and not just a shower. As I ran, the steady rhythm of my feet on the road kept stealing my mind back to Louise. There were so many coincidences. She'd turned up not long after I'd got out of prison. She'd wrangled a job in our office, which meant she had access to all our files, including the missing invoices. Suddenly the cops were sniffing around the place again. Kennedy was involved somehow. Had it been a coincidence that Louise had been at work on the Saturday with Liam, Kennedy and Selgrave, while Connor and I were at the rugby?

There was only one thing I couldn't work out, and that was Louise's ex-boyfriend's involvement in all this. Why had he turned up? Was he somehow tangled up in this too? Was it all a sham? I had a hundred questions and I didn't want to believe Louise had anything to do with me being set up, but I couldn't rule her out, either. I remembered when I'd caught Louise searching articles about me on her phone. The more I thought about the sequence of events, the more confused I got.

Eight kilometres into the run, I felt the first drops of rain hit my face. The road had narrowed and morphed from farming land to large pines still several years from milling. I stopped and paced in a circle in the middle of the road, angry words spilling from my mouth. I still felt frustrated and no nearer to working out who or what was going down.

By the time I got back, I was soaked and exhausted. Paranoia was setting in.

I peeled off my clothes and got in the shower. What I needed was to sleep out the back in the pines again. But it was going to get stormy tonight, so that would have to wait.

Showered, I switched on the TV. I'd just sat down when someone knocked on the front door.

I lifted myself out of the comfort of the sofa and pulled the door open to find Louise standing outside. She was dressed in a raincoat, but still looked half-drowned.

"Hi. Have you eaten?" she asked.

"No. And I—"

"Good." She thrust two large wet pizza boxes at my chest and stepped around me into the hall. She jerked out of her coat and hung it up then unzipped her boots and pushed them to one side. "It's nasty out there."

"This isn't a good time—"

She didn't wait to hear my reasoning. "Are you hiding another woman in the bedroom?" She looked questioningly at me; her eyelashes had droplets of water hanging off them. My gut backflipped.

"No."

She nodded. "Is it that time of the month? You know men have their off days too."

"What?" I had no idea what the hell she was talking about. Her eyebrows lifted. "No, don't be ridiculous," I said, and shut the weather out.

"Why are you here, Louise?" I asked, following her into the sitting room. The pizzas smelled really good.

"You need to eat. I need to eat. Someone had to deliver the pizzas. You've had a shitty day. I thought you might like some company." She walked through to the kitchen and opened the fridge like she owned the house. "Beer?" She held out two cans.

I nodded. *Damn the woman.*

She pulled the tab on the can and took a long swallow. I watched the curve of her throat as she drank, and the Big Guy decided it had been far too long since he'd had an intimate relationship with her. *Fucking traitor.*

I opened a couple of boxes, pushed one towards her end of the coffee table, helped myself to a piece and sat down.

"Have you heard the news?" she asked, folding one leg beneath her as she sank onto the sofa, watching me. She was a riot of colour in her oversized pink jumper from the first day I saw her, teamed with bright blue leggings and red socks.

"About what?" I asked, slightly distracted. My stomach was telling me to eat the pizza, my body was trying to tell me to skip the food and get down to business. My brain, on the other hand, thought I should have declined the pizzas and asked her to leave. My dick was at this stage fighting the good fight, but I feared my brain was going to win out.

"Han's decided to move in with Will. A trial run for a few months, see how it goes. She's asked me if I want to take her apartment. I said yes."

Her grin lit up the room and was reflected in her eyes. The glow that sparked off her would've drawn a small crowd, but tonight it fell short and I was torn between guilt and confusion.

"Well, gee," she said, helping herself to a second slice of the pepperoni. "Don't get too excited about it."

"I told you it wasn't a good time," I huffed impatiently.

She put her slice of pizza down and stood. "Okay. Sorry I intruded. I'll see you at work on Wednesday."

Aw, shit. I wanted her here and I wanted to feel her—in my arms... in my bed—and yet I didn't want her here in case she was tangled up in something, except I didn't know what.

"Wait." I sprung to my feet and followed her. She was stepping back into her boots. "I'm sorry. I'm just not good company right now."

"Don't apologise. It's fine." She pushed her arms into the sleeves of her jacket, flicking water across the floor, and zipped it up.

"At least stay and finish your pizza." My rapidly deflating erection was screaming in protest at my brain about what I was letting slip through my hands.

She opened the door. Behind her, the rain was throwing itself at the house in sheets. "I'll see you at work." She turned and marched out into the torrent. She would be soaked before she even reached her car.

I slammed the door, hoping it would shut out any lingering guilt, and returned to the pizza. It didn't, and I felt like a heel. If Lou had told me yesterday that she had decided to stay in town, I would have been euphoric. But now, I didn't know what to think.

My bad mood continued through the week, and it wasn't helped that every time I turned around, Louise was there doing stuff. Tyler had been shifted home and Louise had taken it upon herself to organise a roster of helpers to do various jobs for him and Julie-Ann: cleaning the house, dropping off hot meals or baked goods, maintaining the garden and driving Julie-Ann to the library or grocery store. Louise had also gathered names of those Julie-Ann could call if she had to go out and needed someone to sit with Tyler. I knew Connor had his name on the list, but Louise had not asked me to volunteer. For anything. In fact, apart from a few unavoidable conversations at work, she was giving me a wide berth. And I didn't blame her. But it wasn't working.

I went to the supermarket, and she was there in the fruit and vegetable corner picking out oranges. I turned and headed for the coffee aisle. She was there choosing her favourite peppermint tea bags. I went to the gym to let one of the personal trainers know his car was going to take several days longer to fix, being that we were short-staffed. I looked over and Louise was working on one of the rowing machines in skimpy shorts and a T-shirt that had *Duck you!* stretched tight across her breasts. As I walked past the flower shop, I glanced in and Louise was standing at the counter talking to Kate. She was everywhere, and I was fighting a losing battle to put some distance between us.

Friday afternoon, I was typing out answers to a questionnaire that she had forwarded to me. Another newspaper or magazine was going to run a piece about the garage and the kart race.

I looked up to see Louise standing in the doorway, a couple of boxes balanced in her arms. I pushed back from my desk to take them from her.

"I can manage."

I snatched them out of her arms.

"With the others is fine," she directed, pointing at the considerable stack of boxes of donated supplies for the derby stacked against the only empty wall in my office. I don't know why my office had to become the designated storeroom.

"I hope you're going to be able to get rid of all these." I added the boxes to the others, returned to my seat and turned my focus back to the questions.

"The more spot prizes, the better," she said, lingering.

Her just being in my office was not good for my resolve.

"Have you got a minute?" she said.

I hit the *save* button on the keyboard and leaned back in my chair, my eyes settled on hers. "Sure."

She crossed her arms over her chest, then uncrossed them. "I want to know if I've done something to upset you."

I'd noticed the way she'd styled her hair today. It was a riot of curls I'd give anything to bury my fingers in. She was stunning. The fact was, I missed her sleepovers. The way she laughed that made *me* laugh, even when I felt shitty. She always made my life look bright. She was wearing pale pink lip gloss and I couldn't drag my eyes away.

She snapped her fingers at me.

I blinked. "What? No, of course not."

"I don't believe you."

"I can't help that."

"Fine. If that's the way you want to play it," she mumbled, then I watched her turn and walk back to her desk and sit at her computer.

It was how I wanted to play it. At least until I knew what her part in all this was.

I just hoped I wasn't making the biggest mistake of my life.

26

LOU

HANNAH WAS LEAVING ALL her furniture and just taking her personal belongings to Will's place. That suited me just fine. I'd arrived with what I could fit in my car, and that didn't extend to furniture. I wanted to stay here in Riverford Valley. It had a sense of community. But there was one person I wanted my staying to mean something to, and he was being a prize idiot.

On Saturday, Hannah closed the café an hour early and I helped her pack her things into both our cars.

"Stay and have lunch with us?" Will asked after we'd carried the last of the boxes from the cars inside.

"Thanks. I'd love that."

Will had a smile permanently stuck on his face today. I felt happy for Hannah. He was a good man; they worked well together and I knew he'd look after her. Hell, everyone in town could tell they were head over heels, and the gossipmongers would already be spreading the news of their living arrangements.

When Will called us for lunch, steaming bowls of thick, creamy pumpkin soup waited for us in the kitchen, along with thick slices of sourdough bread slathered in garlic butter. It smelled divine and tasted out of this world.

"Are you going to watch Reid play this afternoon?" he asked me.

"Nope. Are you?"

"Is it wrong of us to want to stay home? I feel like I just want to be here with Will," Hannah said, looking sheepish.

I shook my head. "Not at all."

"Don't bother with those," Hannah told me when I got up and gathered the dishes. "Not that I'm trying to get rid of you." She stood and crossed to where I was rinsing the soup bowls before stacking them in the dishwasher. "I can finish unpacking, and Will can organise the dishes if you have something else you'd rather be doing."

As it happened, I did. "I'm going to drop in and visit Tyler and Julie-Ann and see if there's anything they need. Then I'm going back to the apartment and I'm going to watch a movie and go to bed early."

"You've made a lot of people happy while you've been in town, Lou. Thank you." She leaned in and gave me a warm generous hug. "I hope you'll seriously consider staying here permanently. The apartment's yours for as long as you want it." She took both my arms and held them.

"I don't have any reason to stay."

She narrowed her eyes at me. "You don't actually believe that, do you?"

I broke free and finished loading the dishes. "I love being closer to you and Will, but there's nothing else keeping me here." I was skirting the elephant in the room and we all knew it. I rinsed a glass and filled it with cold tap water. My throat was suddenly dry.

"What about Reid?"

And there it was.

I sighed and took another sip of water. "I was beginning to think we might be able to build something. But Reid's got a stick up his backside over something and he won't tell me what. He can barely stay in the same room as me."

Hannah shook her head. "He needs to sit and talk his emotions out. He bottles things up until they've become so big there's no way around them."

"Good luck if you're going to suggest that."

"Lou!" Connor called as I made my way across the workshop on Wednesday morning. He was working under a car, replacing a muffler. I glanced around the floor—no sign of Liam or Reid.

"Morning," I greeted, lifting a cardboard box with foil over it. "Sausage rolls this morning."

"Thanks. I don't know what I'm going to do if you ever leave. Heads up—Reid is in one hell of a black mood this morning. Might pay to steer a wide berth if you see him coming."

"Oh?"

"A photographer turned up yesterday with some woman."

I put my free hand over my mouth.

"Something to do with a—"

"Oh, shit. I forgot to tell him they were coming. Sorry if I've made your life hell."

"He'll get over it. The guy took some photos of the both of us and some of Reid on his own. It's all good promo, I'm sure. It'll just take time for him to calm down."

"Perhaps I should work from home today?"

"You'll be fine." He gave me a reassuring smile that somehow made me more anxious.

"Unfortunately, the photographer arrived just after the cops. Didn't help matters."

"What did the cops want?"

"It was all a bit strange. They had a look over the kart and left. Not really sure what they were searching for."

"Not Selgrave, was it?"

"No, Constable Dewinter and that new guy."

"That's odd."

"How's everything going for the weekend?" He wiped his hands on a rag he produced from a pocket and followed the scent of hot sausage rolls across to the reception. "Need me to do anything?"

"Everything is running smoothly. I've notified the ambulance service, and they'll have first-aiders along the course and at the end. I've got eight food trucks at the sports grounds. The local paper is covering it, and the council have approved the road closure times. I've got to notify the residents on the road. Everything is falling into place. We have all the prizes listed and ready to allocate. We've just got the hay bales and signage to see to on Friday and Saturday morning, which I'll need help with. Oh, and have you decided who's driving our kart yet?"

Connor burst into laughter. He pulled the reception door open and stood back for me to walk through.

"What's so funny?"

"Reid really drew the short straw yesterday."

"Short straw?"

"Yeah. It was a three-in-a-row day yesterday." He laughed even harder. "He and I decided last night to draw straws and see out of the three of us who would race it. Reid drew the shortest. He was already worked up from the photography session and the cops."

Now I was laughing.

I glanced around to see where Liam was. "Does Liam know?" I had a niggling feeling that Liam was expecting to race the kart.

"No. I haven't told him yet."

"Can you keep it from him until Saturday morning? And ask Reid not to say anything either."

"Do I need to know why?"

"I just want to check something out first."

"Sure. I'll give Reid a call and tell him to keep his mouth shut. But you let me know what's happening. I don't want to be the last to know stuff."

"I promise." I gave him a scout's honour sign. "Where is the kart? I'd like to get some photos for social media and our website."

"Liam's taken it. Apparently, a friend of his made some decals for the sides. He getting them put on. He'll be back with it by lunch."

I glanced at my watch; nine-twenty a.m. That gave me plenty of time. My mind was working overtime, and I wanted to find out what Liam was up to.

I designed a realistic-looking certificate of compliance for the kart which would give me a reason for visiting Liam's if I got caught. Slipping it in my bag, I processed some invoices, scheduled some social media posts, rang several of the key sponsors and asked if they'd like to present their donated prizes. Then, I hunted up Liam's address on the computer. As soon as the clock struck eleven, I picked up my bag and walked out to the workshop. I had an hour, tops, to find him. Relief washed over me when I saw there was still no sign of Reid.

"Hey, Connor? I'm just popping out. Won't be long."

He waved in acknowledgement, and I hurried out to my car, started it up and reversed out of my parking space. I drove up the main street and turned onto Lake Road, counting the streets as I passed each one. At the fifth, I turned right onto Western Crescent. It was a straight piece of road with houses that were built in the sixties. I suspected the families that lived on this street weren't the type who would be interested in keeping gardens. The front yards sloped slightly to reach the street and there were no white picket fences. A couple had tall wooden fences erected around them that stopped anyone from the street seeing in, while many had no fences at all. The odd tree graced a berm here and there, but most of the lawns were littered with old car bodies, rather than plant pots or flowerbeds.

Liam lived at number seventy-eight. I drove slowly along the street, checking numbers on letterboxes and passing the odd parked car, until I spotted up ahead what I'd been looking for: Liam's truck. I pulled the car to the kerb at least a dozen houses away and cut the ignition.

From my vantage point I could make out it was backed into his drive; the tail gate was down and there was no sign of the kart. There were two other vehicles parked not far from his drive. They looked like the same two that I'd seen parked outside the garage, but I couldn't tell from this angle. If it was the detective and Phil Kennedy, then they were definitely up to no good. I pulled out my phone and snapped a couple of photos.

There was only one thing to do: I'd go and knock on the door. Tell Liam I had his compliance certificate and hope he didn't realise what I was up to. Something caught my eye and I shifted my attention to the property I was parked outside. A sign on the only fenced section on the street stated: *BEWARE DOG*. Right next to the sign, where a piece of the fence had been chewed, was the biggest, meanest-looking dog I'd ever seen. It bared its teeth in welcome. I gulped and wondered just how secure the fence really was.

I started the car again and slipped it into gear, but as I eased my foot off the clutch, the passenger door flung open, I jumped, the car jerked and stalled, the dog snarled and I might have wet my pants a little. I stared at the mysterious person for a fleeting second before realising it was Reid wearing a dark wig. Laughter erupted from me. He snatched his dark aviators off. The look on his face was priceless. A baseball cap and black hoody completed the outfit.

"Reid? What are you doing?" I managed once the laughter had subsided.

"What are *you* doing, is more to the point," he demanded. This was obviously not going to be a friendly chat.

I couldn't tell Reid I suspected Liam was involved in something suspicious and I didn't want Reid getting involved. I, on the other hand, had nothing to lose if I got caught out snooping.

"I'm curious about where Liam lives," I hissed, trying to calm my heart rate down and come up with something convincing while keeping one eye on the dog that was pacing back and forth behind the fence, snarling at me.

"I'm calling bullshit on that one, sweetheart," he said, a sarcastic tone to his voice. He glanced from me to Liam's place and back. "How about you tell me the real reason you're parked down the road from Liam's at eleven-forty-five on a Wednesday morning? And don't tell me you were bringing him lunch."

I turned to look behind me. I couldn't see Reid's truck. It wasn't parked anywhere on the street in front of me, either. In fact, the only vehicles were two cars parked at intervals on the far side of the street, and an old, battered Holden two houses back.

"How did you get here? Where's your truck?"

"I'm in the white Holden." He thumbed behind him. "Stop changing the subject. Tell me why you're here."

"Get out of my car, Reid."

"I'm not moving until you tell me."

I swore under my breath. "I wanted to know where Liam took the kart. Connor told me he had taken it. I wanted to get some photos of it for social media and our website."

Reid stared at me as if he was trying to work out the probability that my story was credible. "So why not wait until he got back to the garage?"

"It was a spur of the moment thing."

He was giving me the stink eye. I ignored him and turned my attention back to Liam's place. The side door on his car shed opened and three men stepped out into the light of day.

"Look!" I pointed at the movement farther down the street.

Reid's eyes slid from me to the road ahead. "The larger one's Phil Kennedy. And that's fucking Selgrave wearing the jacket."

"And Liam behind them."

As we watched, Kennedy and Selgrave walked slowly out to the street, towards their respective vehicles.

"Climb in the back seat! Quick! They'll know us if they see us," Reid ordered.

"Why do I have—"

"Don't argue. Get in the back now, and down, out of sight. Hurry."

I scuttled between the seats and climbed into the back. Meanwhile, Reid attempted to fold himself into the front footwell of the car and bent over the seat. How on earth he managed it, I had no idea.

"Take your jacket off and throw it over you," he barked. "We can't let them see us."

I scrambled around on the back seat, fell into the footwell and tried to pull the jacket free of my arms. I clambered back onto the seat. It was almost impossible.

"Now isn't the time to be flaunting your choice of lace panties," the smart alec drawled from the front. "Can't you move any faster?"

I looked down and discovered my skirt was hitched up around my waist, with my butt almost pressed against the side window. *Good grief.* "For God's sake, Reid, look away." I groaned, wishing I'd worn jeans today. Grappling with the hem of my skirt, I used the other hand to give the jacket one almighty tug. The car swayed as it came free of my arm with a *whoosh*, and I belted my knuckles on the door.

"Is there anything there I can use?" he asked, desperation sounding in his voice.

I found a rug on the floor and, wincing at the pain in my hand, pushed it covertly between the seats.

He draped it over the top half of himself and I held my breath as a vehicle sped past, followed a minute later by a second. How the heck did he fit in the front of my car?

"Lou, see if you can spot what Liam's doing. I'm a bit stuck."

I grinned and lifted my head inch by inch until I could see between the seats. Reid was looking decidedly uncomfortable. "Great view from here." I clamped my lips shut to stop myself from laughing.

"Hurry up! I've got fucking cramp in my right leg!"

"Okay. Keep your pants on. I think he's back in the shed. I can't see him."

With that, he flung the rug off him, pushed the door open and kind of barrel-rolled out of the car onto the road. There was a lot of swearing. "We need to leave now before he comes down this road and sees us."

Reid's wig was now crooked. He had long strands hanging across one side of his face and his own hair was clearly visible above his forehead and around one ear. That was all it took for the laughing to start.

He snarled and I wondered if he was chatting to the dog.

I pushed the jacket off me, opened the back door and crawled out on hands and knees, dropping onto the grass beside the footpath. The dog jumped excitedly at the hole in the fence and did a bit of snarling of its own. I ripped the driver's door open and jumped in, shutting it firmly behind me.

"I'll see you at work, Louise. You have some explaining to do." Reid closed the door with a *humph* and was gone as quickly as he'd appeared. If I laughed any harder, I'd need a complete change of clothes.

I started the car, did a U-turn and drove back to work. I couldn't work out what those three men were up to, and why was Liam spending so much time with the detective? One thing was certain, he also had a lot of explaining to do.

27

LOU

I WAS CONVINCED THE three men were planning something, and I suspected the tyres Liam told me he'd had to change had something to do with it—I wished I could somehow get ten minutes alone with the kart to inspect them. I was missing something. But what? I got my phone out, typed in some key words and hit the search button. Articles on Reid's arrest came up again and I slowly scrolled through them.

I couldn't find anything obvious. Heck, I didn't even know what I was looking for. The mystery of how the cocaine ended up in the car was messing with my head. If someone wanted the drugs, why didn't they just buy them straight from the dealer? Why include a middleman like the garage? I had no idea. I needed to find out more.

Was Reid being set up—or Connor? What motive did Liam have? Did Liam know Reid was driving the kart in the race? And how much did Reid and Connor know that they weren't sharing with me?

A fist knocked on my car window and I jumped. My phone flew out of my hands and landed in the footwell.

Reid was standing outside, frown etched across his forehead, his disguise now gone. What was it with this man? I placed my hand over my heart to try and calm the racing.

Retrieving my phone, I grabbed my things and climbed out of the car, locking it behind me.

"Is there no peace?" I muttered.

When we got inside, Reid called Connor over and ushered me into his office. "Sit down," he ordered.

"No, thanks."

"Have it your own way." He stayed on his feet too while we waited for Connor.

"What's up?" Connor asked, breezing in to join us.

"The door!"

Connor glared at his brother. "Close the fucking door yourself."

Reid paced to the door and shut it. Windows in the office rattled. "Do you know what I caught Louise doing?"

Connor shrugged his shoulders and didn't look particularly concerned.

"Oh, for goodness' sake," I grumbled. "What is this? Tell-tale time at school?"

"I caught her staking out Liam's house."

"Because he was already staking out the property."

Reid ignored me and I noticed the flared nostrils had returned.

I stared at Reid. "Great. You feel better, now you got that off your chest?"

"I'm sure she had her reasons." Connor lifted his brows at Reid. "You done now?"

Reid mouthed something unintelligible.

"Well, if there's nothing else, I've got two hundred hay bales to organise for Saturday," I told them both, and breezed out the door.

But first, I had more questions that needed answering. I stowed my things under my desk as Connor walked back through reception and winked at me. I waited for both men to leave the reception area and I hunted out my phone.

"Constable Gaylene Dewinter speaking."

"Hi Gaylene, it's Louise Adair."

"Louise, what can I do for you?"

"I wondered if I could meet you for coffee or lunch?"

"Not today, sorry, I've got a lot on. I could meet you for coffee tomorrow if it's important."

"It is. And... um, could you come on your own?"

"Okay. Where and when?"

"Do you think we could meet at the park on Cornford Street?" I rattled off a time.

"I'll meet you there tomorrow," she agreed, and hung up, leaving me a little less apprehensive.

I sat back in my chair and noticed Liam was back in the workshop. I watched as he wheeled the frame of the kart through the garage and out the back. The body was gleaming with its bright green paint job, newly covered in sponsors' logos.

My phone pinged. It was a notification from the bank. Someone had deposited money into my account. Interesting. Money going in was better than it coming out, and it wasn't even payday. I swiped the screen and tapped in my PIN and stopped.

Twenty. Thousand. Dollars. It sat there, staring at me. So many zeroes. I gasped for breath. I tapped more links and found it was a transfer from Jayden. For some unknown reason, he'd seen fit to pay back some of the money he'd taken from me.

My eyes welled up as an overwhelming sense of freedom hit me. Twenty grand. It meant I had a good deposit for a flat in Auckland. I could buy some new clothes. At that moment, Reid pushed his way into reception and stopped abruptly.

"What's wrong?" he asked, coming to squat beside my chair. "Are you hurt?"

I shook my head, but I was too emotional to say anything. He lifted his hand and, with his thumb, gently wiped away a tear that was in freefall. I loved this side of Reid. The gentle, caring side that he kept hidden from everyone except his closest friends. I cried harder. I was so damn confused. One minute he was yelling at me, the next he was being all soft and concerned. And with the money—it was too much.

"Jayden," I said, and snorted a nose-full of gunk into some tissues. "I can't believe it."

"Can't believe what? What's he done now?"

"He put... in my... bank account." I blew some more and sniffed. "Money."

"I'm pleased," he said and rose to his normal height. "That dirtbag should have paid you back much more than what he has, but it's a start." He turned and wandered back to his office. I sat there for a hot minute before I got to my feet.

"What do you mean, he should have paid me more? How do you know how much he's given me?" I yelled at him through the dividing window.

"I'm guessing," he shrugged his shoulders and flipped through the pages of the work diary on his desk.

"Really?"

"Yeah."

I had no idea what Reid had to do with it, but I was thankful. I now had a big bit of my nest egg back. I just hoped Jayden was okay and not in some hospital in traction. I sat back down and dreamed of all the things I could do with so much money.

Thursday, I picked up lunch at the café then walked down the main street and across to the park where I was meeting Constable Dewinter. I couldn't see her anywhere, so I took a seat and waited. Ten minutes later, her police car pulled up. She got out, fitted her hat firmly in place and strode across the grass towards me.

I held up a bag. "I picked up something from Hannah's. I didn't know if you'd eaten yet."

"Thanks." She took the bag and peered in. "I'm starving." She sat down alongside me, ignored the chicken sandwich and pulled out the sugar-coated apple-filled donut and took a bite. Her face told me how strongly she agreed with my menu choices. "This is just what I needed." She removed her coffee from the carry tray and took a sip.

"So, what did you want to talk to me about?" She took another bite of the donut, and a large portion of apple oozed out and landed on one pant leg. "Oh, shit. These were clean on this morning."

I handed her a serviette and stifled a snigger as she carefully cleaned up the spilled apple. "I wanted to know about Reid Hamilton."

Her eyes widened and she looked at me as if I was asking her to run naked across the park. "What about him?"

"Were you involved with his arrest?"

"Does he know you're asking me about him?"

Typical police manoeuvre. Answer every question with one of your own. "No," I confessed. "And I'm not going to tell him, either."

She nodded. "I started work here two weeks before the arrest. So, I was called in as a member of the search team." She took another bite of the donut, this time making sure she didn't spill any.

"Who was it who actually found the drugs?"

"One of the constables from Greenhill, I think. Why?"

"Do you think I could talk to him?"

"No can do. I heard he left about three months after Reid got arrested."

That was interesting. "Do you know why?"

"Apparently his wife wasn't well and they shifted further north. Warmer climate," she said.

"And what do you think of the detective in charge of the case?"

"Tony Selgrave?"

I nodded.

"Between you and me, not much of a personality and huge sense of entitlement." She shoved the remainder of the donut in her mouth.

"Would you trust him with your life?" I watched her chewing until she was finished and dabbed her mouth with a clean corner of the napkin.

"I have to. But if you were to ask me if I'd invite him around to my place for drinks on a Saturday night, the answer would be no." She took the sandwich from the bag. "Why are you asking me all this?"

"I'm worried about Reid," I admitted. Nothing like getting straight to the point. "I think he's being set up."

"Set up?"

"I think something's going to happen at the kart race."

"What makes you think that?" She paused mid-sandwich and concentrated on what I was saying. I was half-expecting her to whip out her notebook and start writing.

"Well, Selgrave and another guy have been hanging around the garage when neither Reid nor Connor have been there, and then I happened to be parked on Liam's street recently," Dewinter's eyebrow lifted, "and happened to see them visiting Liam at his home. I don't know what's going on with Liam or what any of them are up to. I just have a bad feeling about it."

She nodded. "Selgrave hasn't had any callouts in Riverford, so he's had no reason to be over here on police business. I appreciate you coming to me about it." She stared at me as though she was putting two and two together and the sums were adding up to more than four.

"I'm sure something's going to happen on race day, I just don't know what."

"Leave it with us. I don't want you doing anything... ah... unusual."

"Unusual? I have no idea what you mean." I feigned innocence, but I was sure she saw right through me.

"I don't want you staking out houses." Her lips were drawn, then switched to a smile. "It's hard enough trying to keep an eye on Reid."

A momentary flush of embarrassment swept through me.

"Well," she said, swallowing the last of the sandwich. "I'd better be getting back. I've got a stack of paperwork that needs attending to. If you hear anything else, let me know first—and remember, no amateur sleuthing. I don't want you getting caught in the middle of anything."

I nodded.

"Thanks for the lunch. I owe you one."

I watched her walk back to her car and hoped I'd done the right thing. Reid would probably never speak to me again if he knew that I'd been meddling in his affairs.

But the truth of the matter was, I was head over heels in love with the man. And even though the feeling clearly wasn't mutual—I wanted to make sure that this time, the real criminals got locked up.

Friday, I worked with Old Man Matheson to set up the staging area, and together we placed several trailer loads of hay bales along fence lines to protect any wayward drivers who missed a corner.

Exhausted, and with all the day's jobs finally crossed off my list, I parked the car outside The Lucky Cat Chinese takeaway and dashed in for sweet and sour pork and fried rice. There was no way I could cook a meal tonight—hell, I could hardly drive, my muscles ached so much from all the lifting. With any luck, I'd stay awake long enough to eat, shower and fall into bed.

I placed my order and took a seat. The door opened and Claire, who owned the day spa and hairdressing salon in town, stepped inside.

"Hello, Louise."

I must have looked as bad as I felt, judging by the look she gave me.

"You realise your hair is full of hay?" Claire informed me. "What on earth have you been doing?"

"Shifting bales for tomorrow."

I ignored my hair—pulling bits of straw free would involve me raising my arms, and that wasn't happening.

"Aren't there enough young men in town to do that?"

"Maybe. But you know what they say about wanting a job done properly."

She smirked.

The door opened again, and this time Kate walked in.

"Hi, Louise. Claire." She gave me a smile and pointed to her hair, and I nodded. She stepped up to the counter and Mr Lucky Cat handed her three containers in exchange for her debit card. I noticed she had a large quantity of food for one person.

"My brother's visiting," she offered when she saw me glance at the takeaways. I nodded. Did Kate have a date or was her dinner guest really her brother?

Twenty minutes later, I was sitting on the sofa in Hannah's apartment, shovelling sticky, sweet pork pieces into my mouth, when the door sounded. I groaned. If I went down and unlocked it, I was at serious risk of not making it back up the stairs.

It sounded again. Twice. *Grrr.* I made my way down and pulled the door open, immediately regretting my decision.

"Reid," I said with no enthusiasm whatsoever.

"You look like you've been sleeping rough. Maybe under a bridge," he said, stepping inside and closing the door behind him. He grabbed my hand pulling me up the stairs behind him.

"What do you want, Reid? I'm too tired to fight."

We reached the top of the stairs, and he pulled me against him. His eyes were sultry and dark, with an evil glint that would have made me orgasm on the spot if I wasn't so tired. He leaned into me, his lips brushing my ear.

"I've come to apologise to you."

28

LOU

THE CAR I WAS driving crashed through the barrier and nose-dived into a lake. My alarm buzzed and I blinked open my eyes. I pulled my other hand from under the duvet, where it had been holding tight to something warm and muscular, and waved it around in the general direction of my phone.

A deep, husky moan sounded next to me. "Put that back."

"Too much of a good thing," I mumbled. I wondered if the car wreck was some sort of premonition about how my life was playing out. My on-again, off-again relationship with Reid was definitely on again, and although it gave me the warm fuzzies, I was also anxious about where we were going. Was our relationship ever going to be anything more than what it was—a convenience? I didn't want that. I wanted Reid in my life. Permanently. But so far, I had no proof he wanted the same thing. Right now, I felt so confused about whether I should leave or not.

Beside me, Reid snaked an arm over my stomach, fingers digging under my waist, pulling me against him. Spooning his erect penis against the small of my back.

"Sweetheart," his deep rumble of a voice added lust to my cocktail of emotions.

"I gotta get up," I groaned, wishing I could sleep the whole day. That we could both stay safe inside this apartment. I promised myself tomorrow, once the race was over, I would sleep for as long as I wanted.

"What time is it?" Reid asked without opening his eyes.

"Five-thirty."

"Already?"

"I can't afford to sleep in this morning—I've got a lot to do." I dragged myself away from him. "You do too."

Last night, as I finished my Chinese, he'd apologised to me for being such an arse about Liam. He'd put me in the shower, and tucked me into bed. Then he'd let me lie back and enjoy the ride while he sent me to orgasm heaven. I definitely loved his apologies. I finally fell into a deep sleep an hour later, dreaming about all the things I could fight with Reid about, so we could have more make-up sex.

His mouth met mine as he kissed me gently and let me go. "I'm taking a rain check," he called as I headed to the bathroom. "Just so you know."

I showered and dressed in thermals with my Hamilton's Automotive T-shirt over the top, pulled my legs into jeans and hunted out my thickest socks. I made toast while Reid took his turn in the shower. It was still outside, and a thin coating of frost blanketed the lawns. It was going to be a nice day. One less thing to worry about.

By the time we got to the staging area, Connor was already there.

"Morning," I greeted, breathing a cloud of misty vapour into the air. My nervous stomach was still doing flips, and I'd already suppressed the urge to throw up more than once.

"Morning." He glanced from me to Reid, who was sauntering along behind. "Where's the kart?"

"Don't panic," Reid said. "Liam's dropping it off at seven." He blew warm air into his cupped hands and rubbed them together.

"Does he know the road will be closed from eight-thirty?" Connor asked.

"He knows," I said. "Do you think the road will be icy? I hope we have enough Portaloos. Do you think the police will turn up?"

"Lou."

I turned to Reid.

"Take a breath, sweetheart. Everything will be fine. I promise."

I nodded, but his words did nothing to reassure me. My stomach was still whirring. "Promise me something?"

"What?" He put his arms around my waist and pulled me in to his body.

"Be careful."

"Scout's honour, ma'am."

I belted him with the palm of my hand. "I'm serious. Be careful."

"I will. Stop worrying." And to silence me, he dipped his head slightly to cover my lips with his.

I sighed. "I'll hold you to that rain check," I whispered.

His mouth curved into a grin.

"After I do the briefing, I'm going to head down to the finish, set up for the prize-giving and meet the mayor." I went through the list of tasks in my head. *Winner. Speeches. Mayor. Prize-giving. Auction... Shit.* My brain had finally turned to mush. I strode over to where the brothers were now roping off the car parking area.

"I forgot the auctioneer," I blurted out, and screwed my face up like I was in pain.

"No problem," Connor said.

"Really?"

"Well, how hard can it be? Annie will do it for you."

I spun around to see where she was and found her talking to Old Man Matheson. "I'll go ask her."

With some arm-twisting and a promise from me to shout her lunch, Annie agreed to run the auction. With everyone on the same page, I walked back to the car. Liam pulled in to the competitors' staging area, towing the gleaming, fluorescent green kart. With its bright orange and yellow flames licking along the sides, it was a miniature replica of a classic hot rod, and I had to admit, it looked pretty sleek.

Liam jumped down from his truck and wandered over to talk to Connor and Reid. I glanced around, noting there were now quite a number of competitors in varying stages of preparedness. If I walked around the two closest cars and trailers and kept a low profile, I could get to the trailer and the kart.

Keeping an eye on Liam, I hurried over to the cars, slipped between the Falcon and Liam's truck, and dug in my back pocket. My fingers grasped the round disc I'd hidden there. The three men were still talking. I leaned over the tray of Liam's truck and slipped a tag underneath the body next to the tyres. It had a good grip on the metal and it didn't budge. Hopefully, anyone seeing me would think I was just manifesting a win. I'd purchased the tag a year ago when I'd thought taking an overseas trip with Jayden was a good idea. I'd intended to throw it away, but I was pleased I hadn't.

I quickly made my way back to my car, pulled out my phone and checked the app. A moving circle radiated out a few metres from where I was sitting. I sighed with relief—if anyone spotted it, they wouldn't know who put it there.

"What are you doing?"

I jumped. My phone hit the dash and fell on the floor as the face of Constable Dewinter leaned towards my open window. She was dressed in casual clothes, with a beanie tugged down over her ears and a red-checked woollen Swanndri jacket zipped up under her chin.

"Nothing." I slumped back against the headrest, trying to recover my heart rate.

She narrowed her eyes at me. "This tracking device yours?"

I looked out the window at the cars arriving, towing karts of all shapes and sizes. "Nope. Never seen it before."

"Right." She dropped it through the window and it landed in my lap. "Leave the policing to us, Louise. Consider this a warning."

"Well, I'm worried about Reid."

"He's a grown man, Louise, capable of looking after himself."

I let out a sigh. I wasn't reassured, but I was at least a bit happier knowing there would be a police presence.

She smiled at me. "We've got eyes on the ground. Constable Thompson is in plain clothes and Constable Martin will be along in another hour. If anything happens, we'll catch it."

"But what if—"

"Everything is under control."

"Won't they suspect you're watching them?"

"It's not unusual that we attend community events. Detective Selgrave will recognise me and Johnny, but I don't think he'll recognise Constable Thompson—he only transferred in two weeks ago."

I watched her wander off, looking at the karts and talking to competitors. I waited around until it was time to give the briefing, then made my way back down to the sports ground.

The route the karts would take was safely lined with hay bales. The food trucks were all set up, and there were picnic tables and chairs scattered around. Some vendors were already serving coffee and breakfast burritos, hot chips and freshly made sweet and savoury scones. Grace was manning a table with Hannah's pies and donuts. The smell was making my stomach rumble.

I glanced around, looking for any sign of Kennedy or Selgrave, but couldn't see them. What did I expect? A flag? A sign stating their whereabouts? I was getting as bad as Reid.

"Louise!"

I spun around at the sound of a familiar voice. "Ed!" I ran over and flung my arms around his neck. "What are you doing here?"

"Thought I'd come see this amazing race you've organised."

"Are you staying over?" I asked, steering him towards a coffee truck.

"Got a spare bed?"

"I've got a sofa. Any good?"

He put his arm around my waist as we walked. "It'll do me. You look amazing, by the way. Positively glowing."

"Thanks." I ordered a latte for me and a long black with a splash of almond milk for Ed.

"I think this country air must be good for you," he paused and studied my face. "Unless you've met someone?"

"Kind of."

"What sort of answer is that?"

"An honest one. I'll fill you in later." I handed him his coffee. "Make yourself at home. I've got to check the juniors are ready to race."

"Go do your thing," he said and lifted his coffee in a salute.

Gradually, more spectators lined the road and spilled into the sports ground while crews made their way back to the finish to watch their entry cross the line. I scanned the crowd for the two-thousandth time, but couldn't see anything of Selgrave or Kennedy.

My phone rang. It was Connor.

"Are we good to launch?" I asked.

"Five minutes to start."

"Okay, hang on, I'll grab the mic and relay what's happening." I rushed over to the flat-deck truck we were using as a prize-giving stage and climbed up and switched the microphone on. From there, I could see the finish line and give a commentary of what was happening.

Then I spotted Kennedy leaning against a food truck, eating a burger. That put two out of the three here—now I just had to find Selgrave.

I could hear the cheers from the roadside as the first karts got closer. Matt from McCarthy's stood poised at the finish line, chequered flag in hand.

It took a good ten minutes before the first entrant peddled across the line, and one exhausted child was helped out and swamped with hugs. The sounds of cheering and clapping filled the air as the child's father ran to shift the kart off the track.

Lots of talking, one hot dog, a carton of hot chips, and a coffee later, the last of the junior racers were rolling over the finish line. The crowds whistled and yelled words of congratulations and I felt my chest swell with pride. Will was handing out bottled water and Ed was giving free T-shirts to the competitors, telling them to wait around for prize-giving.

"Great job," Ed said. He was sitting on the far end of the stage, waiting for me. "That was the best fun I've had in ages."

"I'm pleased you enjoyed it. I expect the adults will be much more competitive." The sun, although weak, was warm enough that I had peeled off my jacket.

"You've done a great job here; you deserve a medal."

"Actually, I'd settle for a long soak in a hot tub and an early night."

"I'd be happy with a beer."

When all the junior entrants had been accounted for—including an eight-year-old who had pulled out halfway down the road because everyone was passing him, and two boys who had crashed into hay bales and demolished their karts—and the tears had been wiped away for some of the younger entrants, it was almost time for the adults to race.

Having Ed with me was a nice distraction from the possibility of drug busts ruining my event, but my nerves were beyond frayed. We were one race down, and still nothing untoward had happened. My phone rang in my hand and I calmed a little when I saw it was Connor again.

"Hey," I answered. "We've got everyone down here. Send the next lot down when you're ready."

"Great. We'll start in five."

"How's Reid?"

"Oh, he's great, but there's been a problem."

I knew it. "What's happened? Is Reid okay? Anyone hurt? Are the police there?"

Connor's laughter sounded in my ear. "Everything is fine. Just a malfunction with the equipment. Reid couldn't physically fit in the kart. He handed it over to Liam to race. How's things at your end?"

I felt the air *whoosh* from me and bent double, one hand on a knee, hoping I wouldn't be sick or faint. Reid was okay.

"I've got the mayor arriving in ten minutes. The kids are all eating or drinking and I'm setting up for prize-giving," I said, checking my clipboard for the millionth time.

"Right," he said. "Let's get this show on the road."

The rest of the event proceeded like clockwork. Relief settled in as Reid took the chaser vehicle following the tail-end drivers, stopping to help get karts back on the road, or pick up the pieces. The adults were twice as competitive as the juniors, and the damage to karts and bodies was considerable. Thank goodness everyone had to wear helmets.

Ambulance officers attended to one teen who'd grazed his knuckles on one hand and another who'd sprained a wrist, but I knew all eyes would be on Liam driving the

Hamilton's kart, with its unmissable flared lime-green wings and spoiler.

Liam came in third, and I saw Kennedy shake his hand and slap him on the back before disappearing into the crowd. I still hadn't seen Selgrave and I wondered if he had stayed away, but I hadn't seen any of the police contingent either. When all the adult karts had either cleared the finish line or been loaded onto trailers, the spot prizes were given out, then I announced the auction for the Hamilton kart. Connor and Liam had wheeled it into prime position in front of the stage and I handed Annie the microphone and she started the auction like a pro. The blue uniform of Constable Martin moved through the crowd at the very back giving a subtle police presence. Once Annie started calling bids, I pointed out the hands as they shot up. She started the bidding at one hundred dollars.

I couldn't see Kennedy or Selgrave bidding. *Damn.* This wasn't going as I had thought it would.

The bids rose to six hundred dollars, then a thousand. There was heckling and laughing in the crowd as Connor encouraged more bids. They continued to come until the price climbed and stalled, to my surprise, at five thousand, four hundred dollars. I noticed Constable Martin disappear and Gaylene sauntered up to the kart and took a look at it. Finally, Annie declared it sold and thanked everyone on behalf of Hamilton's Automotive for participating in what had been one of the most successful and enjoyable events in the history of Riverford.

"Together, we have raised over twelve thousand dollars that will be used to start a trust fund to help those in our community who, for whatever reason, need help with medical appointments."

The crowd clapped.

"And I'd like to thank everyone who has worked to make this possible." Annie turned to look at me. I shook my head. I didn't need public gratification; I hadn't done anything except rally around a few people and ask them to help.

Annie continued, regardless. "And especially all the sponsors who supported the event, but most importantly, our very own Louise Adair who spearheaded this from conception to end." She turned to me. "Thanks to your idea, Louise, our community will benefit from your generosity for years to come. On behalf of everyone here and all the residents of Riverford, I want to say a huge thank you. Put your hands together for Louise!"

I blushed while she hugged me, and then Connor called to me from below the stage and passed up a large bouquet of flowers. I stuck my nose in them. The scent was divine.

"Now I'd ask the wonderful bidder to come forth, and we'll get this transaction processed as quickly and painlessly as possible. To the rest of you, you've now seen what fun it was—I challenge you to plan your fastest kart for next year's race!"

A man I hadn't seen before stepped forwards as the crowd began to disperse. He looked to be in his mid-forties, with thinning hair and a sparse ginger beard. He looked at me and held his hand out.

"Gareth," he said, lifting his sunglasses to rest on his head. "I can't wait to give this to my son on his birthday," he said, pulling his phone from his pocket with his free hand.

"I'm sure he's going to love it," I told him, disappointment sliding over me. If my suspicion was correct, this stranger was buying a kart stuffed with cocaine and Selgrave would be stepping up to pay for it. But there was no suggestion of anything corrupt going on. I checked the dispersing crowd over Gareth's shoulder, half-expecting one of the men to interrupt the transaction and ask to buy it from the winner for an outrageous price.

No one interrupted us. Everyone was helping to pack down the finish line.

Gareth did a quick bank transfer to the Hamilton's Automotive account, shook hands with Connor, Annie and me, and proceeded to push the kart away. The transaction was simple and felt way too easy.

Deflated, I spent the next thirty minutes talking to people who wanted to thank me for running the event, or to know how they could apply for funds.

"Congratulations, Louise. Fantastic day," Gaylene said as she surveyed the food trucks that had opted to stay on for the junior rugby games that were starting shortly.

"Well, I'm still sure something went down."

"Not today, it seems."

I thanked her for coming and watched as she strode off towards the taco truck. My phone sounded from the depths of my pocket. I dug it out and checked the screen.

"Hi Han," I greeted, basking in the afterglow of being an event organiser extraordinaire. There was a pregnant silence on the other end of the line. "Everything okay?"

"No."

I dropped down to sit on the edge of the stage. "What's wrong? Where are you? Do you need help?"

"Louise, he passed about twenty minutes ago."

"Passed?" I still had karts in my brain, and she wasn't making sense.

"Tyler."

29

REID

I'D FINISHED PULLING OUT all the stakes and rope, and stacked the last of the hay bales in a pile, ready for Matheson to collect. It was almost one p.m. and I needed to eat. I was walking back to my truck when I spotted Louise sitting on the edge of the stage. She looked like she was upset, and what made it worse was some lanky-looking Latino kid had his arm around her. I detoured.

"Louise?"

The kid looked up, recognition in his eyes. "You must be Reid. Ed." He held his hand out. "Maker of T-shirts." So, this was Louise's friend. I shook his hand. He might look like a kid, but he spoke and carried himself like someone who was years older. I guessed he must be Lou's age. He stepped back and I reclaimed my girl.

"Hey, you," I stepped into the space between her legs and hooked her chin, lifting it to read her eyes. "Have you been crying?" She was melting my heart right now.

"You haven't heard?"

I shook my head. "Heard what?"

"It's Tyler." She was sobbing outright now, and I took her in my arms. "He's gone."

"Gone?"

Her crying got louder.

I froze. Tyler had passed away? "How do—"

"Hannah just rang. She couldn't get you."

"My phone's in the truck. Does Connor know?"

She shrugged, pushed me back and slipped off the stage to the ground. "I'll put my flowers in the car and then help you with packing down."

"Give me the flowers and I'll put them in the car for you," Ed offered. "Let me know what else I can do to help."

"Thanks, mate. Much appreciated. Louise, why don't you and Ed take a walk around, see that everything is good to leave while I find Connor. Then we'll see what we can do for Julie-Ann." We were supposed to be playing a home game here at four-thirty against the Falcons, but there was no way I could play today. I felt my throat close, and I struggled to swallow. I swiped the back of my hand across my eyes. Reid Hamilton did not cry, but losing Tyler was like losing my father all over again.

Julie-Ann had her younger sister staying for a few days and told us she didn't need more visitors that evening; she'd see us the following day. We all descended on Connor's place for dinner.

"Have you met anyone yet?" Lou asked Ed as she snuggled against me.

"Well..."

321

"You have! Tell me more. I want to know everything about her, and does she know you're spending the weekend with me?"

He held his hand up and folded down his fingers one by one. "Her name is Wendy. She's gorgeous. She's a year older than me and working for a law firm, and yes, she knows about you. And she also knows we're old friends and I'm sleeping on your couch."

"When do I get to meet her?" she asked.

"Next time I visit, I'll bring her. And look at you. I'm guessing you are more than friends?"

"Friends with benefits," she told him.

Connor laughed and muttered something about benefits I didn't catch. Friends with fucking *benefits?* Was that what she thought this was?

"Anyone want a refill?" I snapped and pushed myself off the sofa and escaped to Connor's kitchen.

"You okay?" Lou asked, joining me in the kitchen. She slid her hand across my back up to my neck.

"I'm fine."

"I'm so sorry about Tyler."

"Yeah, it sucks."

She reached out for my hand and gave it a comforting squeeze. "I'm here if you want to talk."

"Thanks."

The service for Tyler was held five days later, at the local high school where Tyler had been a student. Louise had spent the week commuting between the café, the garage and Julie-Ann's. She cooked meals and made cups of tea for the visitors who'd called in endless streams. Connor and I helped with the funeral preparations.

At the funeral, Connor and I both got up and spoke. Several of Tyler's old mates stood up too. His involvement with the community over his seventy-three years was incredible and inspiring. And while I lifted the casket and helped carry it through the school hall, I realised that we might think we go through life unnoticed, but there is always someone who notices a moment of compassion, or the time you gave them a lift when it was raining, or the week the car needed its muffler fixing and you told them they didn't have to pay you until they could afford it. Or told someone they looked beautiful. He'd touched a lot of lives. I wondered what people would say about me when my time was up.

"I'd like to be on my own tonight," Julie-Ann told us, as the last of the mourners left.

"Are you sure?" Lou asked, putting an arm around her and hugging her for what seemed the hundredth time that day.

"Perfectly. Perhaps you could call in tomorrow for a cuppa. I'd just like some time to myself."

"You wouldn't like to come and stay with Connor or me?" Louise asked. "Maybe just for a night?"

"No thanks, love."

She moved to me and put her bony hand on my cheek. "Thank you for everything you've done for Tyler. He'd be shaking your hand if he could."

Connor helped her into his car while I ordered pizza for us to eat at mine. When we arrived home, I checked the mail while Lou carried the pizza boxes. There were several flyers, a windowed envelope from the council, a copy of the weekly community paper, *Riverford Valley Star*, and a large white A4 envelope from a company in Auckland called Brown and Gifford Media. More junk mail, I guessed. Connor and Annie arrived and followed us inside.

I elbowed the door closed behind me, tossed the mail on the kitchen bench and opened the large envelope out of curiosity.

Annie and Louise were already in the sitting room, eating pizza. Connor walked through to the kitchen and opened the fridge door and took out some cans.

"You reading the fancy shit now?" Connor jibed, grin on his face.

Speechless, I stared at the thumbnail image on the cover of the magazine in my hands. *Shocked* didn't begin to describe how I felt at what I saw. An image of a topless me stared back. What the fu...?

Connor, standing beside me, roared with laughter. "Jesus. My brother's a pin-up for *GQ*. Hey, you guys, come and look at this!" He snatched the magazine out of my hands. I was too paralysed to grab it back.

It had been a long, gut-wrenching week and I was not in the mood to be ridiculed by some journalist, let alone family members. Anger simmered beneath the surface.

"*The rebirth of Reid Hamilton*," Connor read aloud. I gripped the edge of the counter. Breathing through the embarrassment, I went to join the others. I'd thought the interview had been for the local paper. I'd foolishly thought they'd pick the best photo to go with the article. *Dear God*, what the hell had I done?

Annie and Lou were sitting side-by-side, turning the pages looking at the photos. How many damn pages were there?

Annie let out a whistle. "Wow. Those photos are something else, Reid. This edition is going to be a sell-out. Connor, why aren't you in here in all your naked glory?"

"You got my car, what more do you want?" My brother was leaning over the back of the sofa, reading the article.

"I never knew oil and grease could make a man look so good." Louise commented to no one in particular.

I rolled my eyes. "Throw it in the fire." I got up and made a grab for it, but Annie was too quick.

"Now, now. Don't be hasty, Reid. Let Louise and me enjoy your beautiful body."

"Wow," Louise hissed. "You sure make those tees look good." The two girls cackled like chooks in a henhouse.

That damn photographer. Damn Louise.

"Five whole pages," Annie declared, flipping from one to another. "Wait until Rachel and Ellie see these."

"It's got a lot of detail in there," Connor commented.

"Not you, too."

Connor looked up. "It describes your life before bars and how much prison life changed you. Oh, and it talks about your struggle to be accepted back into the community. No stone unturned. They obviously inter-viewed others, too."

The magazine article was the tipping point. Unable to contain my annoyance any longer, I spun around to face Louise. "I trusted you, of all people, Louise. Why did you do this?"

Louise looked up at me, mouth open, but nothing was coming out. "I didn't—"

"Don't you dare tell me you didn't know this was going to be printed in some stupid men's magazine."

"Reid, I'm sorry, I—"

"I don't want to hear it. I trusted you, Louise. More than I trusted anyone since I got out. And you do this!" I snatched the magazine up, waved it in the air and slammed it down again. "They didn't get all this infor-mation from me. Who did they talk to? You? Annie? *Jesus*, Connor, did they interview you too?"

Connor nodded.

"Did everyone know about this? Has everyone been laughing at me behind my back? I feel no better than some fucking male prostitute. I can't do this." I was blinded by rage and disappointment. I stormed across to the front door.

"Nobody laughed at you..." Louise reached for my arm, but I shook her hand off, ripped my jacket from its hook and grabbed my keys.

"Anything between us is over. Be gone by the time I get back." I snarled. "The lot of you." And I slammed the door behind me.

30

LOU

WHEN I FINALLY PICKED myself up off the floor and wiped the remaining tears from my face, I was left with the feeling I'd betrayed my best friend and now he was gone. I'd lost him. I'd trusted that journalist and had said things off the record that should have been kept private. I knew how much Reid valued his privacy. But I'd pushed and kept pushing, and now I'd pushed too far. I thought I was doing what was best for the business, but now he'd probably never forgive me for this. I found my phone where I'd left it in the sitting room, and paced while it rang.

"Hello?" a sleepy voice answered.

"Hannah, I'm so sorry to wake you, but I'm worried about Reid." Hannah yawned and, in the background, Will asked who it was.

"What happened?"

"We had an argument and he stormed out."

"Hang on." I heard a door close and a moment later, she was back. "What did you argue about?"

"You know when I told you that photographer took the photos of Reid? And they asked me a heap of questions?"

"I think so. So?"

"I didn't tell Reid, but the journalist was from *GQ* magazine. And they must have interviewed half the town. It's in the latest issue. He got a complimentary copy in the mail today, flew into a rage and took off when he saw it."

"Are you at Reid's? Do you want me to come over?"

"He told me to get out. Told me it was over between us."

"Had he been drinking?"

"He's sober."

"He won't do anything stupid. He's probably just going to go someplace quiet and stew it over until he realises he's overacted. Don't worry about him for now. I'll check in tomorrow and see if he's come home. Can *you* get home?"

"I'm going to call a taxi."

"Okay. Don't worry about him, Louise. He'll work things out in his own time."

I sniffed and another flood of tears threatened to fall. "I don't think so this time. I don't think he'll speak to me after what I've done."

"Give him time. Now, are you sure you can get home okay?"

I nodded even though she couldn't see me. "Yes. And sorry for waking you both."

"Everything will work out. You'll see. I'll pop up and see you in the morning."

"Okay. Night," I whispered into the phone.

"Wait—was it a good article?"

"Well, Annie and I thought the photos were incredible."

"I might have to buy a copy."

"Me, too," I said before thanking her and putting my phone away.

I cleaned the dinner things and, satisfied Reid's home was tidy, shrugged into my featherdown jacket and rang for a taxi. Collecting my purse, I stood and took in the masculinity of the sitting room. The fire had now died, and the cushions were back in place on the two large leather sofas. I wanted to absorb everything that was Reid, in case I never came back. There were large throw cushions the colour of mulled wine on the floor and, at the far end of the room, the huge TV lorded over everything. The curtains were thickly draped and the wool carpet warm underfoot. It was a man's paradise, but it felt welcoming and homely.

The tears welled again, and I focused on committing the room to memory as the headlights of a vehicle shone through the glass panel in the front door.

I sat in the taxi and wondered: was Reid out in the pines, where he'd taken me? It didn't matter. I would ring Connor tomorrow and tell him I was leaving. Hopefully, I wouldn't have to work through my notice period. Reid was never going to ask me to stay.

The driver pulled up in front of the café next to my car. I moped my way upstairs, the streetlights throwing shadows across the floor. I threw my purse on the table, slipped out of my heels and into my pink and white fluffy slippers with the bunny ears, and shrugged out of my coat. I hurried past the hall mirror and caught a glimpse of myself. At my bedroom door, I stopped and backed up. A sad image with red, puffy eyes stared back.

Come on, Louise. What did you expect?

"I don't know what I expected," I told her.

You know none of this was permanent. And you certainly weren't looking for a relationship, so why are you so upset? You're a strong woman who is capable of taking on the world. Forget Reid Hamilton and move on. My mirror image wasn't holding back.

"I know, but we're talking about the Reid on page thirty-seven of *GQ*."

So? He's just a guy.

"A guy I happen to love."

This was just a short visit with Hannah. Now it's time to head up to Auckland, find a permanent job, a flat and get on with life. Come on. Get your colours on and do it! My mirror image was fighting a good fight. I put my hands on my hips.

"I've never had a guy treat me like Reid has. I want more of that."

Which Reid are you talking about? The shouty, cantankerous, moody one, or the other version?

I wriggled my toes and studied the floppy ears on my feet for a long moment, then lifted my head. It was tough debating against myself. "I want both Reids."

Why are you telling me, and not him?

"I don't know." I narrowed my eyes at the woman in the mirror. She gave me the stink eye right back. "Okay. So, maybe because I didn't count on falling in love with him? And I know he doesn't feel the same way."

Now do something about it. Or pack your bags and run.

Shit.

Right.

I'll tell him.

Yes. That's what I'd do. After all, what was there to lose? I gave my reflection a cheesy grin in thanks and marched through to the bathroom. I would go into work tomorrow looking like a damn goddess, and I'd tell him to his beautiful face that I loved him. If I didn't get a response, it was all over.

I bunched my hair and tied it up, washed my face in cold water, then hunted out a thermal mud mask I'd bought but not yet used, and slathered it on.

Yeah! As the mud hardened, I punched a hole in the air and stormed the kitchen for wine and snacks.

In the bedroom, I peeled the covers back on the bed and crossed to the window. I loved the view from the apartment. It looked down on the main street. It was only just eleven p.m. and everything was quiet outside. There was a fog settling in the valley and the streetlights made everything look magical. I'd miss this when I left.

I leaned against the window frame, staring out at nothing in particular as I sipped my wine and felt the mud tighten on my face. I felt like I fitted in this community. Everyone was so friendly and had treated me like I'd grown up in Riverford. A truck drove past, the only vehicle on an empty street. For a moment I thought it looked like Liam's. I sighed heavily against the window creating a film of condensation.

And stared harder.

It *was* Liam!

He had something big and bulky on the back. It was covered with a tarpaulin, but one corner had lifted as he drove and, in the streetlight, I could make out familiar fluorescent green paintwork.

The kart!

I sprinted through the bedroom, grabbed my car keys and rushed downstairs. I fumbled with the lock and jumped in the car. There was a thin layer of frost on the windscreen, so I turned the heater on full blast and threw it into reverse. At the other end of the street, I could just see the taillights turn towards Greenhill. Where the heck was Liam going? And how did he come to have the kart?

I followed his taillights through the fog at a reasonable distance. There wasn't much traffic. I passed a car and a delivery truck both heading back towards Riverford, and saw a car parked in a layby and a motorbike that came up behind and eventually overtook me.

Up ahead, Liam turned off the main road onto a side road about two kilometres short of the Greenhill town boundary. The fog wasn't as thick, and I flicked my lights off before following him. I didn't know the area and I didn't know where on earth I was going. There were what looked like farmhouses dotted here and there—some with lights still on, some just visible in the darkness. And then the fog thickened, and I lost the taillights and everything else.

I wound the window down and stuck my head out. The icy air took my breath away and as I brought the car to a stop, even the sides of the road weren't visible. Flicking my seatbelt off, I opened the door, jumped out and took a step. My foot slipped and I slid until I felt the chill of water through one bunny slipper and long damp grass around my face. *Yuck!* I brushed madly in the darkness. My plush footwear was soaking up water. Why didn't I change my shoes? *Idiot!* I must have been driving perilously close to the edge of the road.

I scrambled the way I thought I'd come until I had gravel under my hands. The road surface had morphed into loose gravel chip and, standing up, I could feel the stones under my slippered feet. I hadn't realised how difficult it would be to drive in the dark with no lights. I got back in the car, put it in gear and crawled ahead, keeping myself parallel with the edge of the road, cursing, because by now, I'd probably lost Liam and my wet foot was starting to freeze.

I cranked the heater a few degrees warmer.

I drove for another five minutes before I caught sight of headlights moving across what I assumed was a paddock. They illuminated a shed and then died. I reached the driveway and edged the car off the road. The shed door opened, throwing light onto Liam as he stepped inside. I turned the engine off, climbed out and made my way to the paddock gate. Who was Liam meeting?

I couldn't get the gate latch open, so I climbed over the fence post next to it and crept closer. The grass was almost chest-height in places and covered in dew. I was going to be soaked by the time I got back to the car. As the shed got nearer, the murmur of voices carried through the air. The door had been closed, and every-thing was in darkness again. Reaching the shed, I put an ear to the tin door. I'd struck the motherlode. I pressed an eye to a slit of light and squinted inside. Figures were grouped in the middle of the shed. Selgrave had to be one of them because I could hear his voice.

"Look what we have here," a voice behind me drawled.

I jumped. My heart almost pounded a hole in my chest, and I thought I might have peed myself as I fell to the ground.

He took my arm, his grip vice-like.

"Ow. Do you need to hold me like that? I'm hardly going anywhere." Little did he know that if he let my arm go, I'd be sprinting like I had a pack of cheetahs after me.

His grip tightened. "That's right sweetheart, you're not going anywhere. Jesus. What's that on your face?"

I lifted a hand and fingered my cheek. Dried mud. Oh, great.

I felt the cold touch of gunmetal against my neck and shivered.

"I'm not your sweetheart," I stammered. I couldn't quite make him out, but I knew I'd heard his voice before.

"You could be," he sneered, the stale scent of tobacco on his breath. He yanked me to my feet and pushed me in front of him and when I tripped, he yanked me back up and dragged me along with him. "I think the boss might want to see what I've found."

Oh, boy. I was in big trouble.

31

REID

MY HEAD WAS FILLED with pictures I couldn't dislodge. I sat in the cab of my truck, my head against the strut between the window and the headrest. A mix of images played like one of those flickering old twenties movies. Tyler's casket with a wreath of beautiful flowers, morphed to Connor and Annie, then to Hannah tightly holding Will's hand. The Lazy Biker and the fight; the kart race, and the faces of the kids who didn't get to the finish line because they'd crashed. The magazine article with its glossy photos and bold heading in gold letters. Louise, cleaning the kitchen at work. Louise, eating a triple chocolate and caramel brownie. Louise, prancing around my kitchen in lacey bra and panties. There were a hundred and one random pieces of shit that weren't important right now, playing in slow motion, and they always circled back to Louise.

I gripped the steering wheel and ran a hand around it. I'd been sitting in the truck out under the trees for almost three hours and, tonight, it wasn't delivering the peace and tranquillity I'd come to rely on. The window was covered in condensation and I didn't have any blankets. The freezing temperature in here matched my heart. It was heavy and numb. What the hell was wrong with me? I had taken my anger and frustration out on Louise and it was uncalled for. I needed to fix things. I needed to tell her I was sorry and to mean it. I'd do it now. I just hoped I wasn't too late with my apology.

I turned the ignition on, reversed out of my parking space and headed for home, heater on full. My phone buzzed before I got to the main road. I dug it out of my pocket.

"Yeah?"

My brother answered. "Just checking on you. Everything okay, bro?"

"Will be shortly."

"What're you planning?"

"I need to go find Lou. I need to have a serious conversation with her and hope she forgives me."

"You'll be a lucky man if she does. I can't understand how you ever thought she had anything but our interests at heart. Especially when you think about all the things she's done for us and the town."

"I know. I've had time to think about it."

"Well, good luck. I'll catch you tomorrow."

I was a jackass. Lou needed a guy who she could trust wouldn't rip her off or leave her. I'd probably just done worse. I had no idea how I was going to convince her I would never do anything like that ever again.

I drove past my place and headed into town. Lou's car wasn't parked outside her apartment. I drove to Will's place. Not there, either. Neither was she at Connor's house: Annie's car was parked in his drive, but not Lou's. Where the hell was she at this time of night? I drove back to her place, kept the engine running and climbed out. I buzzed the door repeatedly. Nothing. Even if she was sleeping, she would have heard that. Odd.

I walked back to the truck. Charlie's bread delivery van pulled to a halt behind me, blocking my exit. He beckoned me over, so I walked around the front of the truck and looked up at him.

"Hi, Charlie."

"You looking for young Louise?" he asked, hanging out the window.

I nodded.

"Yeah. I've just come from Greenhill and she passed me."

"Going in which direction?" Bless the man. He was the salt of the earth, but he was slow with the details. I didn't know how Grace put up with him.

"Looked like she was scooting on over to Greenhill."

"What time was this?"

He looked at his watch. "About forty minutes ago. I know that because I was making good time with the run, and was thinking about getting the Riverford drops done early and getting home for a cuppa before bed.

It usually takes me about twenty minutes to get to the Greenhill town boundary, so that would make it—"

"Where did you see her?" I interrupted.

He scratched his head and rubbed his stubbled chin. "You know that sign that went up a few months back advertising Greenhill's Winter Festival?"

"Yeah," I answered, getting a little impatient.

"Well, about a kilometre past that, there's a right turn heading out the back of Greenhill. Not much up there, mostly farms. Back road to nowhere. Had an uncle used to live up there about thirty years ago and used to go shooting on his property—mostly rabbits, but sometimes the odd deer would come down out of the bush and I'd—"

"Yeah, thanks, Charlie," I cut him off again. Charlie was a talker, and if I let him, I would be here all night. "I'll take a run out there, see if I can find her."

"She had her indicator on to head up that road."

"Okay. I'll shout you a beer next time I see you in McCarthy's."

"Looking forward to it," he replied.

I pulled out my phone and dialled Connor back. He picked up on the third ring.

"This better be important."

"Lou isn't home. I've just been speaking to old Charlie Miller. Said he saw her over Greenhill way—she was going up Harrison Road. Do we know anyone living up there?"

"No, I don't. Doesn't Phil Kennedy have a farm up there? I don't know what he farms, but I think someone once told me he just lets the grass grow. Keeps the visitors out."

"Shit. What the hell is she doing up there?" I let out a long sigh. "I'm going to follow her. See what she's up to."

"Be careful, Reid." There was a pause. "Aw, Jesus. Wait there. I'll jump in the car and follow you out. Don't do anything stupid. And call the cops if you see anything suspicious."

"Will do."

I shoved the truck into reverse, pulled out onto the road and headed down the main street and the road that would take me to Greenhill. All manner of emotions were fuelling the panic that was building. Was she at Kennedy's farm? How did she even know about it? I couldn't let anything happen to Louise. Not now. Not ever.

32

LOU

THE LIGHT IN THE shed momentarily blinded me as I was pushed inside, tripped and tumbled to the ground. I blinked and tried to shade my eyes. The voices of people silhouetted against the light went silent before the thug spoke.

"Lookie what I found sneaking around outside," he boasted. He gave me a kick to the leg which hurt like hell.

"Ow!" I rubbed my thigh and inched away from him. *Damn it.* I was missing one rabbit slipper.

"Get up," he ordered.

I scrambled to my feet, still rubbing my thigh. With my eyes adjusted to the brightness, I glanced around to look at my captor. Gareth? The guy who had purchased the kart at the auction.

In front of us, three men stood in a semi-circle around the kart. Liam was leaning against a tractor, watching. I recognised Selgrave and Kennedy, but not the third man in the semi-circle: a stocky guy wearing a beanie and gloves, holding an angle grinder, totally focused on cutting into the framework of the kart.

The framework?

The drugs had to be hidden in the framework, not the tyres! Why hadn't I thought of that?

"Shit, Louise, what happened to your face?" Liam asked moving closer to me. I couldn't think of an answer to his question. I couldn't even remember the question. I was having enough trouble trying to stop my body from shaking, and I had no way to get a message to Gaylene—or anyone.

"What?" I stuttered.

"Shut the fuck up," Selgrave barked at Liam.

He nodded vigorously.

Selgrave walked towards us, a smile on his face that I didn't trust. I wanted to sit down; my knees were feeling wobbly.

"Liam." Big smile. "You had one job to do, son, and you couldn't even do that, you fucking loser," Selgrave growled.

"Sorry boss, I didn't notice anyone following me."

"I should never have involved you." A shot split the air. I screamed, and Liam crumpled to the ground a few feet from me. "You pay peanuts, and you get the fucking monkey," Selgrave muttered.

"Liam!" I didn't particularly like the guy, but I wouldn't wish him dead. This was not heading in a good direction. No one knew I was even here. This is where I was going to die.

"Gareth," Selgrave ordered, "take another look outside, make sure half the fucking town hasn't followed him." His attention shifted to me. I could see the calculating meanness in his eyes.

"Now, doll face, what are you doing here at this time of the night?" He stepped towards me until he was in my personal space. I shuffled back against the cold tin of the shed wall. He'd replaced his gun in its holster at his hip, but rested a hand on it, pushing his jacket back so I could see it.

I gulped. That was two guns too many, so far tonight.

"I... um... I..." I'd forgotten how to speak.

He reached out a hand and ran a finger down the side of my face until he reached my chin. I screwed my eyes closed. His fingers grabbed my cheek—squeezing. I tried to pull away and he pushed my face away with a flick of his wrist.

"What the fuck is this shit on your face?"

"It's a mud mask, full of minerals that tone and firm your skin, and when—"

"I don't care!"

"Well, you asked." I was babbling. "It was you who set Reid up, wasn't it?"

His laughter was harsh. I now had his full attention, and my nerves were having anxiety attacks of their own.

"He didn't even notice the drugs were planted in that car. He was so easy to take down."

"Why pick on him, though? Or the garage? And why do it again?"

A few feet from me, a moan escaped Liam's lifeless body. I hoped that meant he was still alive.

"Because Hamilton had it coming. Because he always took everything I wanted. A place in the first fifteen rugby team in college. The girls I wanted. Hell, the family I envied. My mum lived in fear of my old man all her married life. My father was a teacher during the day and a drunk after dark. At home every time I did something wrong, it was 'why can't you be more like Reid fucking Hamilton?' He got everything he wanted. And more. It was so easy to set him up, that look on his face when I slapped the cuffs on him and escorted him out to the police car.

The temptation to push drugs was too easy to ignore then. But the kid here," he nodded at Liam, "fucked up good and proper. He got the product, waited for our purchaser to book his car in for something simple and the idiot should have put the drugs in the car. But Reid did that job and Liam was left holding the goods. When you, doll face, came up with the idea to hold a kart race, Liam panicked and hid them in the karts framing and we couldn't recover it until after the race. The rest is history. Just like you're going to be, very soon."

"You know you're going to get caught, don't you? All of you," I spat at him.

I swallowed hard. I had no idea where that moment of bravery came from.

"What are we going to do with you?" Selgrave asked, reaching out and running a finger around my neck. I held my breath. I didn't want to die out here. The thought that I'd never get to see Hannah again, or have earth-shattering sex with Reid bought tears to my eyes. I felt the pressure build in my temples. What did I have to lose?

"Let me go and I'll forget I ever came out here."

"Shut it, doll face. You're too damn nosy for your own good. What the hell is keeping Gareth? Phil, go see if you can find him." He belched orders like I'd expect a bent cop to do.

Kennedy strolled across the floor, pulled the door open and disappeared. Selgrave put his hand on my shoulder and pushed me to the ground. I crumpled.

"Might save you until after our little business transaction is complete. We could have some fun before Kennedy has to dig a hole deep enough you won't be found. And don't think about running—you'd be dead before you reached the door."

I shuddered and scooted myself up against the wall. "I'd sooner be dead," I muttered scanning the interior for exits.

"It can be arranged," he sniped. "Mick. Hurry it up."

I needed to work out some sort of plan, but my brain had disengaged, my legs didn't work and my hands were shaking like I was making a martini—not the stirred kind. The wall offered nothing but frostbite and the concrete floor was like a gigantic block of ice. I had one stockinged foot, one grubby slipper, a face covered in mud, and no chance of being found. I began to shiver. This was how my life would end.

I watched the man with the angle grinder. He'd removed a piece of framework and was making another cut. I glanced at the tractor and assortment of old farm machinery. Yeah, what was I going to do? Run over, climb on the tractor and just drive out? I didn't even know how to drive a tractor.

I watched as Mick put the angle grinder down and started pulling white tubular packages out of the framing and packing them into a carryall.

I felt hopeless and, what was worse, I'd seen all their faces, and I knew exactly what they were doing. I'd signed my own death warrant.

33

REID

I DROVE AT BREAKNECK speed until I hit the turnoff that Charlie had told me about. Ten minutes later, I spotted Louise's car parked in a drive in the middle of nowhere. The bad feeling that was gnawing at my stomach took another bite. I didn't know if this was Kennedy's place, but I suspected it was. The gate was closed and the car was empty. *Shit.*

I kept driving, so as to not arouse any suspicion. The fog had settled low, but there was a clear patch that allowed me to see light seeping out from what looked like a shed, set way up the drive. I hunted for the next driveway, pulled up and cut the lights in what looked like a turning bay for a milk tanker.

I climbed out and ran back down the road. What was Louise thinking, coming out here by herself? Why hadn't she called me? I jumped a ditch and climbed over a fence into the paddock, judging that I was still about two hundred metres from her car. The grass was long and heavy with moisture. Trying to move silently was near impossible.

I cursed myself for being such an idiot. Of course she wouldn't call me. I'd be the last person she was going to contact. *Wait...* I crouched and listened.

A matter of feet from me, someone or something was moving through the grass too. I stilled. The noise stopped. Before I knew what was happening, an arm circled my neck and another reached for my wrist, pulling it back. I was flipped and pushed to the ground on my stomach.

"What the hell are you doing, Hamilton?" a stern female voice rasped, close to my face.

"Fuck! Dewinter? Is that you?" I rasped and began breathing again.

"You're interfering with a police operation."

"I'm going to get Louise. She could be hurt." She could be dead for all I knew, but I didn't want to think of that possibility. I struggled with whoever was holding me down with no luck.

"Louise will be fine if she sits tight."

"You don't know that."

"We do know that. We've been watching Selgrave and this group for the last three months. We know they have the drugs in that shed, but we need to get Mick Dunnet when he comes out with the goods. He's managed to elude us for the last five years. Do not ruin everything by interfering."

"I'm not leaving when they've got Louise in there."

"Don't make me arrest you, Hamilton" she warned. "We've already arrested two men tonight, and I'll happily eliminate you, too."

I didn't need to listen to her threats when Louise might be in trouble. "Okay," I agreed.

"Let him go."

The arm around my throat loosened and I was suddenly free. I scrambled to my feet.

"Don't make me regret my decision," she warned me.

I took off at a run, smashing the grass aside, heading towards the slivers of light spilling from the shed. I heard Dewinter swear behind me and knew she'd be giving directions for me to be arrested. I had to make this quick.

I inched my way along the wall, careful not to step on anything that would give away my position. I stopped and listened again. The voices were further away. I backtracked. The voices got louder. And then I heard it. Muttering. It was Lou's voice! She was talking to herself. Relief washed over me. She was still alive.

I put my mouth up against the wall, careful not to touch it. The last thing I wanted was to be stuck to the shed by my lips.

I crossed my fingers. "Louise?" I whispered, low and quiet. "If you can hear me, say yes." I waited. Had she heard me?

Those seconds I waited with my ear close to the wall were the longest of my life.

"Yes."

It was only just audible.

"Where is Selgrave standing? Give me directions from the door. Is he in front of you, to the left? Right?"

"In front," she said faintly.

"Doll face! Don't make me shoot you." Selgrave roared at her.

"Police are here. Hold tight. How many men do you have in there?"

"Have we got it all?" I heard Selgrave ask. "Where's Kennedy? Anyone'd think this was a fucking tea party."

Lou was silent.

I waited. My heart was pumping. I had to get Louise out. I couldn't wait any longer.

"Two inside. Two outside."

Okay, I had the two men inside to deal with. I reckoned I had brute force on my side, but I would be no match against a gun. "Lou, is there any farm machinery in there, like tractors?"

"Tractor, trailer," her voice was barely audible. "I'm scared."

"Stay calm, sweetheart."

This was all my fault. I had to get her out alive. And then I was going to make sure nothing bad happened to her again. Ever. I just wanted to hold her in my arms and tell her I was sorry. That I needed her to stay. I hunted around and found an old fence batten. If I could get close enough, I would beat them to a fucking pulp. Thanks to rugby, I had sprint speed on my side.

I took off towards the shed door, passing the place where Louise sat. It was now or never. Behind me, I heard Dewinter curse again.

I sucked in a deep breath and kicked out hard at the wooden shed door. It swung open and crunched against the wall. Shots rang out. At the same time, I heard the far door splinter from its frame. I ran for the tractor, rolling and putting the tyre between Selgrave and me. Three shots crossed the shed and Louise screamed. Talk about going in blind. I crouched for a fraction of a second, waiting to get a take on where Selgrave was. Behind me a hail of gunfire filled the shed. More screams. She was still alive. Then I saw him. He was limping and making a dash for the open door I'd just come through.

I launched myself at him as he passed the tractor, tackling him side-on and taking him by surprise. He went down heavily and quickly rolled over trying to get a grip on my jacket as gunshots sounded around us. I felt something hit my leg and it stung like crazy, but I was focused on revenge. We struggled for domination over each other, but I had rage and adrenaline on my side. I rolled him again and managed to pin him down.

He flung his arm back, and his gun barrel connected with my cheek. *Shit.* He rolled me in the second I was distracted, and connected a punch to my gut. I sucked in air and spun him back. He had self-defence training on his side, but I had years of rugby training, plus plenty of weightlifting while I was behind bars. He kicked out with a boot and my leg screamed in pain. I lashed out harder with a fist and hit him square on the jaw.

"That's for not treating Louise like a fucking princess, you piece of shit." I didn't give him the chance to say anything before I swung again, channelling all my rage through my hand. This time he spat blood, and the third time, teeth. "And that's for putting me in a fucking prison, you arsehole."

I was going in for the fifth punch when hands grabbed my shoulders and heaved me up through the air and back onto my backside. My full focus had been on dealing with Selgrave, and I hadn't noticed the place was now crawling with police dressed like black-clad ninjas.

"Reid!"

Momentarily dazed, I wasn't prepared for the body that suddenly lunged at me, knocking me flat against the concrete floor, smothering my face with kisses.

"Lou!" I crushed her in my arms.

"Reid, you saved my life." She took my face in her hands studying the damage. "You're bleeding!"

"I'm okay. My leg hurts like the blazes though. I think someone shot me." We clung to each other until Dewinter strolled over and reminded us there was a squad of armed defenders watching. I staggered to my feet, with a little help from Lou.

"Did that bastard touch you?" I asked Lou. "If he did, I'm going over there and finishing what I start-ed." Behind Dewinter, Selgrave was on his knees with his hands behind his head while the ninjas read him his rights.

"I'm fine. But you're shot!"

I looked down—a red stain was spreading like a flower in bloom across the fabric of my pants.

Dewinter was motioning over a medic.

In the middle of the shed, it was a hive of activity. One officer had Mick Dunnet on his stomach with a knee in his back as another slapped cuffs on him.

"I can't believe you came out here on your own," I said, wrapping my arms around her. "It was pretty damn brave of you, but never do that to me again. My heart couldn't take it."

"Yeah, I know how that feels," Dewinter said in a sarcastic drawl.

I turned my attention to the action around us. A team of medics were working on Liam. "*Shit.* What happened to him?"

Lou looked at me, the quivering of her chin told me she was close to tears. "Selgrave shot him."

"Poor kid. Is he alive?"

Dewinter turned to observe the medics. "He's still alive. Lost a lot of blood, though. They're getting him ready to transport to hospital."

"You okay?" Constable Dewinter asked Louise, noticing her limp.

Louise nodded. "I'm fine. Just bruised."

She was shivering uncontrollably.

"Can we get a blanket over here?" the police officer called. She narrowed her eyes at me, and I guessed I definitely wasn't on her list of favourite citizens right now. I would work on that. "Make that two!" she added.

"Louise... I have to tell you..."

A ninja ran over and handed Dewinter a couple of blankets.

"Here you go." The constable draped one over Louise's shoulders and I pulled it tightly around her and wrapped her in my arms again. Dewinter threw the other around me.

"Louise..." I attempted but was interrupted again.

"How did you know where I was?" Louise asked Dewinter.

"We've been running an undercover surveillance operation on this group for the last few months," Dewinter told her. "It all came to a head tonight. We had to catch Selgrave and Dunnet at the scene, and I'd say we've just taken about two million dollars' worth of cocaine off the streets." She turned to me. "However, I'm not going to live it down at the station when they find out not only did I let Louise slip through my security cordon, but I let you get through as well."

"You couldn't have stopped me," I muttered.

"But how did you know I was here?" Louise asked me.

"Charlie told me. One thing about small towns: everyone knows everyone."

"Charlie?"

"Delivers the bread from Greenhill every night. Grace Miller's husband. He saw your car."

Dewinter cut in. "There should have been a roadblock right back at the highway."

"Louise is safe and that's all that matters."

The cop stared at me and shrugged her shoulders. "I guess. Don't go anywhere though, I'll need to get a statement off you both." She turned and left us alone. Finally.

"I thought she would never shut up."

"Reid—"

"Louise. I need to..." I took her face in my hands. Her lips had never looked so good. But her skin was... kind of brown and flaky under my fingers, and pale where tears had smudged tracks down her cheeks. "Jesus, what is that all over your face?"

She sniffed and laughed, a hysterical kind of cackle. "It's a mud pack."

I was not going to ask.

Instead, I was going to kiss the living daylights out of her. My mouth pressed against hers and she responded like she was starving for air. "I love you, Louise Adair. I always have. And this time, you're not running away. This time, you're staying." I felt her body melt into my arms.

"Try and get rid of me."

34

LOU

"THAT'S A NICE FLESH-WOUND you've got there," the medic told Reid. "If it had been another two inches that way, it would have shattered your tibia and fibula." He cleaned and dressed the wound, told Reid he would need to have it checked out with his doctor in a day or two, along with his cheek.

"Here." He offered Reid two paracetamol tablets and some water.

"Thanks."

The medic checked my bruises—all minor apart from the one on my thigh, now large and impressive. I assured him I was okay. Then Dewinter was back for statements.

"Good news," Dewinter said. "You are both cleared to go."

"Thanks, Gaylene," Reid said. "There's nothing I want to do more."

"I think you should let Louise drive," she said, glancing at the bandaging on Reid's leg.

"No problem. Do you have a colleague who could drive his car back?" I asked.

"Sure. Keys...?" she held her hand out.

"In the ignition."

"Right. Keith!"

A young officer ran over to join us.

"Take Mr Hamilton's vehicle back to Riverford, will you? Park it outside Hannah's Café and slip the keys through the letterbox to the upstairs flat." She turned to me. "Done."

"Thanks."

"I've had about as much excitement as I can handle for one day," Reid said. "Let's go home."

He looked as tired as I felt. All I wanted to do was shower and sleep, and not necessarily in that order.

"Did you mean what you said back there?" he asked as the pair of us limped down the drive to my car.

"Did you mean it when you said you wanted me to stay?" I couldn't believe that he'd finally said it out loud.

"I don't joke when it comes to matters of the heart."

Despite feeling cold and exhausted, a warmth blossomed in my chest and hope unfurled inside me. "Then, I guess it's settled. I'm staying." I was holding his good hand as we reached the car, and he squeezed mine in appreciation.

"Best decision you ever made. And you're not staying in Hannah's apartment any longer that you have to. You're moving in with me."

"You realise this clears your name, now."

"I hadn't had a chance to think about it, but I guess it does."

"Reid?"

"Yes, sweetheart?"

"Are you still angry with me over the article in *GQ*?" There was silence. "I'm really sorry I threw you in the spotlight without warning. I promise I'll try and make things right." It was the elephant between us, and I needed to know that it wouldn't wander at leisure in the future.

He turned in his seat, his face serious.

"You just pulled off an amazing event, Louise, and raised thousands for a town and its people you hardly know. You rallied around a dying man and his family, and took the time to make their lives a little less painful. You did an absolutely crazy, life-threatening thing to try and clear my name—and almost gave me a heart attack."

My eyes were starting to mist as he continued.

"And where do I start when it comes to listing the number of things you've done for Hamilton's? You're a fucking hero in my books, Louise, and no article in some cheesy men's magazine is going to change that."

"But what about those photos? I mean, they're way too sexy for general consumption, but—"

"Images of me are all over the internet. A few more won't hurt." He lifted my hand and gently kissed the back of it. "I love you, Louise."

That did it. Tears ran down my face again, but they were good tears this time. Happy tears. I reached over the console and pressed my lips to his cheek. "I love you, too. Now, let's go home—I want to sleep."

"Nothing I'd like better," Reid said. "But can you do one little thing for me, first?"

I nodded.

"Please, promise me you'll never use a mud mask again?"

I laughed hysterically and promised, as he reached for his seat belt and I started the car.

We finally fell into bed at four in the morning, exhausted, happy and with not a speck of mud to be seen anywhere.

Epilogue

My life could be categorised as *Before Louise* and *After Louise*. I never knew just how much I needed her in my life. She was crazy with her blue hair days and colourful platform heels, and sexy as hell with her skimpy black lace underwear and short dresses. She made me feel like I owned the damn world. I no longer needed to retreat to the pines when things got shitty, because Louise was my retreat, and things never got shitty anymore.

"What are you doing this evening?" I asked her. We were walking to my truck, her hand in mine. The Stallions had just played the last rugby game of the season, and we'd finished with a win.

"I was planning to try out a new relaxation method on my pin-up Man of the Match," she said, shoulder-bumping me, a sly little grin on those cute lips of hers.

"Mmm, I like the sound of that."

It had been a long, rough game against the Bulls, and they didn't go down without a fight. I'd managed to intercept two of their attempts at tries, charge down an attempted dropkick, set up three of our own tries, and even score two others myself. It had been a good physical game to go out on. I'd also made the decision not to play next season. I had a long list of things I wanted to do, and anyway, I was getting too old to be chasing a ball from one end of a hundred-metre field to the other.

The thought of her hands on me, however, brought instant happiness.

"As much as that appeals, sweetheart, I thought we might go into Greenhill for a quiet romantic dinner. Just the two of us?"

"Okay. As long as we have time to work up an appetite before we go."

I grinned, and squeezed her hand a little tighter. "I was counting on it." We both sprinted to the truck.

An hour later, I untangled the linen and dragged myself out of bed. "Come on, we're going to be late. Wriggle that stunning backside into the shower and into something special." We had treasured the delights of each other's bodies for far longer than we should have. Her body was a pleasure I would never tire of.

"Join me?" she asked, flaunting her nakedness at me.

"Are you kidding? We'll never get out of here on time."

She laughed, her syrupy voice making me want her again. A minute later, I heard the shower running.

I was starting to get nervous. I'd made plans that had involved getting Connor, Annie, Hannah and Will's help, as well as swearing half the town to secrecy. So far, everything had fallen into place, but there was always a chance...

I buttoned my shirt, leaving it open at the neck, and tucked it into my pants, then rolled the sleeves up. Slipping my arms into a vest, I looked up to see Lou watching from the doorway. She was wearing a short black dress that sat low on her shoulders and dipped across her cleavage. A bright red pashmina draped around her shoulders. Her legs appeared longer in black heels and her hair was up in a messy bun that didn't quite contain all her hair. Ruby-red earrings fell from her lobes.

"Am I overdressed for Greenhill?" She gave me a twirl, and I grinned in appreciation.

"Wow." I crossed the bedroom. "Is that dress even legal?" I leaned in to her and melded my mouth to hers. She tasted of strawberries. "Delicious. I'll be coming back for more, just warning you now."

"Fine by me. Hope you can make it through the meal," she teased. "Hope *I* can make it through the meal. I love the vest." She ran her hand down my chest.

I tasted the strawberries again, hooked my suit jacket and collected my wallet and phone. I checked the screen and flicked off a quick car emoji to Connor.

"Are we good to go?" It was almost seven.

We made our way out to the truck and headed towards town. As we got to the garage, I pulled the truck to the kerb. It was in darkness. The nerves were buzzing through my body and churning my guts.

"Why are you stopping here?" she asked.

"I need to pick something up from my office. I'll be two minutes."

"Okay. I'll wait here."

"No, you won't. Not in that dress. I'm not letting you out of my sight." I needed her inside with me if this plan was going to work.

"Fine," she muttered, and pushed the door open. I walked around and helped her out. It felt like everything in my life had led to this moment.

"You okay?" she asked.

"Couldn't be better. Let's do this."

I unlocked the side door to the garage, paused for a second and reached for Lou's hand. Would this work? My fucking heart was pounding so loud, it's a wonder she couldn't hear it. I reached out and flicked the light switch. Two single beams cut through the dark interior. One on us, the other landed a few feet away on a small round table that sat against the inside of the garage roller door. The light was so strong that everything else was blacked out and our attention was immediately drawn to the table. I let out a breath. Connor had pulled it off. I owed him.

"What's that table doing on the workshop floor?" Lou asked, peering at it.

"Let's take a look." I pulled her with me, and we walked towards it. So far, so good.

"What...?" She glanced from the table to me and back.

On the table was a bottle of chilled Moët & Chandon, two champagne flutes and a small velvet box. Lou looked up at me, brows furrowed, trying to understand what was happening.

I reached for the box.

"This is what I wanted to pick up." I dropped to one knee, and flipped it open to reveal two equal-sized diamonds, with another two tiny diamonds nestled on each side. She gasped, and her hands flew to her face.

"I'm not going to tell you how much I love you, because I tell you so many times every day, but I want to make you a promise that I'll love you forever and I'll never stop telling you. You deserve it, Louise. I want to get straight to the business end of this, because my nerves are fucking killing me."

She laughed and sobbed and snorted all at the same time.

"Louise Adair. Will you marry me and make me the happiest damn man in Riverford—hell, probably the whole country?"

"Yes." She was nodding and crying, and then her arms were around my neck. It took me a hot minute to realise she had answered me. Had she really said yes?

I stood, took the ring from its cushion and pushed it up her finger to its rightful place, then kissed her like I invented the art form.

"I love you, Reid," she breathed.

"Thank God you said yes!"

She laughed, and I picked her up and spun her around. She squealed and I put her down, kissing her again. I would never get enough of her. At the same time, light flooded the rest of the garage, and the workshop was filled with the sounds of clapping and whistling.

Louise looked around, shocked to see half the town surging towards us, as the first notes of "Crazy Little Thing Called Love" by Queen began to play. Annie and Connor were handing out glasses of bubbly at a makeshift bar, while Matt and his kitchen staff were lifting lids along the trestle tables on the other side of the workshop. Bar tables were sprinkled around the garage, with the centre cleared for dancing. Above them, strings of lights gave the space a party atmosphere. The plan had been executed to perfection.

"Reid, did you organise all this?" Lou asked, stunned.

I nodded. "I did have some help."

"We're not going to dinner, are we?"

"Nope. I think an engagement party would be much more fun—especially when it's ours."

I kissed her again—a slow, lazy kiss that teased her tongue and encouraged my dick to ache, even though he'd been busy all afternoon.

"Congratulations," Gaylene Dewinter held her hand out to me. "Couldn't find two people more deserving of each other."

"Thanks, Gaylene." I had apologised to her for not having more faith in the establishment's ability to save my girl, and she had arranged that Hamilton's Automotive got the contract to service the local fleet of police cars.

"Thought you might like to know there's a rumour floating around the station that you've got compensation coming to you." I had received a letter of apology from the Ministry of Internal Affairs with regard to my wrongful arrest and time in prison. Once again, I'd made national news. And, of course, the arrest of Selgrave, Kennedy and Dunnet had attracted countrywide attention along with seven others who were part of their drug ring and were all serving lengthy jail time. Gareth and Liam had received lesser sentences as accessories and would be out in five years.

"Business is great, I got the girl, so I don't need any payouts."

Dewinter looked from me to Louise. "Perhaps you might know of a charity that would welcome a boost?" I caught the wink they shared.

"Great idea. As it happens, I do."

"Congratulations, both of you," Hannah cut in, handing us glasses of champagne as Will shook my hand and dropped a kiss on Lou's cheek. "I'm thrilled you two made it official."

"Bro!" Connor barrelled up and flung his arm over my shoulder. "You've got quite a sheen going." He grinned, pointing to my forehead. *Cheeky bastard.*

"I was shitting myself in case you lot fucked up."

"When would I ever let my little brother down?" He slapped me on the back, shook my hand and moved on to Lou, hugging her to him and kissing her cheek. "Welcome to the family, Lou. Good luck—you'll need it, with him."

As Connor filled Lou in on how they'd set the garage up, I moved over to talk to Matt and the McCarthy's crew. They'd closed the pub for the night in our honour, and had done me proud. When I walked through the reception to use the bathroom, I stopped to smile at the new Staff Appreciation noticeboard that Louise had erected and pinned my *GQ* photos to. It was all done in fun, and it made me love her even more, if that was possible.

With both Tyler and Liam gone, and work almost tripled, we'd had to employ three full-time mechanics. Lou was also working full-time as our office manager, and she'd hunted the office out and never found the missing invoices. We assumed Liam had taken them.

We danced the night away with great food, music and company, and at two a.m. we said goodnight to the last of our guests. It was just Connor, Annie and us.

"Thanks, bro. That was some party," I told him, as we stood outside in the crisp night air.

"Any time."

They headed off, and I took Lou's hand in mine as we walked to the truck. Her face was flushed from our night of celebration, her lipstick long gone and her hair was loose, but she looked stunning, and I couldn't wait to get her home and undress her.

"I love us," she slurred, and smiled a happy, very drunk, grin.

"You know what?" I whispered in her ear. "I love you more."

"Prove it," she challenged.

"Oh, I intend to do just that," I said, opening the car door for her. And I would never ever stop proving it to her.

Acknowledgements

To say getting this story to a point where I can publish it has been a challenge, is an understatement. This is my first attempt at writing a fun and sexy romance and I'm hoping the world will love it. I hope you'll get a few laughs from the story as you read about Louise and Reid's struggle to get together. As hard as it was, I did enjoy putting it together. As always, thank you to the lovely team of people who have helped bring this book to fruition.

The things I'm grateful for, in no particular order are:

- Pineapple lumps. Their pineappley, chewy, chocolate goodness have kept me at my writing desk and helped tighten the waistband on my favourite jeans, damn it.

- My readers. Please don't stop telling me you enjoy my stories!

- My hubby who is a super hero when it comes to keeping the house liveable while I work my day job and write.

- My critique partners, Helen and Shannon who took the shift in genres without flinching. Helen, it's even more fun to think I've won you over to the romance genre. It was only a matter of time.

- Chatham Island crayfish, or rock lobster. Absolutely no explanation needed!

- My personal cheerleaders, Maria and Karen. I appreciate all your encouragement—keep those pom-poms waving!

- Iced coffee (without the whipped cream,) I love you even with the overhang.

- My editors Daisy and Lucy (from Reedsy). Is it too early in the relationship to tell you I love you?

- My garden. It's the thing that's kept me sane and a great place for plot development—crazy and sane—but not the dead body type.

- Janet Elizabeth Henderson who is the Queen of Rom Coms, in my humble opinion, and who told me I might just be able to pull it off.

- Rainy winter days that gave me a reason to keep my butt in the seat and write.

- To my Dream Team beta readers, Maddison,

Caitlin, Ashlee, Senithi, and Rebekah, thank you for being brave enough to read *Finding Us*.

- And thank you world for caramel lattes! Damn, they're good!

About the Author

Carole Brungar is a New Zealand multi-award-winning author whose novels have attracted international acclaim. She published her first book in 2014, and is currently working on number 13.

Brungar writes love stories set in the 20th Century and contemporary romance. She is best known for her powerful, gritty, and authentic Vietnam War series, which evokes and disturbs the readers. These books have won numerous awards and medals and have been highly praised by veterans in America, Australia, and New Zealand. The Nam Legacy spent seven weeks in the top ten of the NZ Bestsellers list.

With a Bachelor of Communication, Brungar has worked as a communications officer for a city council, a newspaper editor for the New Zealand Defence Force, a journalist and a photographer. In a previous life, she was a national quilt tutor and was one of the first artists in New Zealand to teach mixed media classes via the Internet.

Her hobbies include reading, gardening, climbing sand hills and catching up with friends and family. She also keeps emotional support fish that keep dying under the burden of so much publishing stress. She lives in Horowhenua in a small cottage on what was once an air force runway in the 1940s.